His Wicked Whispers

JEN BRADLEE

His Wicked Whispers

Copyright © 2022 Kirsten S. Blacketer/Jen Bradlee.

Printed in the United States of America.
First Printing, 2022
ISBN: 978-1966905141

Cover Art by The Midnight Muse
Written by Jen Bradlee
Published by BlackShip Press
Kirsten.blacketer@gmail.com
https://kirstensblacketer.com/jen-bradlee/

Dedication

Thomas William Hiddleston, your characters inspire us in ways you could never imagine.

Summer, you made me do this. It's all your fault.

A Letter from the Author

Dear Reader,

Welcome and thank you for selecting *His Wicked Whispers* for your reading pleasure. I truly hope you enjoy the story and fall in love with the characters.

Allow me to preface with a warning. If you're not a fan of anti-heroes with dominating and questionable morals, explicit intimate scenes, or graphic language and violence, then this may not be the book for you. For a complete list of content forewarnings, please visit kirstensblacketer.com/jen-bradlee.

If that's exactly what you're looking for, then allow me to welcome you and proceed. Thank you for choosing The Prince of Whispers as your literary companion.

Sending warm regards and best wishes your way. Remember to be kind and love one another.

Sincerely,

Jen Bradlee

Table of Contents

Year 1442 A.D.
SCOTLAND
Northern Hold
IRELAND
ENGLAND
Balmont Holding
Marian's Cottage
Monastery
Culver
MERADIN
WALES
KEY
Capital ⊛
Landmark
Village •
Port ⚓
N

Prologue

Summer 1442, Meradin

The hooded man stepped from the dark forest shadows. Crispin Saville glanced up as he approached. A hint of moonlight showed through the clouds and the treetops, but it afforded him no aid in uncovering the man's identity. Crispin pulled his hood down lower to ensure his face remained hidden.

"My fee is fifty gold pieces." The man's voice was low and hoarse as though he struggled to form the words on his tongue.

Crispin pulled a small bag of coins from his pocket and tossed it at the stranger who caught it with ease. He clenched his teeth as the man counted each coin. "'Tis all there."

The man snorted and pocketed the coins. "It shall be done."

Crispin nodded with satisfaction. "I expect it concluded within a fortnight."

"You cannot rush a master; any artist will tell you so." The man scoffed and retreated into the forest.

Without a second thought to the transaction, Crispin returned to the inn and slipped into the loud common room. The drunk revelers pushed and shoved, clamoring for ale and female companionship. He slid into a chair facing the front door, his back to the wall, desperate for a distraction.

A buxom maid sauntered toward him. "What can I get for you, love?"

"Ale," he said, barely sparing her a glance. She pouted and walked away, her arse swaying beneath the thin material of her skirt.

He kept his hood up. Even in common garments, his face was recognizable to most in the village. His thoughts drifted to the man he paid. Henry would be disappointed in his decision and the direction of his plans. Not that it mattered. His trusted friend always proved more conservative. He wished his friend was home. It would only be a matter of time before Crispin sat upon the throne, then he could call Henry back to his side. Patience afforded him more opportunities, but it singed his pride to entrust such a delicate task to a stranger, especially in the absence of his friend's counsel.

The thought of relinquishing control set him on edge. He would rather do the task himself, although it would allow too much room for speculation regarding his involvement. His hand flexed with the need to move to action. There were several ways to burn off frustration, were there not? He knew exactly where to find an eager participant with little effort.

His gaze settled on the wench who brought him his ale. Yes, she would do quite nicely for the evening. She came eagerly when he called.

teeth.

"You know damned well what you have done!" The king rose from his seat and slammed his fist down on the massive wooden desk. He stalked around it, approaching Crispin. His dark gray eyes shone with exasperation and conviction.

Crispin swallowed hard and straightened, keeping his attention fixed on the far wall. He refused to make eye contact with his father. Why should he care what the peasants or lords thought of him? He was the rightful heir to the throne, chosen by God to lead them. He smirked, allowing his arrogance to bolster his courage.

"She informed me she was unattached. How was I to know she was the visiting duke's wife dressed in peasant rags?" Crispin dropped carelessly in the chair beside him, swinging his legs over the arm.

"Do not pretend you had no inkling as to her identity. Why must you constantly behave like a self-indulgent child?" The king leaned against his desk, arms crossed, his gaze narrowed on Crispin.

"Because I am—at least according to you." He grew tired of the lectures and his father's constant ridicule.

"Crispin." The king rubbed his forehead. "This is precisely why I sent Henry away. If you do not learn to control your baser impulses, I will be forced to cut you from your inheritance and give the crown to the next in line, your cousin Fredrick."

His head snapped up at the mention of Henry and the implication of the king's words. "Father, you cannot be serious. You would deny me the throne? My cousin, the bumbling fool, has neither the presence of mind nor the fortitude to rule a nation."

The old man shook his head. "I have done all I can to lead you, to show you how to rule as a true king should, but you simply refuse to acknowledge the basic tenets of leadership."

"I have done all you have asked of me, Father." Crispin ground his teeth and shot to his feet, pacing the worn rug. "Surely you must see this is ridiculous." He ran his hand through his hair tempted to tear it out in frustration.

The king's gaze followed him. His lips pulled in a thin line and his face remained stoic. "I have tried to be a good king and father, but as of late, all my attention has been dedicated to appeasing nations you have insulted with your careless and selfish behavior. The people have suffered because of this, and I must set things to right. Unfortunately, disinheriting you may be the only course of action to ensure the safety of my people and the realm."

"You cannot take what is mine!" Crispin's voice rattled the ceiling timbers. "It is my birthright! I will have what is owed me." He jabbed his finger at his father, punctuating each word.

"It was not your birthright; it was your brother's!" His father's restraint finally snapped like a dead branch beneath a boot.

"My brother is dead!"

"Crispin!"

His mother's voice boomed behind him, making him turn. She stood inside the door, her hands clasped before her. The dark blue gown emphasized the color in her cheeks and the dark auburn braid wrapped intricately around her head. The stern set of her lips and the concern in her eyes enhanced her regal bearing. Crispin cursed himself for not realizing she had entered the room, but then she made it a point to tread lightly until the opportune moment. He dropped his hand and met her gaze.

"Mother." He greeted her with a slight bow. Fury still raged inside of him, boiling and roiling in his mind full of dark thoughts. He would definitely need a good, mindless fuck to release all this repressed anger. Maybe he would start a fight; sometimes that worked just as well. He allowed himself a small, wicked, satisfied grin.

"I know the gleam in your eyes, my son. It betrays the mischief in your mind." She cocked her head and stepped closer to him, cupping his face with her palms.

Crispin leaned into her warm touch. Her unwavering belief in him touched his calloused heart, but it never swayed him. He stiffened and reached up to slowly draw her hands from his face.

"I appreciate your concern, Mother." He took a measured

step out of her reach. "But I am a man grown, I believe I know my own mind."

She nodded with tears glinting in the corners of her blue eyes. "'Tis what concerns me, darling."

The king held his hand out to her, and she joined him, leaning into her husband's warm embrace. They formed a united front. Crispin crossed his arms, irritation flooding him.

"We are sending you on one last quest to see if you truly are ready to take your responsibilities seriously." The king spoke with confidence and conviction. "This is your last warning. Failure will result in your banishment."

Crispin arched his brow, silently challenging his father. "Is this the worst you can do? Banish me from my home and abrogate my God-given rights."

"I will strip you of your title, your station, and your wealth, and cast you out of my kingdom. Then you may live as you choose. As you are right now, you are unfit to wear a crown."

His father's words stuck like an arrow piercing his heart. How did they expect him to change overnight? Could he even change at all? Crispin refused to let emotion creep into his expression. He affected a cold mask of indifference.

"What is this quest?" His voice remained level and calm while the storm raged in his breast.

"A taste of what you can expect if you fail."

"I beg your pardon?" Crispin glanced between his mother and father. "What will this accomplish?"

His mother spoke this time. "You will travel within our borders, unescorted and penniless, with only the clothes on your back and the people you meet for companionship."

"And you expect me to survive when they discover who I am?"

"You are not permitted to reveal your true identity. You are to survive using only what you bring with you as a man alone against the world." The king's limiting instructions seemed ludicrous.

"Father, surely you jest?" Panic crept into his chest, constricting his heart with its iron grip.

"You know I am not one for games and tricks, Crispin." He narrowed his gaze. "Those are traits you favor. I doubt they will serve you well on your quest."

"When may I return?"

"When you have learned what it is to lead and serve in tandem. When you realize a king has duties which lie beyond these walls and his own selfish indulgences." The king's voice grew more passionate with each statement. "When you fulfill your destiny and become the man I know you can be."

Crispin's hands clenched into fists as he listened to his father's words. He would do what he must. Deep in the corner of his mind, he realized the futility of arguing. He was not a good man at heart and refused to conform to the mold in which his father expected him to fit. He nodded even though he burned to argue the uselessness of such a challenge.

"Yes, Sire." His jaw clenched. If he unleashed his anger now, his father would surely banish him without a second thought. It was for the best he follow their request. "Is there anything else you require of me before I take my leave?"

"Know that we do this out of love," his mother said softly. "Be the leader we know you were born to be."

With a stiff nod, Crispin turned his back on his parents and strode from the room without a backward glance. If they were so eager to be rid of him, who was he to defy their orders? He swiftly returned to his chamber and found himself alone.

The wench had gone. He cursed. Part of him had hoped to find her still wet and willing in his bed. He ran a hand over his face. The night had quickly turned sour.

He changed into sturdy traveling clothes and packed a small satchel with some essentials. He hoarded some coin, so he tucked what he could into his pocket for safekeeping. Strapping the belt around his waist, he buckled it and slid his sword into the scabbard. He tucked the daggers away, one into the sheath at his hip and the other in his boot. One could never be too prepared.

Crispin headed for the door, snatching his heavy woolen cloak from the hook and draping it across his shoulders. He took one last, long glance at his warm bed and his opulent room then disappeared into the night.

***

The dirt and stones scuffed his boots as he ambled down the moonlit road. *Where are you when I need you, Henry?* Crispin lost patience two villages ago. He had been denied a horse, so he walked from the castle he once claimed as his home. The villages near the castle knew his face, so he had wandered into the night in a dark state of mind knowing he must find shelter far from the familiar.

The glimmer of lantern light through the trees signaled a village. He sighed. Hopefully, this one had a whorehouse. He needed a warm body and a good fuck to ease his tension. He rolled his shoulders. A bath would not be remiss, either. Perhaps he could charm one from the wench he intended to persuade to share his bed. Crispin had not checked his coin, but he thought it would be wisest to save what he could.

Crispin grinned when he saw the telltale sign of a brothel. He slipped in the door and took an empty seat by the fire, waiting for service. One of the wenches approached him, sliding her hand up his arm and over his shoulder.

"What can I do for you, love?" she asked, her voice husky. She was plump and ripe, her reddened lips begging with a soft pout.

"I shall take an ale and whatever else you are offering." He charmed her with a smile.

The wench slid into his lap and toyed with the hair curling at the nape of his neck. "With a smile like yours, 'tis a wonder you have to pay for women to grace your bed."

"Perhaps I tire of the games that requires." He slid his hand along her hip, under her skirt. "How about you retrieve my drink," he whispered as she leaned against him. His fingertips glided over her cleft. "Then I can show you what other games I know."

She moaned as he touched her. *Wet and willing.* He smiled. She would suit his purposes quite nicely. He removed his hand and helped her stand. She wobbled a moment before disappearing into the back to fetch his drink.

Crispin glanced around the room. Men and women mingled in various stages of undress. He chuckled. It was almost freeing for once in his life to be in a room and not be the center of attention. He noted the women's sly looks in his direction. He grinned. Perhaps this would not be so bad after all.

The wench returned, handing him a goblet filled with amber liquid. He took the drink and downed it in one swallow. He reached up to pull the woman into his lap when she was suddenly snatched away.

"Oi, let me go," she demanded, pulling against a tall, brawny man's hold. He had a scar running along his right cheek and a dangerous gleam in his eyes.

"You are mine tonight." He pulled her tight against him, his voice harsh and demanding.

"I am otherwise occupied." She tried to jerk from his grip, but he brought her up short.

Before Crispin could interject, the back of the man's hand connected with the woman's face, knocking her to the floor. Eyes wide, she clutched at her cheek and scurried backward away from them both.

Crispin stood, infused with rage. Such an action was not to be tolerated. "Leave her!"

The whole room fell silent.

The man turned to Crispin, rage contorting his face. "What did you say?"

"I told you to leave her alone." Crispin rested his hand on his dagger. "She is with me."

"She is my whore." The man spat on the floor. "Stay out of it."

"Do you belong to him?" Crispin addressed the cowering woman on the floor. She shook her head vehemently. He glanced back at the man. "Seems like the lady disagrees with you."

"Lady? She is a fucking whore." His guffaw echoed through the room.

"That does not mean she deserves any less respect."

Crispin's body pulled tight in response to the tension brewing in the room as it readied for a fight. He licked his lips. "Get out."

"Who do you think you are barking orders and issuing commands? The king?"

Crispin thrust his jaw out. He grew tired of the man's insolence. In one swift motion, he twisted the man's arm behind him and threw his weight into his back, sending him crashing to the floor. When the man scrambled to get up, Crispin kicked his backside, knocking him over again. As the interloper attempted to stand, two men came up to them.

"Janos, go home. You have had enough to drink tonight," one of them said. The other reached for the hulking brute's arm, but he jerked it from his grasp.

"You and I have a debt to settle." He pointed at Crispin then stumbled out of the building. The other two men followed him, making sure he had gone.

Crispin offered his hand to the wench, helping her to her feet. He gently moved her hand and saw the red welt below her eye where the brute had struck her. He clenched his teeth.

"Are you well?" His soft question made her relax beneath his touch.

"Aye," she replied with a shaky smile. "You saved me. I thank you."

"I can think of another way for you to show me your thanks." Crispin slid his hand over the top of her breasts, cradling one in his palm. She moaned as she met his gaze.

"Of course, good sir." She licked her lips. "It would be my pleasure." She grabbed his wrist and pulled him toward the stairs.

A hand clamped down on Crispin's shoulder. He turned, coming face to face with one of the men who had tossed out the rabble.

"We are going to need you to leave as well, sir." His stern tone invited no argument.

"You cannot be serious." Crispin shook his head in disbelief. "Can I not at least reap the reward for rescuing this fair wench?"

"Not unless you would have me summon the sheriff. We

cannot allow such troublesome clients to remain in our establishment."

Crispin bit his tongue before he betrayed his true identity. It would not do for him to be cast from his father's house, a whorehouse, and his homeland in a single night. He swallowed his scathing retort and turned to the wench clinging to his arm.

"My regrets, darling. It seems I must take my leave." He pulled her in for a kiss, tasting what might have been, and released her. She pouted, the disappointment evident in her expression.

"I believe I can find my way out." Crispin glanced at the men moving to follow him. He walked out the door, drawing it closed behind him.

The night lay shrouded with a thick, misty fog, dimming the glow of the lanterns outside the brothel and encircling the rest of the small village. He ran his hand through his hair. *So much for a willing woman and a warm bed.* Agitated, he ruffled his hair again.

Crispin stepped down onto the street when four men stepped from the darkness, surrounding him. The two flanking him grabbed his arms, while the third wrapped his arm around Crispin's throat from behind. He thrashed against their grasp, but they were huge, hulking beasts. He was outmanned and outmaneuvered. *God's blood, teeth, and bones.*

"You and I have unfinished business," the fourth man said, stepping into the light, allowing Crispin to see his face.

"You bloody bastard." Crispin struggled against their hold. "I will have your head for this. Do you have any idea who I am?"

"The pompous arse who stole my whore." Contempt dripped from the man's words. "I do not give a cock's crow who you are." He threw a punch, and it landed in Crispin's stomach, knocking the air from his chest. "But you are going to pay."

Crispin jerked, trying to break free, wheezing. The man holding his head released him but stood like a solid stone wall against his back. He had to defend himself, but there were too many of them and they were far too strong for him to take them on alone. Three more blows landed in succession, two to his midsection and one cracking across his jaw. Pain shot through him as the warm, metallic tang of blood filled his mouth.

"That the best you got?" Crispin spat. He knew it would only enrage the beast more, but he never backed down, even in the most hopeless situations.

The man threw another punch, square in the chest over his heart. Crispin thought it ceased beating with the blow. The world spun as he gasped for breath, doubling over. The men held him steady. Crispin coughed, spewing blood onto the man's shoes. The assailant grabbed a handful of his hair and jerked his head back. He winced before narrowing his gaze. Never show weakness.

A yelp of pain from the man on his right was followed by Crispin's sudden release. A moment later, the second man released him, clutching at his arm as he stumbled backward. The man behind them backed away as if sensing something was not right. Crispin stumbled forward, trying to catch his breath. His eyes watered from the pain throbbing in his head. He glanced up and saw the man who had been pummeling him standing as still as a marble statue. The shaft of an arrow glinted in the lamp light from where it protruded from the man's chest. The beast pitched forward, and Crispin scrambled out of the way, slamming onto his back on the ground.

He lay there, staring up into the starlit night catching his breath. A figure stepped into his view wearing a dark cloak with the hood pulled up.

"Are you going to lay there and bleed?"

Crispin's head pounded. Those blows must have affected him more than he had thought. Was it a woman's voice? Surely not. He tried to sit up and wobbled at the motion.

"Help me up, damn you." He held out his hand.

With a derisive snort, the cloaked savior helped him to his feet. Crispin draped his arm across the man's shoulder, steadying himself.

"Come, we must away before the soldiers arrive." The stranger's voice was strong and steady, but it most definitely belonged to a woman.

"Wait." Crispin protested, but the stranger pulled him

deeper into the shadows.

"There is no time." His savior helped him onto her horse then swung up into the saddle behind him. With a nudge, the beast was off, hurtling through the darkness.

Crispin's head ached. The jolting pace of the horse did nothing to ease his discomfort, but it could have been worse. The stranger's arms around him made him acutely aware of the lithe body pressed against his back. It was a woman, he would stake his life on it. In silence, they rode into the night away from the village. He would demand answers once they reached wherever the hell they were headed if he survived the ride.

Chapter Two

What in Saint Jude has gotten into me? I must be daft. Ruby shifted her weight behind him in the saddle. He groaned. It was too late to turn back now. She could not very well dump him along the side of the road. She needed to be sure his injuries were treated. *What is the point of saving him, only to let him die in the forest?* She should drop him at the nearest monastery. Let the monks care for him. It did not matter; they were nearly to her campsite.

Ruby nudged her mare into the thick copse of trees. *We should be safe enough here tonight.* The soldiers would find the bodies soon enough and make the connection. Her name was all but emblazoned on every one of them.

"Whoa." She reined her horse to a stop and slid from the saddle. When she reached up to help the injured man down, he pushed her hands away.

"I can dismount a horse." He swung down and stumbled as his feet hit the dirt before falling on his arse. "God's bones!"

Ruby chuckled. "Would you like help, or can you manage on your own?"

"Do not dare laugh." He struggled to his feet, brushing the dust from his backside.

"I would never." Ruby fought the impulse even as she spoke. She left him to gather his wits and led her horse to a small grassy spot, tying the reins to a low-hanging branch to let her graze. When she returned to the site, the man she had rescued sat on a log, rubbing his jaw.

Ruby set to work, quickly building a small fire. When it blazed to life, she glanced at him and found him watching her intently. She pulled her hood back and met his gaze.

"I knew it." He grunted and clutched his side.

"Knew what?" She cocked her head, slightly annoyed by his

attitude but amused nonetheless.

"You are a woman."

"Did you mean to insult me?" Ruby arched her brow before rising to her feet and crossing the space between them.

He eyed her carefully as she sat beside him. "'Tis common knowledge women are the weaker sex."

"And you believe such cow dung?" Ruby noted his indecision as it flickered across his face. This man was not stupid, that much was certain. Shrewd and calculating, he took a solid measure of her in silence as though weighing the repercussions of his reply. Saints alive, he was a handsome devil. His curly, dark hair barely brushed his collar. Her fingers itched to glide through it and see if it were truly as soft as it looked. His blue eyes darkened to the color of stormy summer skies, and they pierced her soul like a bolt of lightning splitting a tree.

"Never mind." She cleared her throat. "Allow me to examine your injuries."

When Ruby reached for his face, he jerked away from her touch. "I do not require your mothering."

She grabbed his chin, forcing him to meet her gaze. His eyes shot open wide. Something stirred in their depths. Anger, surprise, lust...She pushed the observation away and turned her attention to the gashes on his cheek. Releasing him, she turned and retrieved a scrap of cloth and a small flagon of brandy from her leather satchel. Ruby wet the rag and pressed it to his injuries. He sucked in a breath.

"I know it stings. Do not be such a bantling." She gently cleaned each wound, paying careful attention to the sharp angle of his cheekbones and the carefully trimmed facial hair around his mouth. He was most assuredly a lord of some kind. Everything about his bearing bespoke wealth and propriety, down to his finely cut garments, although his attitude was nothing short of contemptuous.

"You have lovely eyes."

Ruby inhaled at his soft compliment and met his gaze. He had been studying her, almost as intently as she had been observing him. Her cheeks warmed under his scrutiny. Ruby pressed the rag to a cut on his lower lip.

He winced at the sting. "What is your name?"

"Ruby." She forced herself to concentrate on the task at hand and not be distracted by his seductive voice.

"'Tis an unusual name. From where do you hail?"

"Dorringbrooke." The lie came easily enough as it had a hundred times before.

"Ruby of Dorringbrooke." Her name slipped from his tongue like molten silver into a cast, leaving an impression upon her soul.

She shivered at the wicked thoughts filling her mind. Lunacy! Wanting a man she had just met, a man who obviously held secrets of his own.

"Are you cold?"

"Nay." She turned from him to retrieve another rag. When she turned back, he took the flagon from her hand and took a long drink. "What shall I call you?" She arched a brow in surprise at his lengthy drought of her brandy.

"Tristan." He wiped his mouth on the back of his hand.

"From where do you hail?" Ruby crossed her arms.

"The south." He took another drink. "'Tis all you need to know."

"Oi, enough." She snatched the flagon from his hands. "'Tis the last of my brandy."

"My head feels like it has been bashed in with a rock; have you nothing else to soothe my pain?"

"'Tis nothing but a few scratches. You will survive." She tucked the flagon away.

"Where did you learn to shoot?" His silken voice glided over her, drawing her attention back to him.

"What does it matter?" Ruby purposefully avoided his intoxicating eyes. She did not need a distraction or a complication, and he was a dangerous, distracting complication. The sooner she left him to his own devices, the better off they both would be.

"You are a maid, living in the woods, alone." He mused aloud becoming more irritating by the moment. "It seems you are going to great lengths to remain hidden. And you did kill at least two men tonight. Perhaps you are a member of the Guild."

"And if I were, I would not tell you." Ruby shrugged her shoulders. "Get some rest." She stood and walked to the other side of the fire. After unrolling her blanket, she lay down upon it.

He wanted to know more about her. Although he teased her about being a member of the secret, mythical group of assassins and thieves, it only lead him to wanting real answers. Ones she was unwilling to give. Best to ignore his curiosity for both their sakes.

She heard movement and glanced through the flames. He sat on the ground, leaning against the log, watching her. *Saints preserve me. This man could be my downfall. Why did I save him?*

Ruby knew the answer to her own question. It was not in her nature to leave a soul in need. She rolled onto her back and stared up into the starlit sky. With a prayer to Saint Jude, she willed herself to sleep, painfully aware of the man on the other side of the fire.

Chapter Three

Crispin could not move. His entire body ached and throbbed. Every movement sent waves of excruciating pain through his chest. Even training as a knight had not left him in such agony. He lay on his back, staring up into the gray, morning sky. Then he glanced at the fire. No flame remained, not even a wisp of smoke. When he gently rolled over, he groaned. His body protested as he stood.

One glance around the small camp told him she had gone. He frowned. It came as no surprise, but a twinge of disappointment stung somewhere in the vicinity of his heart. He had found the infamous Lady of the Forest. Her bright eyes betrayed her intelligence, and her skill with the bow told him the truth of her identity.

Perhaps it was better if they went down separate paths. A shrewd, lovely woman such as her could pose a threat or, at the very least a distraction, neither of which he desired at the moment.

"You survived the night?" a voice echoed behind him, making him turn.

Ruby leaned forward in the saddle, watching him, her hood back revealing deep auburn tresses curled over her shoulder in a thick braid. Her hair shone with threads of gold and fire, even in the morning gloom. He took a step closer. She could easily pass for an elegant lady of court had she not been garbed in men's clothing and armed with a bow. What a juxtaposition. Her eyes narrowed at his scrutiny.

"Do you have a problem?" The corner of her lips tilted up.

"Nay." He shook his head. "I should be on my way." He glanced around, quite at a loss for which way to go.

"Follow me." She reigned her horse around.

"Where are you leading me? To my slaughter." He could not help but tease her.

"To the road." She ignored his jibe. "Is that not what you were searching for?"

"Aye, it was." He took a few steps then stopped, realizing their arrangement. "Are you truly going to make me walk?"

She turned in the saddle and met his gaze. "Aye." Ruby's smile caught him off guard, but her eyes twinkled with mischief and challenge, making him wary.

"Minx," he muttered under his breath. "I should tame your tongue."

"I beg your pardon. Did you say something?"

"Nay, lead on, my lady."

Crispin walked behind the horse for a while, lost in his thoughts. Then he stepped in it. Horse shit. He picked up his foot and shook it, trying to wipe it off in the tall grass.

"God's teeth, blood, and bones!"

Ruby turned around. "What now?"

He glared up at her. "I swear you are enjoying this torment, are you not?"

"You seem to be perfectly capable of walking. I see no reason why I should coddle you as a child." She chuckled, her gaze narrowing on his face. "I expected your face to be more...purple."

"I do not bruise," he growled, still irritated. She insisted on testing his patience and his restraint. Part of him wanted to drag her off the bloody horse, pin her against the nearest tree, and fuck her senseless. Thinking of it sent a shiver of desire coursing through his body.

"Everyone bruises." She cocked her head with evident skepticism.

"I do not." He walked up to the horse and laid a hand on the beast's neck. His gaze lingered on her thigh, then traveled up the length of her body. "The last time I got into a fight I took a blow to the face. Within two days the redness was gone. By the end of the week, no one would have known I had been struck." Crispin watched her expression. She hid her emotions well. It was her mouth which drew his attention. She worried her lower lip between her teeth. When she released it, he groaned.

"When was this?" she asked.

"A fortnight ago." He grinned at the raucous memory.

"Why am I not surprised?"

"At what?"

"The fact remains. Someone struck you only a fortnight ago, and you believe yourself to be impervious to the laws of nature."

He arched a brow. "You do not think highly of me, do you?"

"The more I learn, the more inclined I am to think you are of a certain breed." She mimicked his expression. "Sweet words and smoldering eyes will not win my favor."

He dropped his hand and backed away. "You could do with a few manners as well."

"Come." She nudged the horse to walk again. "The road is just ahead. I have a prior commitment to fulfill. I would hate to keep you from your whores."

He shook his head. It seemed as though she already painted a vivid portrait of him in her mind. Perhaps if he was more focused on...wait, why the hell should he care what she thought of him? Ruby may have saved his life, but that was the end of their attachment. He could see the road on the other side of the trees. Part of him remained curious; who was she truly and what could she possibly be doing alone in these woods? The Lady of the Forest was most assuredly a mystery as the stories claimed. One worth unraveling.

"What commitment could you possibly have?" He found himself asking the question even as he convinced himself the answer was not necessary to his survival.

Ruby stopped beside him, meeting his gaze. "A serving girl who worked for the king was in desperate need of help. I found her near the lake with a dagger pressed to her breast, ready to end her own life." She took a deep breath as if trying to calm herself. "The prince used her for his amusement, and she now bears his child."

Crispin's heart stopped. His mind raged in revolt. It was not possible, but then again, he knew deep inside it could very well be true. He had never known, never cared to know what happened to the women he bedded once he was finished with them. In his defense, he was always careful not to spill his seed inside of the women he took to bed. The possibility of this woman carrying his bastard was truly slim unless she could prove she had given herself to him alone. A mixture of shame and anger roiled in the pit of his stomach. He stomped it down, willing his conscience into silence. He never dallied with virgins, ever. Had the woman lied to gain sympathy from a kind stranger? Nothing would surprise him, especially when it came to power, politics, and gold.

"Who is to say the girl is not lying?" He regretted the question as soon as it left his lips.

Ruby slid down from the horse's back and rounded on him with glorious indignation. He backed up until he slammed against a tree. Livid, she jabbed a finger into his chest.

"You men never understand, nor do you truly want to." Her jaw clenched. "You woo them with pretty words and promises, fuck them for your pleasure, then run like cowards with your tails between your legs with no thought to the consequences of your actions." Her hand tightened in the fabric of his tunic, holding him steady as she shredded him with her words. "The poor woman is now left to deal with your by-blow, her image forever tarnished, any hope for a good match crushed by your inability to restrain yourself. Do you ever give a thought to the lives you ruin with your actions?"

Crispin knew she was referring to the prince and noblemen in general, not him specifically. He saw the fury blazing in her sherry-colored eyes and the blush staining her cheeks. Her grip held him fast against the tall elder tree. If she knew the truth of his identity, she would run a blade through his heart without hesitation.

As if realizing her actions, she released him and stepped away. "I beg your pardon."

"I take it you do not think fondly of our prince." He

straightened his tunic.

The passionate hatred flared to life in her eyes once more and she thrust her jaw forward. "If he would ever leave the safety of his castle, I would hunt him down and end his reign before it has a chance to begin. He should be put down for the wild mongrel he is. I am not the only one who believes so."

Crispin swallowed the lump in his throat. How was he supposed to react to such a vehement display of loathing? She confessed treason to him, a stranger. But more so, this made him a target. Who else thought these things of him? As the question churned in his mind, he forced his expression to remain impassive despite his discomfort.

"You think I am a traitor?" Ruby studied him, her golden eyes searching his face.

"I said nothing of the sort," he replied, choosing his words carefully. "However, you would do well to keep such thoughts to yourself from this moment hence. One misspoken word to the wrong person could land your pretty neck on an executioner's block." He reached out and brushed a curl from her cheek where it had fallen loose from her braid. "That would be quite a waste."

"Flattery, again." She scoffed. "You have no shame, sir."

"My lady, you have saved me once. Can I not return the favor?" His words held a ring of truth, he realized. Crispin was not merely playing a game to save himself. Even knowing this woman would kill him in a heartbeat, he still desired her.

"See to it you do not cause problems in the next village." She turned from him, picking up the reins and mounting her horse. "I will not be around to save you again." With a wave of her hand, she bid him farewell and urged the horse into a trot.

Crispin leaned against the tree and watched her leave, completely unprepared for the pang of loss lodged in his chest. He frowned, disappointed in himself. He was the prince of Meradin, and she wanted him dead. Remaining with her would have been a volatile proposition. One misstep, one misplaced word would have shattered the shroud of anonymity. It was better they parted ways.

Crispin emerged from the tree line and ambled down the road. *My kingdom for a horse.* His body still ached, but the exercise did wonders for his mood. With the dangerous and distracting Ruby placed firmly behind him, he focused on his next goal—a hot bath and a warm bed. His loins ached, but something told him a whore would do nothing to appease his hunger. An auburn-haired vixen would haunt his dreams this night.

As he walked, Crispin considered the conundrum of the expecting servant girl, and his mood took a significant dive. 'Twas true, he never cared what happened to them after he bedded them. He used them, all of them. But was that not what he experienced at the hands of others? Callous disregard and greed. Everyone he met wanted something from him, not only the women he bedded.

Every single person at court wanted something from him. He was the prince. He possessed influence at court. There was not a soul he met who would not desert him if he could not provide them with something of value. They coddled him, acquiesced his every desire in the hopes of repayment. There were no kind gestures at court, only political games. Crispin was no more than a whore himself. He spat, disgusted by the thought.

Suddenly weary, he quickened his pace in search of sanctuary for the night, wishing he had stolen at least a kiss from the Lady of the Forest to sate his hunger.

Chapter Four

Ruby was pleased with Anna's progress. The servant girl had been terrified when she discovered she was with child. Ruby vowed to help her find a safe place to have the baby and find a loving family to care for it. Being an outlaw who moved frequently had its benefits. She came to the aid of many people who could not help themselves for fear of retribution.

Nearly a year before, she had helped the shoemaker and his wife. She discovered they could not conceive a child, and his wife was at her breaking point. Most women often felt as though they were worthless if they could not bear a child. It seemed fate had put Ruby in the path of both the shoemaker's wife and Anna. They had taken the poor girl in without question, given her work, and offered to raise her child as their own. Both would benefit from a seemingly disastrous situation.

Her conversation with Tristan earlier instilled nagging doubt in her mind. Anna never mentioned the details of her situation, nor who had ruined her. Ruby had heard of the prince's reputation and assumed Anna had fallen beneath the seductive charms of the rogue. She asked Anna who the father was, and her reply stunned Ruby. The girl had no idea who was the father of her unborn child. With a few comforting words, Ruby left Anna in the care of the shoemaker and his wife. Her heart wept at the consequences of the indecisive, fickle nature of mankind and their desire for pleasure.

When she returned to her campsite, Ruby gathered the provisions she had hidden in a hollow tree trunk and filled in the fire pit. She glanced at the spot where Tristan had slept. Her heart lurched at the thought of him. Where was he now? Probably at the whorehouse in the next village. Men were nothing if not predictable. A shimmer in the grass caught her attention.

Upon inspection, she found a small dagger, gold inlaid with jewels. A rich man's bauble. Either he had stolen it, or it was his by rights. The question haunted her. If it belonged to him, then who was he? She tucked the dagger into her satchel. It would fetch a pretty price and feed a whole village for a year. She shook her head.

Ruby smiled as she led her mare back to the road and mounted. She followed the king's road in the direction of the monastery. As much as she wished to stay, she must keep moving. There were others who needed her help. When the gray stone towers came into view, she pulled a small bag from her satchel. She tied the reins to a small post and approached the door of the monastery. Before she could knock, the door swung open.

A monk stood beneath the arch, his hood drawn up and over his head, obscuring his face. He clasped his hands before him. "My child, what a blessing you have come." His deep, raspy voice offered a strange comfort.

"Brother James." She greeted him with warm affection. "I pray you and your brothers are well?"

He stepped outside but kept his face hidden in shadow. "The Lord has blessed us, my child. What brings you to our humble monastery this day? Have you brought us more healing balms from Marian?"

"Nay, but I will be sure to see if she has prepared more of the salves you require." Ruby held out the small bag. "This may help in some way."

The monk took the bag in his gloved hand and poured the contents into his palm. The jingle of gold coins echoed between them. "My child, you truly are a gift from heaven." He replaced the coins in the purse and tucked it into his robes.

She smiled at his compliment. "I wish there was more I could do. Your brotherhood does so much for the poor and injured." Before she could rethink her decision, Ruby reached into her cloak and removed the jeweled dagger she had found on the ground. "Take this as well."

"We live to serve those in need." He bowed slightly and took the dagger. "As do you, in your own unique way."

The monk's words touched her, and she nodded in thanks. At least he understood what she was trying to do. The people needed a new direction. Their cries for help had fallen on deaf ears for far too long.

"I shall return," Ruby promised as she turned to leave.

"You are always welcome if you seek sanctuary." His words gave her pause. She glanced over her shoulder. He stood in the doorway, his fingers grazing over the jeweled hilt of the dagger. This monastery held special significance as a place of refuge and healing. The monks took in those who sought to be healed, either in body or in spirit.

"May God grant you mercy, Brother James." Ruby picked up the reins and mounted her horse. She cast the monastery one last look before turning her attention toward the path.

A rumbling protest from her stomach made her pause. She grabbed the bread from her satchel. Using her dagger, she scraped the moldy spots off and took a bite. It had been a while since she restocked supplies.

As she rode, she laid her plans to slip into the village and replenish her food stores. A jolt of hope caught her unaware. Would she see Tristan again? Did it matter if she did? They were a volatile combination. His eyes screamed with panic when she spoke of her hatred for the prince. Did he know him personally? If he did, why would he warn her to not speak so freely of her dislike? Ruby had more questions than answers, and it made her nervous. Perhaps she should seek him out.

And do what? Her mind raged. *Kiss him? Fuck him?* Ruby shook her head. He twisted her conscience into knots. Even now, her heart and mind demanded she stay away from him, but the rest of her screamed for release. She had never been with a man before, never even thought about giving in to the urge. But there was something about Tristan that stoked these wanton desires.

"You cannot betray your heart for one night of pleasure." Ruby scolded herself. "If you do, then you are no better than he is. Focus on your responsibilities."

As her mount continued on at a slow walk, she tucked the remainder of the bread back into her saddlebag. "It will be dark by the time we reach the village." She smiled as the plan fell into place. "Perfect timing."

Chapter Five

One room remained at the inn. Exhausted and aching, Crispin had no reservations about paying full price for it. After requesting a bath and a meal be delivered to his room, he sat in the common area and enjoyed a pint while he waited. He watched the peasants as they bustled around the room. It was not the nicest inn, but he was supposed to be living among the common folk. This seemed to be the most reasonable compromise. He wrinkled his nose in disgust at the people milling about the room. There must be a point to all of this chaos. Crispin swallowed the last of his ale as a boy of ten approached him.

"Your room is ready, milord," he said with a quick bow. "If you will follow me."

Crispin trudged up the stairs behind the boy. He entered the room and grinned upon finding his meal and bath awaiting him.

"Good lad." He handed the boy a coin. "That will be all." The boy nodded and left.

Crispin stripped his clothing off and tossed the garments on the chair next to the fireplace. As he eased himself into the scalding water, he sighed as his body immediately relaxed, soothed by the heat. Crispin leaned his head back, closed his eyes, and for the first time in more than a day, indulged in a few moments of peace.

The sound of a door slamming intruded on his peace, and he wrenched his eyes open to find Ruby in his room. With her back pressed against the door and her finger to her lips, she pleaded for his silence. He sat up, the now-tepid water sluicing around him. Her eyes widened at the realization of the situation. She froze. He grinned as the soft glow of a blush stole across her cheeks. *So, she is not the icy maiden she appears to be.*

A knock at the door broke his thoughts. "One moment," he called. Crispin braced his hands on the sides of the wooden tub and lifted himself from the water. Without grabbing a drying cloth, he padded, dripping wet, to the door where Ruby stood, her jaw agape and her eyes as large as the full moon. He moved her against the wall and opened the door, hiding her behind it. A soldier stood in the hallway, his expression stern.

"I pray this is of great importance?" Crispin asked, boredom and irritation lacing his words.

"I beg your pardon, my lord," the soldier stammered, taking notice of Crispin's state of undress. "Have you seen a woman pass through here?"

"I wish I could say I have. A woman to warm my bed might cure my ill temper. But sadly, I have not." Crispin fixed his most intense, princely glare on the soldier.

The man stuttered and took a step back. "I am sorry to have disturbed you, my lord." He turned and walked down the hall as though the Hounds of Hell nipped at his heels.

Crispin closed the door and locked it. He met Ruby's gaze. "You have a penchant for finding trouble. Tell me, do you actively seek it out, or merely tumble into it by chance?"

Ruby shrugged, her gaze skimming across his face, daring to venture lower, but hesitating at the last moment. He chuckled at her attempt of dismissive indifference.

"I will leave you in peace, as soon as I am sure the soldiers have gone," she assured him, her voice barely above a whisper. "I thank you for not betraying my presence."

Crispin pinned her against the wall, his hands on either side of her hips, his thighs brushing against hers. "Did you know I was in this room or was it pure coincidence I happened to be the poor fellow you stumbled upon?"

"I knew you were here." She tilted her chin up, meeting his gaze squarely. "The stable boy is a friend. He saw you enter the inn. I hoped you would show a little compassion since I saved your life."

His gaze narrowed at her presumption. "Do not mistake my

interest in you for compassion, Ruby. I have never been a thoughtful or compassionate man."

"What could you possibly want from me?" she asked. "I have no coin, no wealth, nothing to satisfy your greed."

"Is that so?" He brushed his fingertips across her jaw and down her neck. She was softer than he had imagined, and his cock hardened at the solitary touch. "I think you underestimate your value, my lady." His hand stilled instantly at the cold press of a blade against his inner thigh.

"One more move, bastard, and I shall send an entire kingdom of whores into mourning."

Her threat hung between them. Crispin watched her closely. He saw the lust in her gaze, but she fought it. Why he could not fathom, but he would not tempt her resolve at this time. He dropped his hands to his sides.

"I yield." Even though he no longer touched her, his heat radiated around them, binding them closer together even without physical contact. He bit his lower lip in agitation. Her gaze fluttered to his mouth, and her breath hitched, breaking on a small gasp. He grinned and stepped back. "Please, join me. You are welcome to use the bath if you are so inclined."

Ruby shook her head. She approached the table where his dinner sat and glanced at him in question. "May I?"

Crispin nodded and watched with satisfaction as she took large, ravenous bites. His appetite shifted. He glanced down at his aching erection in despair. There would be no relief for him this night. It was obvious he would need to woo her into his good graces should he desire to take her to bed. Such an entanglement would prove dangerous. He shuddered to think what she would do to him should his identity be revealed. Even if they indulged in some bedsport, he would be gone long before she realized he was the prince she loathed so vehemently. He snatched his hose off the bed and pulled them on. She ate in silence, occasionally sneaking a glance in his direction.

"Enjoying the meal?" He laid upon the bed.

"Aye," Ruby replied around a mouthful of food. She swallowed and turned toward him. "I believe the guards must have taken their leave by now." She rose from the table. "I thank you, again."

In an instant, Crispin leaped to his feet, his body between her and the door. The surprise on her face reminded him of a hare cornered by a fox. He took a step closer to her. She licked her lips and rested her hand on the dagger at her hip.

"Stand aside." Ruby stalked forward, pushing against him, hoping he would move.

Crispin snatched her by the waist and backed her up, tumbling them both onto the bed. He grabbed her wrists, pinning her hands above her head and securing her beneath his weight.

"Why must you be so stubborn?" His voice grew husky as she writhed under him.

"Why must you restrain me?" She arched a brow. "Remove yourself. Release me."

"So you can draw your weapon against me again? I think not." Crispin groaned as she struggled beneath him. "The next time you threaten me with a blade, you had better be prepared to use it."

"I was." She thrust her jaw forward. "Next time, I will not hesitate."

"I doubt that." Crispin shook his head. He enjoyed ruffling her composure. "Your words tell me one thing, but your body betrays you." He slid his knee between her thighs until it rested against the warmth of her cunt.

Ruby gasped at the sensation of him pressed against her. Heat and desire boiled inside him at the challenge. He loved riddles, and Ruby proved to be a riddle he craved to solve. The game would be dangerous, but he continued with the intention of claiming victory.

"If you want to stay, I promise not to ravish you." A wicked smile curved his lips. "Unless you beg me."

"I would never beg." Ruby's eyes glimmered in the lantern light.

He tsked. "So confident in your resolve, are you?" Crispin leaned closer and inhaled her scent, trailing his mouth over the bare spot below her throat. "Tell me you do not want me, and I shall release you. On my honor, I will not accost you." He pulled back and met her gaze once more. "Mark my words. If you consent, you will burn for my touch until you cannot take it a moment longer. Then I will give you the release you crave."

"You pompous, arrogant knave." She stared at him. "You speak to me as if I were one of your whores. You will never hear me beg."

The urge to kiss her overwhelmed him. Nothing would have pleased him more than to make her eat those words. His cock ached from want of her, even though the threat of a single mistake could bring her blade to his throat—or worse. He whispered in her ear, "I have seen you watching me from the corner of your eye, hoping I would not notice. But I have. I offer you one night. One night to do with me as you wish."

Her body stiffened beneath him. Crispin pulled back, admiring the soft flush suffusing her skin creeping into her cheeks. He wondered if any man had ever spoken such words to her before. A pang of jealousy struck him; he pushed it away. The fight was pointless, as the alchemy between them simmered with inevitability. When he wanted something, nothing stood in his way. Fear and uncertainty lay beneath the desire in her eyes. Reluctantly, he released her and rolled off to the side where he lay, staring at the ceiling.

"I should go." Ruby scrambled to her feet, rubbing her wrists and smoothing her clothes. She pressed her hands to her cheeks. "Again, I thank you." She reached for the door.

"Stay." His soft tone surprised even him. "Please."

Her head whipped around. Crispin turned his attention back to the ceiling and closed his eyes, propping his hands behind his head. That was all the propriety she would receive from him. He was a prince, heir to the throne. Never in his life had he uttered that word. So what the hell made him use it now? He pushed the nagging question aside in a vain attempt to relax, waiting for the sound of the door to close when she left. It never came.

The bed dipped as she sat next to him. He refrained from

indulging in a grin of victory, forcing himself instead to control the lust burning through him.

Ruby sighed and dropped something to the floor before settling on the bed beside him. Without another word, she came to rest with her side pressed to his. Silence descended around them, and despite his arousal, Crispin drifted into the first peaceful sleep he had since he was a child.

Chapter Six

Ruby arched into the warmth. If this was truly a dream, part of her longed to remain forever and forego the realities of the world. Tristan's wicked whispers replayed in her mind, tempting her to sin. She remembered lying down next to him and...wait, was she was still lying beside him? She shifted, but her body refused to budge. Something heavy and warm held her tight.

At some point during the night, they had become intertwined. Tristan was pressed against her back, his arm thrown across her stomach, his legs tangled with hers. His insistent erection rubbed against her arse making her moan.

Tristan's grip tightened, pulling her more firmly into contact with the full length of his body. She bit her lip, suppressing a whimper. He had been right about one thing. She did want him, in every way a woman could possibly desire a man. Her thoughts drifted to the night before, when he had her pinned beneath him. Never had she dreamed being dominated by a man could be so arousing. She had nearly succumbed to his sinful invitation. One night with him, one night to do as she wished.

He had wanted to kiss her; she saw it reflected in his actions, in his eyes. Part of her wanted him to seize the opportunity. Why did she want to give him so much power over her? She worked hard to be independent and protect herself as her parents instructed her. Was she truly willing to throw it away for a man she knew practically nothing about?

*No, but one night...*She squashed the thought like a beetle beneath her boot. It did not stop her from wondering if his kiss would be like the rest of him—confident, selfish, and intoxicating. Ruby had been kissed before, but the single occasion was uninspiring, leaving her feeling dirty and ashamed. Something about Tristan, the way he carried himself, the way he spoke, promised his kiss would be life-changing.

Tristan's breath caressed her bare neck, brushing across her shoulder. Her body thrummed in tandem with her racing heart. Ruby's flesh prickled, aware of his every breath, every touch. She closed her eyes, savoring the moment. Once he woke, the fantasy would shatter. Her breath came in soft pants. She attempted to steady herself, focusing on nothing in particular, anything to distract from the man holding her.

The soft press of his lips against her bare skin made her shiver. Ruby feigned sleep, forcing herself not to react. His feather-light kisses brought her closer to the inferno. His hand drifted across her stomach under her tunic, brushing against the underside of her breast. She sighed as his hand closed over it. Her body screamed in reaction. All she had to do was roll over and claim his lips. Surrender to his touch, his seductive embrace. She rubbed her arse against him again, inadvertently encouraging him. He groaned and slid his hand down her body, cupping her quim through the hose. At the touch, Ruby's eyes flew open. She whimpered.

"My sweeting," he whispered in her ear, drawing the lobe between his teeth. His fingertips rubbed against her in slow circles.

My sweeting. He thought she was one of his whores. Ruby scrambled from his embrace and out of the bed. One thing she knew for certain, he would use her like the countless women before her. She glared down at him, crossing her arms. Tristan lay on his side, his head propped on his hand.

"What in the name of the saints do think you are doing?" Ruby set her jaw. He looked so comfortable, so at ease, she longed to smother him with a pillow. He truly had no conscience. She had been right to push him away.

"Tell me you did not enjoy my touch," Tristan prompted, a sinful grin playing on his lips.

She shook her head and gathered her belongings. "I shall take my leave."

"The sun has barely broken the horizon." He glanced toward the window.

"All the more reason for me to leave."

"I shall join you." He jumped from the bed and stood in front of the door, blocking it. She stared at him in disbelief.

"Why do you insist upon forcing your company upon me?" She crossed her arms, praying he did not touch her again. Her body still sang to the memory of his touch, begging for a release she knew only he could bring. "Who are you?"

"Does it matter?" His blue eyes flashed with...was that fear?

"It does." She propped her hands upon her hips. "You are not an outlaw, not a tradesman or a farmer, which leaves only a man of wealth, something you clearly do not possess. Judging by the lack of calluses on your hands and the fine cut of your clothes, I can only guess you are of noble birth. But, saints above, why are you stumbling across the countryside without a horse, with very little coin, and no direction?"

He hesitated for a brief moment before nodding. "My father cast me out," Tristan ran his hand through his dark curls. "He told me not to return until I learned how to behave as a proper son and gentleman."

"So indulging in fights and frequenting whorehouses is your solution?" Ruby scoffed. "How typical. Every nobleman I have ever known thinks his shite smells of roses. He believes he can come and go as he pleases, while he steps on the backs of the poor to elevate himself. Your kind makes me violently ill." She pushed past him and reached for the door latch.

"Where will you go?" Tristan's voice remained steady.

"None of your bloody concern." She grit her teeth to keep from railing him further.

"I love when the fire comes shining through." He stepped closer, making her back up. His proximity confused her senses, and she fumbled with the latch.

"Stay away from me."

"Or you will cut me as you vowed to do before?" Tristan chuckled. He grabbed her waist, pulling her against him and pinning her hands behind her back. "I can be of service to you, my lady." His whisper sent a shiver of lust singing through her body.

With him so close, Ruby found it difficult to concentrate. All she had to do was claim his lips and be done with it. One taste would never be enough. If she crossed the line with him, she would never forgive herself. He embodied everything she abhorred. His arrogance spoke of his entitled beliefs and dismissive attitude.

Against her better judgment, she found herself nodding and he released her. *What am I doing? This is insanity.* "Under one condition." Ruby jabbed her finger into his chest.

He stared down at her. "Your wish is my command."

"Never touch me again."

Tristan smiled and stepped away. She scowled. How had she let him persuade her into this ridiculous agreement? *Not persuade, seduce.* She scolded herself as he dressed. Within moments, they left the inn, the rising sun guiding their way.

Chapter Seven

As they approached a small cluster of buildings on the outskirts of town, Crispin noticed they avoided the direct route along the main road. She led them through the woods along a narrow trail, probably in the hope of bypassing the soldiers who still searched for her.

Ruby was a walking contradiction, a woman of spirit and honor who hid in the forest as an outlaw. He was unsure whether to be impressed by her actions or horrified at her blatant disregard for the law. One thing was certain: he wanted her. He wanted to know what she tasted like, what little noises she would make when he touched her intimately, if she would cry out with abandon when he took her. Perhaps she was yet untouched? The thought aroused him more than he cared to admit. Surely she could not be a virgin. He made it a point to avoid inexperienced women, but the thought of claiming unspoiled goods made him hard. He licked his lips as he watched her hips sway.

A young man, no more than sixteen years, approached them. A strong youth by the look of his build. Then Crispin saw the forge through the door of the building in the distance. A blacksmith's apprentice. The lad stood silently as Ruby greeted him.

"Good morrow, Matthew," she said, her voice cheery.

"M'lady." Matthew acknowledged, twisting his hands in his leather apron, concern and fear in his voice.

"Has something happened?" Ruby laid her hand on the young man's shoulder and followed him toward the barn.

"Father and I were taking our wares to Culver when we were ambushed by bandits in the forest on the King's Road." Matthew glanced at Crispin, then back to Ruby. "It was the same bandits who attacked us last time. Father stood his ground, but there were too many of them. They beat him and left him for dead."

"Is he...?" Ruby's voice grew hard. Crispin saw the anger simmering beneath her concerned expression.

"Nay, he survived. He is confined to his bed. Mother is tending to him."

"How did you escape unscathed?"

Matthew pulled his tunic open, exposing his lean chest where a bloodstained bandage stood out against his pale skin. "They left me a reminder as well." He covered his chest. "Then they took everything. Without them, we will be unable to afford food and supplies for the winter."

"I must speak to your father." Ruby's tone reflected her resolve.

"He has not woken yet." Matthew shook his head. "They need to pay. All of them. This is the last time they will ever steal from us, I swear it." A glimmer of cold malice overtook his eyes as he spoke.

Crispin recognized the hatred and anger bubbling up inside the boy. He had felt it many times himself, but never for the altruistic reasons Matthew did. While he wanted revenge, Crispin craved the power which came from the embracing darkness, the black part of one's soul wanting nothing more than to make a man bleed.

Ruby grasped Matthew by the shoulders. "You must remain here with your family. What would they do if you were captured, or worse, killed? 'Tis your responsibility to protect your family while your father recovers."

"But they deserve to suffer as we are."

"Aye," Ruby agreed without hesitation. "Which is why I will venture into their lair and retrieve the goods they stole."

Crispin arched a brow but said nothing. It was not as if he had not expected her softhearted nature to give in to the boy's unspoken plea for help. But he never anticipated her rash decision to voluntarily seek out the lion's den. It seemed she craved death's embrace.

"M'lady, I thank you, but I cannot ask you to face these

thieves to retrieve a few swords and pieces of armor."

"Nay." Her eyes narrowed as she spoke. "They will find much more than their pilfered goods missing when I have finished with them. Your family is not the first to have suffered at the hands of these bandits. For the last several years the king has done nothing to ensure the safety of his people."

Crispin bit his tongue to keep from speaking. The metallic tang of blood filled his mouth, and he savored the pain it brought. He would not expose himself now, of all moments. Only a fortnight ago, he heard the petitions from the peasants and merchants, begging his father to bring an end to the ceaseless attacks by several groups of bandits throughout the kingdom. While his father sympathized with them, his only solution had been to increase the guards on patrol and put a higher bounty on the bandits' heads. Had Crispin been on the throne, he would have acted with harsh, swift justice and strung up the thieves' bodies at the crossroads serving as a warning to all. Then he remembered his father's words. *All my attention has been focused on appeasing nations you have insulted with your careless and selfish behavior.* He pushed the reminder of his failings away and rested his palm on the hilt of his sword, observing Matthew and Ruby.

She laid her hand on the young man's shoulder. "Trust me in this, Matthew, all will be restored." Ruby motioned toward the stable. "Is Ginger still here?"

"Aye." Matthew held the door for her. "She is tucked in the back stall, the one hidden in the corner."

"I thank you for keeping her safe last eve."

"For you, m'lady, no request is too great."

Ruby led her horse from the stall and out into the yard behind the stables. Crispin picked up the saddle and bridle and followed her. He moved to help her, but she brushed him away with a flick of her wrist.

"I am perfectly capable of saddling my own horse." Ruby glanced at him over her shoulder, her gaze sharp and sparkling with pride.

Crispin stepped back, allowing her to do it herself. He admired the way she took control, knowing exactly how she wanted things done. A smile crept across his lips, and he wondered how she would feel if he took control and made her cry out in pleasure. Made her beg for more.

"M'lord."

Crispin turned to see the youth had saddled another horse and offered him the reins. The dappled gelding was well-built and handsome. "His name is Ghost, m'lord."

Crispin stroked the horse's velvet muzzle and took the reins. He nodded to Matthew as he moved to mount. He swung up into the saddle. Matthew adjusted the girth, making sure it was secure and the stirrups set to the proper length. When he stepped back, Crispin nudged the horse forward, coming alongside Ruby, who sat on her mare with a smirk on her lips. He wanted to steal it from her with a sound kiss.

"We shall return, Matthew. Keep watch for us." Ruby reined her horse around and headed into the forest.

With a nod to Matthew, Crispin followed her, urging Ghost to catch up. They rode side-by-side for a moment before she spoke.

"You could have thanked him, you know." Her attention remained focused on the trail before them. "It would do you no harm to learn some manners. Your parents must have been remiss in teaching you proper etiquette."

Crispin swallowed a harsh retort. *If she only knew.* "My parents did not neglect to teach me manners. I choose to willfully ignore them. Pleasantries are a sign of respect. In my opinion, respect must be earned, not handed out like sweetmeats to children."

"Where do you hail from?"

"The capital city of Culver." He watched her from the corner of his eye. "My father conducts most of his business inside the castle."

"So your family is on pleasant terms with the king and queen?"

"Aye." He shifted his gaze ahead, scanning the horizon through the trees. "They are part of the royal court."

"Do you not include yourself among their ranks?" Her

question reflected curiosity and a tinge of bitterness.

"I did until my father decided I would learn more outside the city than I would wasting away at court." He cleared his throat, hoping she believed his half-truths. Crispin danced perilously close to the truth, but he knew if he offered anything less, she would never believe him. His clothes, his demeanor, his weapons all spoke of his status. It was as close to a confession as he dared. The whole truth would give her incentive to plunge her dagger through his royal heart.

"Do you know the prince?" Ruby's inquiry held only contempt and hatred.

Crispin glanced at her. "We are acquainted."

She nodded, her lips pressed into a thin line. Her hand tightened on the reins a fraction. Ruby disliked the prince immensely—she had said as much before—but why? What had he done, besides enjoy the benefits of his position and a few whores, have a bit of fun, and cause a little mischief? It was his prerogative as royalty, was it not?

Before he could stop himself, Crispin replied, "You have said before the prince should be put down like a wild dog." She nodded. "What makes you loathe him with such a passion?"

"He shows no reverence for the lives of his people, for the work they do to keep this kingdom thriving. He whores and gambles, wreaks havoc on the lives of those he encounters, and shows no remorse for his actions. He disregards consequences as beneath him and considers himself to be above reproach, thereby believing he is immune to the harsh realities of life."

"You have seen the evidence of this first hand and assign yourself his judge and executioner?" He bristled at her callous assessment of him.

"I have heard the tales from those who have encountered him at his finest." Her sarcastic contempt held firm. "You know him. Can you honestly confirm these accusations are false?"

Crispin dared not incur her wrath. "Nay, he is as you say," he replied slowly, "but such is the fault of most noblemen, including myself. We indulge in things we should not, and because of our rank, someone must pay the price for our hedonism. 'Tis the way of the world."

Ruby glared at him. "You defend him because you are his friend?"

"Nay, I defend no one but myself."

"You are a selfish, conceited bastard, did you know that? You are no better than he is." Ruby kicked her horse into a canter, leaving him behind.

She had a point, the same valid point his parents offered when they threw him out of the castle and into the night without any form of assistance. He was spoiled, indulged and coddled from birth. No amount of depravity, hedonism, or mischief alleviated the darkness in his soul.

Perhaps the crown would be his salvation, a way to finally reign in control of his desires. Crispin would regain his place in court, but until then, biding his time with Ruby would suffice to quell the dissent in his soul.

Although he would never admit it to her, she had shown him things about himself that made him question the direction of his future as the ruler of Meradin. He nudged Ghost into a canter, following Ruby's lead. There had to be a way to convince his father he had indeed seen the errors of his ways and ensure his inheritance. If he could convince Ruby of his change of heart, perhaps he could also instill the same confidence in his parents. He grinned as he caught up with her, emboldened by the challenge awaiting him.

Chapter Eight

They rode until the sun began to drop beyond the horizon. Ruby stole glances at Tristan as they rode deeper into the forest. She noticed the tension in his shoulders and his fierce grip on the reins. The closer they came to Culver, the more anxious he became.

"Are you concerned someone will recognize you?" she asked, noting the way he twisted the rein in his left hand when she spoke.

He met her gaze, his expression unreadable. Even with his hood drawn up, shielding most of his face, she saw the cold detachment. Tristan was an intimidating, mysterious man. She knew from the moment she saved his life in front of the whorehouse he was a nobleman. But his insistence to keep any details of his prior life secreted away left her with an unease she could not shake.

A shiver racked her body, and she pushed the thoughts away. Nobility never sat well with her. Even her adoptive family kept her safely out of their influence, living in the forests, scavenging and foraging. They ensured she could care for herself. Until some bandits murdered her adopted father, Guy. That day, she swore to avenge her family and never put her trust in anyone. Especially those who held power or influence. She glanced at Tristan again. He sat tall in the saddle, his jaw set as he stared ahead.

Her hand guided the reins against the horse's neck, leading her to the right into a dark copse of trees. She assumed he would follow. Having Tristan with her for this task would prove much simpler. Although Ruby did not trust him, she was reasonably certain he would aid her in this fight.

They climbed a small hill with scattered brush and trees at the top. She had been there before, earlier in the spring. The cave was well hidden and surrounded by a marsh and patches of quicksand. One false step could be treacherous. They could easily wait at the top of the hill for the men to leave before darkness settled.

Ruby had been watching them for several moons, but tonight felt different. At a distance, she could pick the bandits off, but as soon as she fired the first shot, they would know her location. Her best course of action would be to wait until they left the cave and then take back the loot they had stolen from the blacksmith and any other treasure the thieves might be hoarding.

"Whoa." Ruby brought her horse to a stop beside a large pine and slid from the saddle. She tied the mare to the tree, then without a sound, she crept up to the crest of the hill. A sheer drop on this side of the hill created a perfect horseshoe-shaped valley at the base. The cave lay nestled into the hillside with the swamp surrounding it. She could barely make out the tracks leading to the mouth of the cave.

Tristan came beside her and glanced down at the scene below. She lay on her stomach, watching for signs of movement near the cave. He sat next to a tree and leaned against the trunk. All he had to do was glance to the left and he could see down into the valley. She studied him for a long moment. His disheveled hair gave him a roguish appearance accentuated by the scruff on his face making him look more rugged. A few more days of living in the wild and he might finally blend in with the peasants.

"You have a plan I assume." He glanced at her. His blue eyes pierced hers. "Or are we waiting for a royal invitation?"

"You sure you are not the king's fool?" She cocked her head as she rose and moved to sit next to him at the base of the large oak tree. It was wide enough to block both of them from being seen from anyone in the valley.

"I very well may be." His voice flowed over her. They were so close. Too close. The heat of him warmed her through even though they never touched.

Ruby licked her lips. Her body ached to be near him. She despised the war raging inside her. Her mind commanded she keep her distance, but her body recalled the bliss from that morning, waking in his arms, to his touch. She shivered at the desire pouring through her like the warmth from a drought of mead. What if she surrendered to him? Would it truly be the end of her to concede to the pleasure of his touch? She jerked her thoughts away from traveling down such a dangerous path. No matter if he helped her with the bandits, he was still the last man she would give herself to willingly.

"So this plan of yours." His gaze fixed on her. "Care to share the details with me?"

She swallowed, shaking the distracting thoughts from her mind. "Each evening they leave before dark. They prefer to hunt at night."

"As do I." Tristan bared his teeth in a wicked smile.

Pure lust shot through her. How could she want a man so desperately when she knew exactly what he was? A rogue. A selfish, hubris-laden son of a noble! She stomped on the desire screaming inside of her. It whimpered in response. She cleared her throat. "Once they leave, we shall raid the cave and retrieve everything they have stolen."

"What if they return?"

"Then we shall kill them."

His brow shot up. "You never cease to surprise me, my lady. I did not take you for someone who thirsts for bloodshed."

"You know nothing of me."

"'Tis true," he agreed, his voice pensive.

"These vermin have been a menace to the people for far too long, and the king's men have done nothing to halt their attacks. They must be dealt with."

"You believe you are up to the task then?" Tristan watched her closely. "Tell me, lovely Ruby, how many men have you killed?"

For a moment, she stared at him, distracted by his compliment, then struck by his question. "Too many." She fingered the bow at her side.

"I do not mean with an arrow at a distance." He leaned closer, his gaze riveted to hers, his blue eyes piercing her own.

Her heart fluttered and pounded. He continued, his voice low, his words deliberate. "I mean, have you ever plunged your blade into their chest, felt the grind of bone against the blade, and watched the life drain from their eyes?"

Ruby opened her mouth to answer but snapped it closed. The truth was, she had never killed a man thus, but she could not bring herself to confess it. She was not proud of the fact she had killed at all, but something in his expression made her long to earn his approval. But such a desire was ridiculous. Why should she care what a pompous noble's son thought of her? She pressed her lips together.

"'Tis as I thought." The corners of his mouth twisted up.

"Does it matter?" she snapped.

"It does. What will you do if one of your rescues goes awry and one of the bandits has you pinned, prepared to rape you or worse? Your bow cannot save you. Will you let him take you any way he wishes and then steal your last breath with agony and pain?"

She stared at him, her jaw clenched tight. "I shall defend myself as necessary."

"Even if it means slitting his throat?"

"Aye."

His eyes narrowed. "I do not believe you. I could take a blade to your throat right now, and you would let me live."

Ruby slapped him, the crack of her palm against his cheek louder than she anticipated. His smile widened, his eyes shining with suppressed laughter as they focused on her. She raised her hand to strike him again, and his grip encircled her wrist firmly.

Within a breath, he straddled her thighs, his hands around both wrists, pinning her against the tree. The bark dug into the flesh, pinching against the braces on her forearms. Ruby jerked against his hold, trying to free herself. His grip tightened.

"Get off of me," she ground out between her teeth.

"I told you." He leaned closer, his breath whispering across her cheek. "You could not take me."

"Let me at my dagger and I shall prove it." Ruby met his gaze. Her mind raged, screaming at the imminent danger. But her body betrayed her, arching toward him, her breasts brushing against his tunic.

"Not today." His lips claimed hers.

The kiss shot directly to her head. Pleasure surged through her, mingling with her anger, and indecision swirled through her mind like a whirlpool. The more she fought him, the harder he leaned against her, sliding his body along hers creating a delicious heat between them. Sparks of desire ignited inside of her. Even though she did not want him, she craved what he offered. A hunger she did not even recognize had awakened.

The pressure of his kiss shifted as he tasted the seam of her lips. Ruby opened her mouth in a gasp of surprise, and he took advantage, slipping his tongue into its moist warmth. She thrashed against him, indignant at his actions. A slow heat unfurled in her belly, reaching up and out, fogging her thoughts, stealing her will to fight him. His tongue slid against hers, and she moaned against his mouth, her resolve crumbling to ash. She met his passion, tasting him for herself, the flavor of mead and temptation drawing her deeper. His grip on her loosened as she arched against him, wanting more contact.

He nipped her lower lip between his teeth and drew it into his mouth. She groaned as he released her hands and cupped her face between his to kiss her again, deeply. Ruby clutched at his shoulders, digging her fingernails into his cloak.

"Such fire," he whispered against her lips. "You burn for me, do you not?" He slipped his fingers over her throat, trailing down to the string at the top of her tunic. With one hand, he loosened the knot and pulled the material back, exposing her chest and the soft curve of her breast. His eyes held hers. Her breath came in rapid pants as his touch drifted lower. He was right; she was on fire.

"Shall we let it consume us?"

Ruby nodded, mesmerized by the dark promise in his eyes. His fingertips brushed over her nipple, sending a bolt of pleasure like lightning through her body. She cried out, and he covered her mouth with his, swallowing it with a passionate kiss. His palm cradled her breast as his thumb brushed back and forth over her nipple. She slid her hands into his hair, tangling her fingers in the mass of riotous waves.

He moaned, almost a growl, as he kissed her and ground his hips against hers. Tristan pinched her nipple, causing her to squeal in protest at the unexpected assault, but the kiss never ceased. It went on and on, even as the pleasure pain of his ministrations faded and, at the same time, they made her ache for more.

A shout from the valley below made her still beneath him. Tristan kissed her once more and slowly pulled away, his breathing rapid. He leaned his head against hers. The echo of men talking filtered up the valley to where they hid. The reality of the situation came rushing back to her; where they were and what they were supposed to be doing. The chilling realization sobered her.

"Get off of me," Ruby growled, trying to sound harsh, but the tremor in her voice betrayed her, as did her body, still trembling with need.

Tristan took her chin in his hand. "Do not think for a moment *that* was enough to quench my thirst. I will have you, body and soul, before this is over." The sincerity in his eyes thrilled and terrified her. His cock pressed against her thigh. A few moments more of his seduction and she would have given him what he wanted.

"Never." The word sounded weak, even to her ears. Tristan was a hunter, a predator to his core; it reflected in every decision he made. He would never relent in his quest, and try as she might, Ruby could not deny the attraction simmering between them.

He offered a lopsided smile as he climbed off of her lap and shifted to glance down into the valley. Ruby struggled to her feet, brushing the dirt from her leggings. She heard the thundering of the horses leaving through the valley entrance.

"They have gone." He turned back to her.

Ruby nodded, picking up her bow and quiver from the ground. She saw him step closer and turned her back to him. His lips brushed against her ear as he leaned against her back. She nearly swayed against him but stopped herself.

"Once we are away from here, I will strip you bare and taste every inch of you. I long to know if your cunt tastes as good as your sweet mouth." He kissed her neck below her earlobe, and she suppressed a shiver. He was sin incarnate. The devil sent to tempt her.

Ruby cleared her throat and turned to face him. "Are you quite finished? We have a quest to complete." With those parting words, she walked away, making her way down to the cave nestled in the valley below. Ruby sensed he followed, but she knew something even more unnerving. If he kissed her in such a manner again, she would let him do so much more, and she would be lost forever.

Chapter Nine

As they wove their way down the hillside, Crispin regarded her carefully and rubbed a hand over his grizzled chin. He wanted her; there was no longer any doubt in his mind. After finally tasting her, he wanted to explore her hidden curves with his tongue and stake his claim. Her body responded to his touch, his kiss. But many of the women he bedded in the past responded in much the same manner. Would he tire of her as quickly once he fucked her?

They crept closer to the cave, relying on silence and caution. She lit a torch in the small pit the bandits abandoned, which glowed with the embers of a dying fire. Ruby held the light aloft and motioned for him to follow her into the cave. He nodded, part of him unsure why he would risk his neck for some blacksmith and his family. Putting someone's needs ahead of himself was not something he was used to, but it was not necessarily a bad thing according to his father. He pushed the thoughts away, attempting to suppress any ideas of changing his nature. A man never truly changed. Those souls touched by darkness carried it until their dying breath.

"Here." Her voice drifted from the back of the cave. "I found the entrance."

Crispin crossed to where she gathered the stolen gear into large sacks. He opened one and stowed weapons and armor in it. Out of the corner of his eye, he watched her. Her auburn hair fell from its knot and trailed over her shoulder. His cock hardened at the thought of wrapping it around his fist and pulling her head back, exposing her slender throat. He shook his head. Thoughts of them together would serve only as a distraction. The thrill of being an outlaw alongside her proved intoxicating. He could almost envision himself indulging in such a profession for the long term, at least until his father learned the error of his ways and begged him to return home.

Crispin licked his lips. That was where the true power lay, sitting on the throne. His father had not been wrong in his assessment. Crispin needed to walk among the common folk, see the day-to-day activities of his people while living as one of them. It had been humbling and enlightening, not that he would ever admit it to his parents or any other living creature. He could use everything he had seen and experienced to his advantage in an effort to show his father he had taken his punishment to heart. Allowing himself a small smirk, he continued packing the valuables into the satchels. A noise from the mouth of the cave brought him to a halt.

"Shit." He snatched the torch from her hand and shoved it into the dirt.

"What are you...?" Ruby quieted as he stepped closer, pressing her against the wall and into the shadows.

"They have returned," he whispered against her ear. Her scent, the melding of her body to his, nearly made him groan. "Take your dagger in hand, be ready for when they enter. When I give the signal, attack. Nod if you understand me."

Ruby nodded, her breath brushing the hair below his ear. Had they been anywhere but here, he would take her. Crispin refocused his attention to the blood pounding in his veins, channeling the energy surging through him into the fight he knew was inevitable.

"Where did you leave it, you simpering fool?"

"What did he forget this time?"

The bandits' conversation echoed off the cavern walls. Crispin palmed the dagger, readying it in his grasp. The voices came closer as a man carrying a torch entered the cave followed by two more men. They had seen at least a half dozen leave, which meant three remained outside. The man holding the torch approached where Crispin and Ruby stood hidden in a gap along the cavern wall. As soon as he was within arm's reach, Crispin slipped his hand around the man's throat. Surprise caused him to drop the torch.

"Now," he shouted to Ruby as the other two men raced to aid the one in his grasp. Without a moment's hesitation, Crispin thrust his dagger up into the man's heart, twisted the blade, and then ripped it out. Ruby jumped onto one of the other men, knocking him to the ground. The third man charged Crispin, slamming them both into the wall. Crispin struggled for a moment then plunged the dagger into the assailant's side repeatedly until the man dropped to his knees.

A glance at Ruby showed her staring down at the man lying dead at her feet. Crispin met her gaze. She snatched the torch from the ground when they heard the other men at the mouth of the cavern.

"What goes on here?" one of them called.

"Just taking back what you stole," Ruby yelled, tossing her hair back. "You will pay for your crimes, you sniveling whoremongers."

Three men approached, their attention focused on Ruby. One of them grinned, his mouth as vacant as his stare. "Well, well, look what we have here. The Lady of the Forest, notorious outlaw. I thought we were on the same side."

"We may both be wanted by the Crown, but I will never be like you." She bared her teeth in a sinister smile. Crispin's heart twisted with a longing he could not describe. He watched the men approach and gripped his dagger tighter in his fist.

"Then we will have to take care of you, aye, boys?" The man lunged at Ruby, who returned the attack with equal fervor. The other two charged for Crispin.

Dodging the blow from one man, Crispin ducked to the right as the other man collided with him, knocking the dagger from his hand. The second man came up behind him and wrapped his arm around Crispin's throat. He brought his arm up, slamming his fist into the man's face. The assailant released him in a worthless attempt to staunch the blood pouring from his nose and mouth. Without a pause, Crispin snatched his dagger from where it glinted on the floor and spun around, catching the second man in the stomach with the blade and slicing his abdomen open. Crispin finished them off by driving the dagger up into the back of the first man's skull. He stepped over the bodies, searching for Ruby.

The bandit pinned her against the wall, his hand wrapped around her throat. She gasped, one hand tugging at the man's wrist. Crispin paused halfway to her aid when her other hand came up, drawing a dagger across the man's throat. He wheezed as he released her, stumbling back and clutching his throat. Blood spurted from the wound, coating Ruby's face and garments. When he finally dropped to the ground, she stood victorious, weapon in hand and drenched in his blood.

Crispin rushed to her side. "Are you injured, Ruby?"

"Nay," she replied, her voice hoarse but steady. She turned to him and wiped her face with her sleeve. "Are they all dead?"

He took careful measure of her. She was neither in a panic nor a rage. Her voice remained steady and calm as if he had merely inquired about the weather. He laid his hand on her shoulder, unsure of what to say. She was strong, much stronger than he once assumed.

"Come, let us gather up the goods and the horses. There is no reason to linger." With a slight tilt of her lips, she pushed past him and continued collecting anything of value.

They worked together, silently, until everything was loaded onto the bandits' horses. His mind spun with questions. Who was this woman and what had happened in her past to make her the complicated, mysterious Lady of the Forest? She defended the weak and the poor, the hardworking peasants and their families, the unfortunates and the outcasts, but, without a moment's hesitation, she took a blade to any man who broke her code. Ruby was a treasure indeed, an enigmatic gem, and her story must be tragic to make her both equally dangerous and lovely. Walking away would be the hardest thing he would ever have to do. But before this adventure was over, her secrets would belong to him...all of them.

Crispin led the horses as they returned to their mounts on the hillside. "Do you think we will return to the smithy before dawn?"

Ruby swung into the saddle. "Aye, we still have plenty of darkness before the sun betrays us."

He strung the horses together and led them behind his

gelding. Ghost served him well, a steady and reliable horse. He would speak to Matthew about a long-term arrangement. Such a horse would make a fine mount when he returned to the castle.

They wove through the trees, navigating their way back to the smithy in silence, and all the while, Crispin formulated a plan to finish what he and Ruby had started beneath the tree on the hill.

Chapter Ten

The blacksmith's home sat over the hill and down by the stream on the outskirts of the small village where Ruby found Tristan the day before. They led six horses strung behind them laden with heavy bags, so progress was slow, but at least the extra bounty would help Matthew's family recoup any coin they might lose while his father recovered.

Ruby glanced over her shoulder at Tristan, swearing his attention remained fixed on her as they rode. When he met her gaze, she turned away. He was dangerous in so many ways. If she had any sense, she would cut all ties, send him on his way, and never speak of him again. The possibility of him betraying her remained. He could easily take her captive and turn her in for the reward, or worse, he could discover the truth of her past, then all would be lost. Those who had attempted to kill her before would pay handsomely for the opportunity to finish their quest.

She wiped her hand across her brow. The blood had dried, making her skin itch. She felt no remorse for what she had done. Her actions were justified, at least in her mind, by their nefarious intentions. One detail haunted her, if only slightly. When she drove her blade deep into her assailant, she saw the life flow from his body into a pool at his feet and the vacant stare claim his frenzied eyes.

It had been her life or his, and she did what was required in order to survive. There were no tears, no thoughts of remorse over the decision or his death. She remembered Tristan's accusation of not having killed a man thus. Now, his words took root in her soul for she learned of their weight on her conscience. A glimmer of darkness threatened to overtake her. Ruby shook her head. *No regrets tonight, save one.*

As they rounded the last bend, the lanterns outside the

blacksmith's forge came into view. The kiss she and Tristan had shared lingered in the back of her mind. She wondered what would have happened had they not been forced to break apart. Tristan was hiding something; she knew that much. He would never tell her if she asked directly, but perhaps she could convince him to divulge his secrets in the right setting. As they approached the house, Matthew met them in the yard.

"You have returned." Matthew took her horse's reins as she dismounted.

"Aye, and I have recovered your items." She gave him a firm pat on the shoulder. "We shall unload the bags and take care of the horses."

"As you wish, my lady." Matthew backed away. "Allow me to get you something to eat, and I shall prepare a bath for you as well if you would like."

"That sounds wonderful. I thank you." Ruby turned to see Tristan watching her from atop his horse. He sat casually leaned over the pommel of the saddle, his expression unreadable. She glanced away. "We should get these horses inside."

Tristan dismounted, and without a word, he helped her unload all the sacks and place them in the smithy's storage room. She led their mounts into the barn, while Tristan led the remaining horses to a pasture behind the house.

"What think you, Ginger?" Ruby stroked her horse's muzzle. "Should I trust him?" The horse gave a soft nicker as she loosened the saddle and slipped it from the mare's back. She placed it with the other tack and returned to find Tristan working with Ghost, who was tethered next to Ginger.

His gaze met hers over the gelding's back. The corner of his lip tilted up in a lopsided, careless smile. Her heart twisted and jumped at the innocent action. She wanted more than to kiss him again. What in heaven's name was she thinking? They had known each other for less than a sennight. She successfully defended herself against his advances a handful of times already. Why would she throw herself into his arms so easily? Ruby heard tales of men who returned from battle, scarred and weary, wanting to lose themselves in the arms of a woman, at least for a short time.

Was this similar? A culmination of the day's events making her want to quench the fire burning in her blood?

"Who were you before?" His question startled her.

"Does it matter?" Ruby swallowed and hid behind Ginger, brushing the horse with slow, deliberate strokes. Part of her wanted to tell him, to trust him, but she could not. Not when she knew he was not being completely honest with her. He must have done something terrible to be cast from his family. Before she could bare her soul to him, she had to know.

"It does not matter, but I would still like to know." His voice drifted over her like a ribbon of silk, lulling her into a false sense of security. Ruby recognized she was being played for a fool. She decided to play along and allow him to believe she was clay in his hands, willing to be molded.

"I was a lady once, from a good family." She offered him part of the truth. "They were taken from me, and now I do what I must to survive."

"Have you no other family?"

"Nay. When my parents died, who I was died with them."

"Who were they?" He stood closer now, still brushing the gelding, but his attention centered on her.

"They were good, God-fearing people who did not deserve the fate which befell them." She winced at the harsh tone of her voice. Perhaps she should stop, the information provided should quench his thirst. His hands came to rest on her shoulders.

"You did not deserve your fate, either, Ruby." He spun her around and tilted her chin up with his fingertips, forcing her to meet his piercing gaze. She wanted to drown in those deep blue pools. Tristan asked too much of her.

"Come now, you think I shall fall into your arms so easily?" She jerked from his grasp and stepped away. Taking the horse's bridle, she led Ginger to an empty stall in the back of the barn.

Tristan put Ghost into the neighboring stall and took a step toward her, but a voice from the doorway stilled them both.

"Your bath is ready, my lady." Matthew approached with a pile of clothes, some drying cloths, and a jar of soap. "'Tis the least I could do to repay you for all you have done for us."

Ruby smiled at the boy. He had been so thoughtful, so gracious to offer her this much in return for what she believed to be her duty. "I thank you, Matthew."

"I shall show you to your bath." He led her from the barn. A passing glance at Tristan told her he was far from finished with her. Ghost nudged him and snorted. He stroked the horse's pale muzzle as if communicating with the animal. His gaze followed her as she walked out of the stable and into the night.

A single lantern hung from a hook beside the house. The bathtub sat enclosed by a makeshift curtain, blocking it from view. The steam rose from the water, curling in invitation.

"This is wonderful."

"I would have set it up in the house, but my Pa..."

"I understand. This is perfectly fine. Gramercy, Matthew." He left her, and she closed the curtain behind her.

Ruby removed her ruined clothing and tossed it on a pile next to the wooden tub. She stepped into the scalding water, relishing the heat. As she sank into the water, it soothed all the aches she had not even realized she possessed. She dipped below the surface, rinsing the blood from her face and body before washing with a dollop of the soap from a small crock. It smelled of rosemary and lavender. She scrubbed the dried blood from her hair, her face, her arms, and hands. Closing her eyes, Ruby leaned her head back against the tub and let the tension fade away, if only for a stolen moment of peace.

Chapter Eleven

After quickly splashing his face and wiping the blood away with some warm water the boy provided, Crispin leaned against the roughhewn fence behind the stable. He spied the little space where Matthew prepared Ruby's bath. The curtains were backlit by the lantern, and from this angle, he saw everything with perfect clarity. He watched as she stripped off her tunic and toss it to the ground. Then she toed off her boots and shimmied out of her leggings, adding them to the pile. Her silhouette left little to the imagination. Crispin groaned, hard and aching for her. Seeing her thus only intensified the feeling tenfold.

She stepped into the bath. When her sigh of delight echoed in the darkness, it proved too much for him to endure. Crispin pushed away from the fence, taking silent, purposeful steps toward her little oasis. The sound of the water sloshing in the wooden tub and splashing over her head as she rinsed the soap from her hair grew louder with each step. He paused outside the little makeshift curtain. Her soft sighs of contentment made his cock twitch. He watched her shadow dance as she bathed, her hands gliding over her body. His hands clenched into fists as he fought the desire raging through him.

Ruby settled her head back against the tub, submerging her body beneath the water. The throaty moan she released shattered what remained of his reserve. He pulled the curtain aside and stepped into her tiny sanctuary.

Her head snapped up in surprise, her hands covering her chest instinctively. "What are you doing? Get out!" She looked delicious, completely drenched, the water running in rivulets down her pale skin. He wanted to trace each trail with his tongue.

"You and I have unfinished business, my lady." He wrapped his hands around her wrists and pulled her from the tub. Her breasts fell free when he did so, and his blood heated at the sight of them. Slightly fuller than he had expected, they complimented her curves perfectly. Her rosy nipples perked at the kiss of the cool night air. He held her wrists tight as she tried to jerk free. His cock strained against his breeches, begging for release.

"You would rape me to get what you desire?" She sneered at him, tugging against his firm grip. "You are no better than the bastard I killed in that cave."

Crispin tsked. "I never take what is not freely given." He pulled her close, pressing her naked body against him, and pinned her wrists at her sides. Defiance shone in her eyes. "Tell me you do not want what I offer. A night of pleasure the likes of which you have never experienced."

"'Tis not saying much," she replied with a half-choked laugh.

"Untouched?" His interest doubled. "You are a wealth of surprises."

"Release me, Tristan." Her words were direct, but he heard the tremor in her voice.

"Your lip trembles." He brushed his fingertip across the seam of her mouth. "Do I frighten you? Or does the thought of me claiming you make you shiver in anticipation?"

Her eyes narrowed. "'Tis the cold night air, you calf-brained fool."

"Then allow me to remedy our situation." He dropped her wrists and hoisted her over his shoulder.

"Put me down this instant!" She beat her fists against his back. Crispin pinned her legs with one arm and slapped her bare arse with his free hand. She yelped and struggled harder against him, making him tighten his grip to keep her from falling. Crispin crossed the yard with determined strides, entered the barn, and headed directly for the empty stall where he had seen Matthew place a pile of linens for them to spend the night. Several of the blankets lay spread over a fresh pile of hay.

Ignoring her protests, Crispin slid her down from his shoulder. His hands rested on her hips, holding her still.

"How dare you!" Ruby struck him.

Crispin's cheek stung from the blow, but he remained steadfast, meeting her gaze. Her eyes sparkled with fury and a familiar heat. Long ropes of her auburn hair hung in wet hanks against her pale skin, the water trailing over her breasts and down her stomach. Ruby stood before him, exposed and furious, and yet he had never wanted a woman more than he did at that moment. He cocked his head and admired her glorious indignance, his hands steady on her hips.

"Release. Me." Ruby enunciated each word, but she made no effort to move as if she could sense the danger in her position if she chose to do so. Her intelligence served her well.

"Or what?" He bared his teeth in a wicked smile. "You will kill me? You have no weapon; you are at my mercy."

"If you dare defy my wishes, then I will make you pay with blood." She met his grin with one of her own. Oh, how he wanted her.

"Oh, my darling, you may wound me a little, but you will never kill me. Know this...any pain you inflict, any blood of mine you spill, will only make my victory over you that much sweeter in the end." He slid one hand down to grasp her arse as he brought the other up, threading his fingers in the wet hair at the base of her neck. "I can see the fire in your eyes, the heat and passion burning in their depths. Can you deny this pull between us?"

Her stare could have frozen a hot spring. "You know nothing of my desires."

Crispin slid his hands over her waist until his thumbs stroked the curve of her breast. She drew her lower lip between her teeth but said nothing.

"Come now, the kiss we shared earlier this evening, you cannot deny you want to feel these delights again." His thumb grazed the tip of her nipple. It tightened at his touch, puckering to a tiny bud aching for attention. He longed to take it in his mouth.

Ruby gasped, swaying against him. Her expression softened a little as he continued his slow exploration with his fingertips.

He traced where her damp hair left a trail of water along her collarbone, over her shoulder. She never blinked, but her body betrayed her. Her skin quivered beneath his touch, the heat from her body creating tension between them. He slid his hand into her hair, his fingers delving into her wet tresses, gripping the back of her head. She tensed for a heartbeat, and he grinned before claiming her mouth in a ravenous kiss.

He braced himself for her retaliation, perhaps a strike, a bite, something, but the anticipated protest never came. Crispin tasted her lips, teasing them with his tongue, willing to explore every part of her with his mouth. She opened, allowing him entrance, and his mind whooped in triumph. He held her head with one hand, the other slipping down to cup her arse again. She gasped against his mouth as he slid his fingertip along the sweet little crease where her backside met her long legs.

Her hands drifted to his waist, unfastening his belt, then unbuttoning his doublet. She pushed the material from his shoulders without breaking the kiss. It slid to a heap on the floor. He pulled the tunic over his head, bringing a mewl of disappointment from Ruby at the loss of contact. Dropping the tunic, he buried both his hands in her hair and pulled her against him.

Fuck. He swore as her breasts pressed hot against his chest. She pushed his hose down over his hips, letting his cock spring free. He wiggled out of the offending clothes and kicked them away. Her hand wrapped around his cock, her touch bold and demanding.

"This is not how a virgin behaves." He groaned when she stroked him, her talented fingers driving him wild with lust.

Ruby's lips turned up in a mischievous grin. She stepped forward, moving him back, one pace at a time, until he hit the wall. She pinned him there, her hand gripping his cock. Her knee slid between his, pressing her cunt against his leg.

Whatever reservations she held before must have slipped out the door. The woman before him burned with desire. Her touch singed him. He stroked her jaw with his thumb.

"You have a determined look about you, my lady," he

murmured. "What wicked intentions have you in regards to my person?"

He dropped his hands to her waist as she leaned close, her breath trailing over his neck as she moved. Her nipples grazed against his chest, making him even harder. The pressure on his cock increased as she firmly stroked him.

"I am no innocent. I have been the eyes and ears of these woods for years. Do you think I have not seen a tryst behind the tavern or a whore being taken as I watch through the window of the brothel?" Her words caressed his ear.

"Temptress. So you know what power you wield over me." The minx possessed wicked secrets. The thought made him ache to bury himself inside her. He would make her cry out beneath him and spill her secrets with each panted gasp. Crispin lifted her by the waist. She released her grip and grasped his shoulders, letting his cock nestle between the warm junction of her thighs.

With two strides, he laid her down on the blanket and covered her body with his own. Her hands trailed over his shoulders and arms, nails raking against his skin. The wet strands of hair fanned beneath her head. She glowed; a lovely, flush of rose suffused her skin.

Crispin kissed her, hard and punishing. He nipped her lower lip, pulling it between his teeth. She arched against him when he palmed her breasts and squeezed, pinching her nipples between his fingers.

Ruby gasped, breaking the kiss. He trailed his tongue over her skin. She buried her hands in his hair when he took a nipple in her mouth and suckled. "Oh, God." Her grip tightened, pulling his hair.

He trailed each kiss lower, over the smooth curve of her stomach. Crispin glanced up to admire her amber eyes turned dark, mouth parted in wonder. Her body trembled beneath him, and a rush of power surged through him. He nudged her thighs apart, baring her, and she whimpered when he blew on her hot center. Her delicate pink folds glistened.

"You are wet." He glanced up at her again. "Allow me to quench my thirst on your sweet nectar." Before she could protest, he drew his tongue across her swollen lips. She cried out at his touch, but he tightened his grip, holding her firmly beneath him as he devoured her. Her flavor burst on his tongue. He teased the tiny pearl hidden in her folds, and she arched against his mouth, her hands tangled in his hair.

"I...I...just..." She stuttered, unable to find the right words. He continued his attentions, redoubling his effort with every moan. He kissed the inside of her thighs, then crawled up the length of her body and kissed her mouth again.

Ruby squirmed, flushed and panting, her eyes wide. She rested her hands on his shoulders, toying with the curls lying against his neck. She licked her lips, leaving them moist and glistening.

"When I take you in my mouth—" He brushed his fingers over her damp skin. "Suckling on your sweet center, I adore how you arch against me, wordlessly begging for more. I should slip my fingers inside your sweet cunt and make you come apart in my arms, screaming and writhing beneath me." He cupped her sex, sliding his fingers between the slick folds, dipping a finger inside of her tight heat. "Only after will I relent and take you completely."

"Wait." Ruby's plea stopped him. He met her gaze, his hand caressing her intimately. "Allow me." She pushed her palms flat against his chest.

Crispin released her and stood, frustrated at the loss of contact. When she pushed him down and straddled his lap, he hesitated for a moment and settled his hands on her hips. She leaned down and kissed him, dispelling whatever doubts lingered in his brain. He preferred to be in control, but her bold insistence surprised him. Not that it mattered; he could have her on her back beneath him within seconds if he truly wished it. His cock brushed against her damp curls, and he groaned.

"I do not believe you are as pure as you claim." He narrowed his gaze at the grind of her hips against his.

"My life depends on being aware of my surroundings." Her hands closed over his and drew them up from her hips to cup her breasts. As he savored their weight in his hands, she arched back, dropping her hands to her sides.

He reached between them, placing his cock at her entrance, teasing her. Her head snapped up, their eyes locking. She took him slowly. He held his breath as he slid inside her wet heat. Her body trembled as he thrust further into her.

Ruby bit her lip as a cry ripped from her throat, and her whole body tensed. Crispin moved his hips in a slow circle, enough to feel her tighten around his cock. She collapsed against his chest, her fingernails biting into his arms.

"Close your eyes." Her whispered request made him pause.

"Why?"

"I beg of you."

The sound of her plea, hoarse and broken, made him relent. Crispin closed his eyes. The soft slide of her fingers teased his flesh as she grabbed his wrists and brought them together. Crispin's body twitched in anticipation. His eyes flew open at the unrelenting tug of leather tightening around them.

"Ruby, what in the devil's name are you about?" He jerked his hands, but the knot tightened enough to prevent him from pulling free. He hummed with anger enhanced by a fleeting surge of fear. How dare she trick him, let alone bind him. His mind raged, *do not surrender*, but his cock hardened in response to her slippery ministrations. Where she was leading him, he did not know nor did he care to discover the destination in such a manner. "Release me, woman, or suffer the consequences."

Chapter Twelve

Ignoring him, Ruby tied the loose ends of the leather to a post holding the feed trough. He caught her nipple in his mouth and tugged. She yelped but ensured the knot was tight before turning her attention back to him. She pressed her palms against his heaving chest. He wore an expression of murderous retribution.

"You do not enjoy being rendered helpless, do you?" She raked her fingernails over his torso. His cock pulsed inside her. It had hurt at first, but only for a moment, the pain ebbed as she seized control. His blue eyes flashed with lust and anger. "You have never stopped to consider anyone but yourself. 'Tis time you learned a harsh lesson." Ruby bent down, taking his nipple between her teeth and rolling it.

Tristan released a guttural noise from somewhere deep inside of him. "You have no idea who you are toying with."

"I know exactly who you are." She grinned and rotated her hips. "A spoiled, self-indulged noble with no respect for a hard day's work and the necessities of life."

His breath hitched as she moved, lust glazing his eyes again. He tipped his head back, his mouth falling open. "Fuck's sake, woman, you have no right."

"Oh, I have every right." She savored the sensations building inside of her. "You wanted me. You can have me, but it will be under my conditions." As she rode him, Ruby found a rhythm that brought the pleasure surging to the surface. He filled her perfectly, and she reveled in her moment of triumph. A tight heat coiled in the pit of her stomach as she ground herself against him.

Tristan bucked his hips, struggling and pulling against the leather bonds holding his hands together. Ferocity overtook his gaze, a torrent of lust raging in the depths of his eyes. His fury empowered her.

She quickened her pace, slipping her fingers down to rub the sensitive nub he laved earlier with his tongue. Her breathing quickened as she moved, her body straining toward some unknown height. Then her body exploded as a wave of warmth and pleasure overwhelmed her. She rode him until the sensations dimmed to a mere glimmer of what they were.

"Did you find what you sought?" Tristan's voice broke her entrancing delirium, his tone sharp and sarcastic. She opened her eyes and caught him watching her, his brow arched.

"Aye," she murmured. Her limbs hung heavy in the aftermath of her climax.

"Release me," he demanded, his voice even.

"Why would I do that? I have you exactly where I desire you." She teased against her better judgment, eyeing him with suspicion. He seemed deceptively calm, considering she tricked him and then used him for her own pleasure.

"Release. Me."

Ruby slipped off his cock, backing away so they no longer touched. She must release him at some point; no lengthy passage of time would dim his anger toward her. Although she played a dangerous game, she acknowledged there would be consequences. His gaze leveled with hers. His anger shifted into something much more unnerving, but she could not place it.

Crispin pulled at the bonds, his wrists twisting and straining against the leather. The wooden beam groaned under the pressure. She stared at him in awe as the muscles in his arms bunched and stretched beneath his skin. It amazed and terrified her. If he broke free, he would punish her. She licked her dry lips.

With a snap, the restraints fell away. *Nay, 'tis impossible. He cannot be that strong.* She scrambled backward, attempting to get her footing when his hand shot out, and he snatched her around the waist, pulling her against him.

Her back pressed against his chest, his arms like leather restraints around her midsection and breasts. Ruby swallowed and a shiver raced through her, part fear, part arousal. He was not a man to suffer her actions without reserving the right to pay her back in kind. She jerked against his hold, but he held her steady, the heat from his body seeping into her, causing her to burn for him again.

"The next time you restrain me, it would be wise to use chains instead."

"How did you...?" The question died on her lips as he ground his hips against her arse and settled her in his lap.

"The leather was cracked, weakened by the sun." He nipped at her throat. "And your knots leave much to be desired. Did you enjoy yourself?" His whispered breath caressed her ear. "You must have. The way your body tightened around mine as you took your pleasure. Tell me, did you enjoy mimicking the whores you spied on?" His free hand brushed the hair from her face and exposed her neck.

"I am no whore." She bristled at the insinuation.

"I never said you were. I asked if you enjoyed what you learned from them." Tristan took her ear lobe between his teeth. The pain snapped through her straight to her aching core. Was he trying to torture her? Ruby struggled to remember his question. His teeth grazed the soft skin of her neck. "Did you enjoy it?"

She whimpered in response, distracted by his sinful mouth. Her body ached to receive him again. She twisted, trying to free herself from his grasp, but he held her tight.

"Hush now, wicked girl." Tristan cupped her breast. "Is this not what you wanted? A man to fuck you, to take you hard and fast without mercy? Would you rather I show you gently, showering you with tenderness and sweet words?" His hand cupped her chin and held her steady as he trailed his mouth along the column of her neck. "Shall I show you the difference?"

Ruby would never be able to resist him after what she had done, what they had done together. If tonight would be her solitary experience with pleasure, better it be at the hands of a master. Mustering her strength and burying her pride, she nodded.

He twisted her in his lap and kissed her. The desire swelled again, and she straddled his thighs. His hands rested on her hips as he rubbed his cock against her sensitive cleft. Ruby pressed closer, gripping his shoulders as if clinging onto the edge of a precipice.

"Show me," she whispered into his mouth.

Tristan laid her down on the blanket and thrust into her with one smooth motion. She cried out again, not in pain this time, but in pure pleasure. Her body ached and throbbed, stretched full to bursting, but she welcomed the sensations washing over her as he moved. Beneath him, it felt different, more sensual, more full, more everything. His kiss drove all thoughts from her mind, and he thrust into her, over and over. A slow, spiraling heat churned deep inside of her, as before, but stronger, growing with a momentum she could not comprehend.

"Release your thoughts." He tasted her lips again. Just kissing him intoxicated her. "Let me hear your whimpers, your cries. Do not restrain them." He shifted his hips, delving deeper.

"Oh, saints..." The cries fell from her lips, and he swallowed them with his kiss.

He quickened his pace, pounding into her harder each time. Ruby's pleasure hurtled toward her like an arrow aimed at her heart. The sensations crashed over her again, this time in waves, making her scream. Tristan muffled her cry with his mouth, unrelenting in his movement. She closed her eyes, seeing flickers of light in her mind as the sensations took control of her body.

Tristan's body tensed as he broke their kiss and panted against her cheek, thrusting one last time before pulling out of her. The heat of his seed spread across her stomach as he found his release. She met his hooded gaze, and a small smile played at the corners of his lips before he collapsed beside her.

Ruby took a rag from the pile and cleaned herself. Unsure of what would happen next, she regarded him cautiously from the corner of her eye. Tristan lay naked and replete, his eyes closed, his arm thrown over his head. Almost peaceful. She moved to stand when his hand closed around her wrist.

"Lie down." His eyes were still closed. How did he know...? It did not matter.

"I must retrieve my clothes."

"Lie. Down." He pulled her arm twice, punctuating each word.

With a sigh, Ruby lay beside him, pulling a blanket over her body. She closed her eyes, exhaustion weighing her down. His arm slid beneath her shoulders, pulling her against him, and she smiled at the intimate action. He leaned his cheek against her forehead, his lips brushing her hairline in a soft kiss. Such a tender gesture for a man like him, selfish and proud as he was. She sighed. Something shifted inside of her, a kindling of emotion unknown to her.

Snuggling into his warmth, she allowed him to pull the blanket across them both. Later. She would ponder the repercussions on the morrow. Sleep claimed her, and Ruby surrendered willingly.

Chapter Thirteen

A harried voice shook him from slumber's grip. Crispin cracked his eye open to find Matthew standing in the stall's doorway. The poor lad's gaze remained on the ground at his feet.

"There are soldiers outside." Matthew proffered a bow. He twisted his hat in his hands nervously.

He glanced at Ruby who lay curled against his side, asleep. The blanket dipped low, revealing both of their undress. He understood now why the boy avoided direct eye contact. Then the implication of the lad's message struck him.

"Matthew, why are the soldiers here?" He prayed the hasty bow had been out of embarrassment. Crispin ensured his voice remained low to avoid waking the woman in his arms.

"They seek your presence." An embarrassed blush stole across the youth's cheeks. "Your Highness."

"God's teeth, blood, and bones," he swore under his breath. The boy knew his identity, and somehow his father's soldiers found him. He gently disentangled himself from Ruby and stood. A long glance confirmed she remained asleep. He inhaled sharply. This revelation would not endear her to him, especially after the night they spent together. He could still taste her on his lips. One night with this treasure would never be enough.

"They await your presence in the yard." Matthew seemed uncertain of how to behave now he knew of his true identity.

Crispin pulled on his hose, tunic, and doublet. "There is no cause for concern, lad." He leaned against the wall to pull on his boots. They needed to move this conversation away from where Ruby slept. If she should hear the truth, she would never again allow him close, except perhaps to run a blade through his blackened heart.

"Why did you not tell me, Sire?" Matthew met his gaze as Crispin stepped up to him.

Putting a hand on the boy's shoulder, Crispin shook his head. "There are things I could not reveal...to anyone." He stole a glance at Ruby. When he met the boy's gaze again, Matthew nodded, seeming to understand the unspoken explanation. He exited the stables and stepped into the yard.

A half-dozen soldiers stood at attention when he appeared. With a wave of his hand, they fell at ease and watched him, curiosity blazoned on each of their faces.

"You have found me out." Crispin focused on the captain of the small unit. "What is the meaning of this? Has my father come to his senses and requests my immediate return, or has he finally given the order to arrest me?"

The captain gave him a queer look but brushed it aside quickly. "Sire, we bear news of the king."

"Well..." Crispin trailed off, waiting for whatever message they wished to impart. He folded his arms across his chest while his thoughts drifted to the woman asleep in the stables.

"The king is dead."

Crispin snapped to attention. The words were clear enough, but they embodied a world of consequence. That meant...he bit back the smile threatening to commandeer his lips. A pang of remorse at his father's death stabbed his breast but faded at the sudden implication of the news. *The crown is mine.* The wheels spun in his mind.

"How?" Crispin asked.

"They believe it was murder, Your Majesty."

He swallowed the bile in his throat. "Was there any indication as to who might have done this terrible thing?" Crispin struggled to maintain the façade, the role to which he had become accustomed. Questions flooded him and the only way to discover answers would be to return to the palace. Not that returning would be a hardship for him. There lay his destiny, spread out like a banquet, awaiting his joyous return.

"Nay, Sire." The captain remained impassive and focused. "The people have not been informed of the king's passing yet, at least not formally. 'Tis hard to keep the gossipmongers at bay." He cleared his throat. "The queen requested we find you with all speed.”

“How fares my mother?”

“She is in despair and refuses to speak to anyone until you are returned.”

Crispin acknowledged the man. “As is expected. I shall go to her.”

“Your Majesty, we must make haste.”

Crispin nodded, not trusting himself to speak. A twinge of regret stabbed him in the chest. Regret he had been absent when his father drew his final breath. There had been no love lost between them. *Not since Francis*...he slammed those thoughts into the dust. This proved far more fortuitous than he could have hoped. He believed his plans had been foiled when his father ousted him into the night. But perhaps, they persisted in his absence?

“I must gather my belongings.” He dismissed them and turned back to the barn. How would he convince Ruby to accompany him?

He could use force, tie her up and carry her back to the palace across his saddle. Thoughts of her in his bed in the palace brought his cock surging to attention. His brazen outlaw would attempt to kill him when she discovered his true identity. Was the woman worth the risk? He noted Matthew standing in the doorway of the barn, his face pale.

“I beg pardon, Your Majesty.” The lad bowed and stepped aside. “I could not...” The boy’s words faded into the background as Crispin stared at the empty stall and pile of blankets atop the hay. Ruby had fled.

Crispin rounded on Matthew, rage flooding him. “Where is she?”

The boy flinched and bowed his head. “I tried to stop her, Sire, truly.” He wrung his hands together. “She slipped out the back of the stable in naught but a blanket.”

“Did she take her horse?”

“Aye, my lord.”

“God’s blood!” The fury surged through him, enhanced by the disappointment and betrayal. Had she overheard Matthew?

She must have. Why did she choose to flee instead of confronting him? Perhaps the soldiers' presence. It mattered little, she was gone. He kicked a wooden bucket across the floor, startling the horses.

Crispin turned his attention back to Matthew. "Saddle Ghost and bring him into the yard."

Without protest, Matthew rushed past him to retrieve the gelding. He heard the boy working as he gathered his sword and dagger, fastening them around his waist. The temptation to chase after her tormented him. A selfish whim, a decadent desire ruled solely by his cock. He shook the thoughts of her from his mind. Ruby would have to wait. Crispin focused on his priorities: return to Culver and claim his throne. Then and only then, could he search for the woman whose secrets outnumbered his own.

Ruby would face him again, on his terms, in his domain, and not even the devil himself would be able to salvage her soul when Crispin was through with her.

Chapter Fourteen

The tree branches raked her skin, tearing at her stolen clothing as she pushed her mare through the forest at a dangerous pace. Ruby dared not glance over her shoulder once she left the blacksmith's stables. She had to put as much distance between herself and the prince as she possibly could. *The prince.* Shaking her head, Ruby focused on the path before her. Once she reached a small clearing, she slowed Ginger to a walk and kept to the outer edge of the field.

Only then could she let her mind revisit what had happened earlier. How could she have been so blind? All the signs had been in front of her the whole time, not to mention his name. *Tristan sounds suspiciously like Crispin. Prince Crispin.* She swore under her breath, a long string of words that would make even the most callused whoreson blush. Ruby slumped in the saddle, remembering the night they spent together, the indescribable bliss she experienced at his hands. A shiver wracked her body, not out of disgust or fear, but desire.

Damn the lying jackanape! He had known from the beginning of their acquaintance how adamantly she loathed the prince and desired nothing more than to drive her dagger into his chest. She winced. *Aye, perhaps it was the reason why he did not tell you, daft fool.* But he did not run when she said it, nor did he have her arrested and tossed in the dungeons. *Why?* There were too many questions floating around her head.

Ruby approached a small cottage tucked near the edge of the clearing, alongside a less traveled road. Beyond the hill lay Skye Lake. There was only one person she could trust, the only person who would understand. She prayed Marian was home.

Sliding from the saddle, Ruby tethered the horse to a post outside the cottage. She licked her lips, fortifying herself, and raised her hand to knock, when the door opened. A pair of friendly hazel eyes set in a well-seasoned face met hers.

"Ah, my little gem," the older woman said with a chuckle. "Come in, child, come in." She stepped aside, welcoming Ruby into her home.

The small cottage's simplicity and warmth embraced her as she stepped into the room. A savory stew simmered on the stove; its tantalizing scent curling around her. Her stomach growled in response. She pressed her hand to her middle and glanced at the older woman, embarrassed.

"Sit." Marian motioned to the chair by the table. For a woman of her age, she moved with a nimble grace and purposeful steps. She was not stooped as many older women may be but stood tall and proud. Father Time had been kind, and she looked younger than most women of her age even with her gray hair pulled back into a soft plait over her shoulder. Soft lines framed her eyes and mouth when she smiled. Marian ladled the steaming stew from the pot hanging over the fire into a small bowl and retrieved some bread from the shelf beside the hearth. Setting the meal before Ruby, she slid into the chair across the table and eyed her kindly. "Eat, child."

Ruby devoured every morsel. Her full stomach warmed and the strength infused her whole body. She sighed, contented.

"Dare I ask what mischief has found you this time?" Marian's tone made her glance up. Those wise, loving eyes missed nothing it seemed.

"I believe I have made a terrible mistake, Mother." Ruby buried her face in her hands. She took several deep breaths and then lifted her chin with pride. Marian came to her aid years before, when her husband had found Ruby as a child standing amidst a bloody field of bodies and charred wagons. The couple took her in, clothed her, fed her, taught her to survive and how to fight. Most importantly, they taught her how to make a difference.

"Well, it could be worse, you could have been arrested." Marian attempted to soothe her.

Ruby's laugh came out choked. "I rescued a man several nights ago. Saved him from being slain outside a brothel."

"As we taught you to do—help those who cannot help themselves."

"It was Prince Crispin." Ruby's voice trembled. Marian's eyes widened slightly, her withered hand clenching into a fist and releasing repeatedly. She pressed on. "I gave myself to him."

Marian's jaw opened and closed a few times, no sound emerging. With a heavy exhale, she finally found her voice. "You had better start at the beginning, child."

Ruby took a deep breath and confessed everything. Her mother sat in silence, nodding only to communicate her attention as she told her story. All the worry, the fear, the desire poured out as she spoke. Her words lay drenched in the pain, stinging like the kiss of a blade against her flesh. As she finished her tale, Marian reached across the table, laying her hand on Ruby's, and met her gaze.

"You have had quite an adventure this time, my dear." Marian patted her hand. "So you discovered his deception and slipped out the back of the stable?"

"Aye." Ruby twisted a piece of bread between her fingers. "I feared what he would do to me. Or what I would do to him if we were to meet in a confrontation. So I ran and hid." Her voice cracked. "I have not feared for my own safety since the day my parents were murdered. Until this day."

"You followed your instincts as Guy taught you, and I am proud of you for heeding your intuition." Marian released her hand and reached for a flask of wine. She poured two goblets and handed one to Ruby.

Taking a heavy mouthful of sweet red wine, Ruby savored the tang of the drink on her tongue. Even though a weight had been lifted from her shoulders by telling her story, her heart ached, a deep, longing ache that terrified her.

"How was he?"

Ruby choked on the mouthful of wine. She swallowed it in haste, gasping for breath. "I beg your pardon?"

"The prince. Is he as good a lover as the gossips say?"

Heat crept into her cheeks, and she turned away from Marian, overwhelmed by the images flashing into her mind—his mouth on her, her on top of him, him taking her fast and hard, making her cry out with pleasure. She pressed a cool hand to her flaming face. "He is a callous, self-indulgent, spoiled, self-righteous, pompous, philandering—"

"Ruby," Marian interjected and Ruby snapped her mouth shut. "You forget I raised you. You cannot hide it from me, and you do not have to do so. Do you regret what transpired?"

"Nay." The confession left Ruby's lips without hesitation, without thought. She gasped at Marian's knowing grin.

"Has he confessed his undying love to you then?" Marian busied her hands grinding dry herbs with a mortar and pestle while they conversed.

"I doubt that man loves anything or anyone more than himself." Ruby sighed, lounging back in the chair. "I fear he may have used me to quench the desire simmering between us. Had I not fled, I may have become as unfortunate as poor Anne. A castoff burdened with a bastard."

"Did he set chase once he realized you had gone?"

"I saw no one following." Shaking her head, Ruby frowned. She prayed he would forget her like he did all his lovers. She heard enough stories to know Prince Crispin had a string of whores long enough to wrap around the king's castle a hundred times. The thought hurt, but deep inside, Ruby knew it was for the best.

Marian watched her with eyes as sharp as a hawk's. "Would you risk all you have worked for to have another night with him?"

"He does not love me. Why should I waste my time pining for something that can never be?" Ruby shook her head. "Nay. I cannot give a man such power over me."

"Sex can be a powerful motivator, my dear." Marian smiled. "It can easily be a reward or a weapon. Its powers have been utilized by women for centuries."

"How can I grant him control of my body without losing my heart?" Ruby's mind spun in circles at Marian's words.

"I think your heart has already decided to take the chance."

Ruby buried her face in her hands. "Why must these things

be so complicated?"

Marian rested her hand on Ruby's shoulder and patted with gentle reassurance. "This is one of those lessons of life. I am merely giving you the information you need to better equip yourself for the battle ahead. He knows you are an outlaw. The Lady of the Forest. They will come for you, and you must be prepared to face him when the time comes."

Ruby nodded with determination. "What shall I do until then?"

"What I taught you to do. Help those who require aid, defend the weak, and make a difference in the lives of those less fortunate."

She smiled at her teacher and surrogate mother. "Gramercy, Mother."

"You are a true gem, priceless and multifaceted. I am honored to have you in my life and my home." Marian stood and pulled Ruby to her feet. "Come, rest yourself."

As she reached the small bed, she turned. "What about Ginger?"

"I shall care for your horse, now lie down and rest. I will make you a sleeping draught when I return." Marian scurried out the door, leaving Ruby alone with her thoughts.

She lay down on the bed and curled beneath the blanket, facing the wall. Staring at the splintering wood in the rafters overhead, Ruby wondered at Marian's response. Why had she not been more upset with her poor choices? They may be as close as mother and daughter, but secrets remained buried deep inside Marian. Perhaps one day Ruby could draw them out, but until then, she carried her own secrets.

Her eyelids grew heavy, and she heard the soft click as the door closed behind Marian when she returned. Ruby could not keep her thoughts from drifting back to Prince Crispin, *Tristan*, the man who wove a spell with half-truths and seduction. She had been an indulgence, a warm body for his bed, nothing more. What he did now was no concern of hers. But her mother's advice on the power of sex stuck in the back of her mind. Could she truly use intimacy in such a way? Especially with someone who could never truly love her.

Ruby dashed away the tears on her cheek with an angry swipe of her hand. Prince Crispin commanded a whole kingdom of willing women to keep his bed warm. She would be damned if she let him have her body and soul as well.

Chapter Fifteen

The last time he stood in the throne room, his father threatened to take that which he desired most. In a twist of fate, less than a sennight later, he stood in the exact spot with his dream now realized. Crispin shook his head. Fortuitous indeed. He assumed his plans crumbled the night he was banished from the castle, but it seemed someone possessed a similar notion, aligning their goals, and implemented it without his aid. No matter who had done it, they saved him a world of trouble. He longed to uncover their identity and thank them properly with a visit to the executioner's block.

While the murderer's actions brought Crispin to the throne, he harbored no doubt those plans extended into Crispin's reign. He trusted no one save Henry, who proved himself worthy with years of friendship and companionship. How he ached to see his compatriot restored to his side. It would be the first command he set forth as king to call his friend home.

Perhaps there was another he could trust, one as pure as newly fallen snow in winter. An image of Ruby, her face flushed, writhing beneath him, flashed into his mind. He pushed it away. She would never trust him after his lies and betrayal. Why would he even entertain such a desire? *Because she desired you before she knew the truth. She expected nothing from you, even after your identity was revealed. She gave you something precious. Something that can never be bestowed to another.*

Crispin sat on the throne, leaning back comfortably in the sturdy chair. He must think clearly to avoid any impulsive decisions. With a flick of his hand, he summoned the servant. "Fetch me some wine and send for the fastest messenger in the kingdom." The servant bowed and disappeared into the anteroom.

Another servant stepped forward. "Presenting Her Majesty,

the Queen Mother." As the servant moved aside, Crispin spied his mother entering the chamber.

His mother approached, her head held high. She curtseyed before him, dipping low out of respect. "My king." She stood and met his gaze. "I beg to converse with you alone." Her eyes held his for a long, tense moment.

"Leave us." With a wave of his hand, he dismissed the servants, guards, and courtiers in the room. When the door closed behind them, Crispin settled deeper into the throne. "You have my undivided attention, Mother."

Her hair lay perfectly coiled beneath a sheer net, her garments pristine, and while her eyes were swollen slightly from weeping, they held a strength in their depths. Her appearance reflected the true strength of a monarch regardless of her broken heart.

"Are you well?" The question caught him by surprise. A twinge of guilt pierced his iron-clad heart.

"I am." Crispin had returned, bathed, dressed in his finest mourning clothes, ate a quick meal, and paid his respects to his father. His mother remained in her chamber during that time. Instead of seeking her out, his steps brought him to the throne room. She sought his presence when he should have directly attended her. 'Twas her summons which brought his swift return. Perhaps he could not bring himself to face her after his shameful behavior. Or he knew she would see through his carefully molded mask of indifference.

"Did you learn anything while you were out there?" Her words were precise and crisp, leaving no way to misinterpret them.

"Directly to the heart of the matter. I expected no less from you." Crispin stood and stepped down to face her, eye to eye. He placed his hands on her shoulders and smiled. "I have, Mother, and you need not worry about my state. I understand now what it means to rule as Father would have wanted."

She arched her brow. "Have you changed so much in such little time?"

"Nearly making death's acquaintance can alter one's

priorities rather quickly."

"You were nearly killed?" Her face paled at his words.

"Several times, but do not fret. As you can see, I am hale and hearty, with only a few scars to show for my adventure."

"What of your carnal appetites? You are king now, but even so, I will not stand for you whoring your way through the servants."

"No more, Mother. This I can promise you."

"Very well then." Only those who knew her well would note the surprise and skepticism conveyed by her raised brow.

She must have expected him to rage and fight, but Crispin knew the expectations placed upon him and forced a serene smile. He would grant her this request. In the back of his mind, he had already begun to strategize how he could bind Ruby to him indefinitely.

"Who is she then?" His mother's question startled him.

"I am not sure I understand—"

"I recognize the gleam in your eyes." She cupped his cheek. "There is a woman. Who is she?"

"No one of consequence," Crispin replied a bit too quickly. He cursed himself for the slip of his silver tongue.

His mother smiled but did not respond. She dropped her hand with a nod.

"You should rest, Mother. The funeral will proceed on the morrow." Crispin stepped back, placing distance between them.

She nodded and turned to leave. His heart ached to see her in pain. Of everyone in his life, he held his mother dearest to his heart. Crispin loved her, and although he never spoke the words, he knew she was aware of his adoration. When Francis died in the fire, his father spent his rage on Crispin while his mother showed nothing but compassion even though she lost her beloved firstborn son. While his father never believed Crispin would live up to the bright promise Francis had shown, she held out hope Crispin would blossom in his own right. But nothing could change the past. Francis was dead, and he would never be his brother.

The door closed with a firm thud, and Crispin collapsed on

the throne. He rubbed the crease between his brows.

"My wine!" In an instant, the servants and courtiers flooded the chamber, followed by the guards who resumed their silent positions again. One stout servant bent low as he offered the goblet.

"Taste it first," Crispin commanded. The servant obeyed without hesitation. When nothing happened, Crispin took it and drank deeply, the strong wine soothing his irritable conscience. One could never be too careful.

How did his mother know of Ruby? She could not unless she divined it from the spirits. His mother was always intuitive, which made lying to her complicated. He would have to tread carefully if he intended to bring his newfound treasure home.

Ruby. Her name echoed in his mind. The damned woman left him the moment she discovered his identity. It was obvious she intended to abandon him completely, which both irritated and intrigued him.

"Summon the fastest messenger in the kingdom, and bring me the head huntsman and the captain of the guard." Crispin finished the wine and handed the goblet to the servant. "Another."

He leaned back in his velvet-covered throne, hands steepled, his fingers rubbing across his lips as he pondered the conundrum before him. Within a fortnight, he would be anointed and formally crowned, then he would be king in every respect. Such an honor would require him to secure those whom he could trust in positions of power beside him. Those above reproach.

Two men entered the chamber and knelt before him. "Your Majesty," they said in unison.

"Rise." The men stood at attention, awaiting their orders, and Crispin smiled in delight at their unwavering acquiescence. "I wish to issue a warrant. Have you heard of the Lady of the Forest? The vigilante who considers herself a savior to the poor and downcast?"

"Aye, Sire," the huntsman spoke, meeting Crispin's gaze. "I have seen her myself." A grin split his lips. "The Lady of the

Forest is quite a tempting vixen."

"That she is," Crispin mumbled beneath his breath then replied louder, "I want her arrested."

"What are the charges?"

"Theft. Murder. Treason."

The men exchanged glances, their eyes wide. "As you wish, Your Majesty."

"I shall offer a reward of a hundred gold pieces to whoever brings her to me. Alive. I do not want her harmed in any way, am I clear?"

The men nodded and turned to leave when Crispin dismissed them with a flick of his wrist. He took the proffered goblet from the servant and drank. The wine wet his lips and his tongue darted over them, catching the remaining liquid.

Taking a quill and paper, Crispin scrawled a note to Henry and poured the wax to hold his seal upon the missive. As he pressed the seal upon it, the messenger burst into the room, his breathing labored from the haste at which he reported to the summons.

"You wished to see me, Your Majesty." The man knelt before the throne.

"Take this to Henry Balmont in Wales. Make haste. When you return, you shall be rewarded for your swift service." Crispin handed him the letter.

"As you command, Sire." The messenger tucked the letter into his doublet and bowed before leaving the room.

When Henry returned, their work would truly begin. He required the companionship of his best and closest companion. His father sent Henry away after their perceived mishap at the French court. Soon they would be reunited. Crispin longed to tell his friend of the spirited Lady of the Forest.

He allowed himself a secret smile, remembering the taste of her, the sound of her moans, her whispered desires, and the smooth silk of her skin against his. Crispin shifted in his seat, inconspicuously tugging at his hose in an attempt to relieve the ache in his cock.

A whore could give him release, but he did not want a

whore. He desired only Ruby. No other woman would suffice. He curled his hands around the arms of the chair. Now he possessed his throne, and soon he would have his crowning jewel.

Chapter Sixteen

The chain clanged against the shackles binding her wrists as the two guards escorted her into the throne room. Ruby ignored the curious glances of the servants and courtiers as she passed. Holding her head high, she focused her attention solely on the guard leading her. She had been staying with Marian for nearly a fortnight when they captured her near the lake. Her instinct had been to fight or run, but she knew they would catch her in due course. Her body ached from the quarrel with the soldiers. She bested four of them with her blade before the remaining half-dozen men subdued and restrained her. The purple bruises on her knuckles probably matched the ones on her arms and back.

The funeral for the king and subsequent announcement of the impending coronation of Prince Crispin had been the talk of the kingdom. Whispers about the mysterious and mischievous prince abounded. Ruby kept her mouth shut; however, her mind reeled with questions of her own. Curiosities concerning the prince were best left unspoken and unexplored.

A guard opened the massive doors to the throne room and motioned for her to approach the king. The moment she entered the room, his gaze followed her, intense, not quite a predator observing its prey, more like a god awaiting a sacrifice. She suppressed the urge to avoid his gaze and held it in pure defiance. As she advanced, the blue of his eyes shone brilliant, drawn out by the deep sapphire of the broach on his doublet.

The flutter of desire she failed to smother roared to life. *I will not give him the satisfaction of seeing my desire.* Ruby stopped at the base of the raised dais, her heart in knots, but her face remained impassive as she held his stare.

"My lady." Crispin appraised her from head to foot. "You have been brought here on charges of theft, murder, and treason. Have you anything to say in your defense?"

"Rot in hell." Her lip curled in a sneer.

His smile transformed into a feral grin. Ruby swallowed the lump that was her heart, currently lodged firmly in her throat. She refused to bend to him, or break, and tilted her chin higher, letting her pride speak louder than her words.

Crispin turned his attention to the attendants and guards. "Leave us; seal the doors. Let no one in or out until I command otherwise."

Everyone in the room vacated with haste, the last bolting the doors behind them. Crispin and Ruby held their ground, the only souls remaining in the room. He crossed the space between them and stopped before her.

"Did you believe I would forget your confession so easily?" His gaze roamed her face, making her breath catch. "I warned you of allowing such treasonous thoughts to cross your succulent lips."

Ruby inhaled, recognizing the subtle aroma of cedarwood and the underlying scent she knew belonged to him alone. "You should have made your identity known."

"So you could plunge a dagger through my heart?" He tsked, tilting his head to the side as he observed her. "You made your dislike for me clear the first day we spent in each other's presence. Had I told you then, would you have let me live or put me down 'like the wild dog I am'?"

She flinched at her own words being used against her. He warned her such treasonous thoughts could return to haunt her. "Had I known then what I know now, aye, I would have run you through." Ruby met his gaze and held it. "You were a coward to hide behind those lies."

"I was under explicit instructions not to reveal my identity to anyone—not that it matters—but that is my defense." He fingered the chain binding her wrists together. She stepped back jerking it out of his reach. "I gave you all the clues you required to figure it out." Crispin paced in a circle around her.

Ruby felt his appraisal. "What will you do? Hang me?"

"I should. You are a danger to the crown."

She scoffed. "Like bloody hell."

"You threatened the king."

"You were a prince, and I did not threaten you directly."

He stopped before her again. "Aye, that may be true, but I saw the murderous glint in your eye. You would have killed me. I cannot let it go unpunished."

Her hands clenched and released as she struggled to control the rage boiling inside her chest. "Who are you to judge me?"

"I am your king." Crispin captured her chin in his hand and held her steady, peering into her soul. "Kneel before me."

Ruby jerked from his grasp and hesitated momentarily before dropping to her knees with a grunt. "If I am for the block, for heaven's sake, drop the blade. I have no desire for your riddles and games."

"Oh, my sweeting, you shall be punished for your crimes; be sure of that." He sat down on the velvet padded throne. "When you rise, you will do your duty to your king. You shall be mine in every possible way. Surrender to me, Ruby, and I shall give you what you deserve."

Her eyes locked with his. Somewhere deep inside a hunger clawed from the darkness, craving escape like a dragon from captivity. Pride was a damnable thing. It prevented her from taking what he offered, warring with the desire to surrender pooling in the pit of her stomach.

"And if I refuse?" The question fell from her lips without a thought for her well-being.

"Then I shall have to convince you." He leaned forward. "I can be quite persuasive."

"Of this, I have no doubt." She pondered his proposition, pausing long enough to make him shift in his seat. "I have one condition."

Crispin nodded for her to proceed, his eyes dark and lips parted.

"I will not be a whore for you to parade around the castle, use for your own pleasure, and then cast aside when you have finished with me."

"I am the king. I shall do as I please." He grinned. "What do you propose?"

Ruby rose to her feet, chains dragging across the floor, and stepped onto the dais, bringing them face to face. "Make me your queen."

Crispin's laugher echoed through the chamber. He leaned back and stared at her, the corners of his eyes crinkled in mirth. "What makes you believe you are worthy to be my queen?" He met her challenge and topped it with his own.

The chains hung heavy on her wrists as she touched his lips with her fingertips. His blue eyes darkened to a midnight storm. He wanted her; the air crackled with the tension surrounding them. She played a dangerous game, but what did she have to lose? Death next to love was a trivial thing. She welcomed death. This man, however, terrified her. The way he made her feel, the cravings he unleashed with his touch, his kiss. If she was going to sell her soul to the devil, then she would reap all the benefits.

"Take me as your queen, or take my life. Those are my terms."

He nipped her finger between his teeth and grazed the pad of it with his tongue. A delightful pleasure-pain shot like an arrow to her core, making her wet. Silence stretched between them as their gazes remained locked.

"What do I get in return for such a boon?" Crispin's breath drifted over her skin. She shivered.

"All of me." Ruby's cryptic reply hung in the air. She prayed her strength would not falter.

A predatory smile stole across his lips. With a nod, he straightened. Ruby dropped her hand and stood aside.

"Guards!" The main door opened when he shouted, and four guards entered the room, standing at attention awaiting their orders. "Take her to my chambers, fetch a bath and some suitable garments for her to wear, and remove these chains."

"At once, Your Majesty." The captain of the guard removed the shackles from her wrists. "Follow me." He led her from the throne room.

Ruby paused outside the doors and glanced over her shoulder. Crispin stood as regal as any king, watching her with an expression she could not decipher. A delighted grin broke upon her lips, and she offered him a bawdy wink. His mask slipped, if only for a moment. But it revealed the truth. Her soul might belong to the devil, but she held the key to the kingdom of Meradin.

Chapter Seventeen

Apprehension clawed at him, tearing apart his heart. Crispin paused outside the door to his chambers. Her bold demand had been rash, but he admired her tenacity and courage. When the ultimatum left her lips, his response came without hesitation from the pit of his gut. There was no one like her in all the kingdom, nay, the world. No one with the fire and the spirit she possessed, no one who challenged him as she did. Her name suited her for she was a prized jewel, perfectly fashioned for a king. Now she belonged to him.

He pushed the door open. The servant tending to his treasure turned and curtseyed, quickly exiting into the antechamber. Ruby turned to face him. Her curly, damp auburn hair lay loose, flowing over her shoulders down to her waist. Her eyes twinkled in the firelight, her brow arched slightly. The pale shift she wore was damn near transparent in the light of the fire, showing her shapely legs and generous curves.

"Have you found everything to your liking?"

"Aye." She stepped closer, gliding like an ethereal creature from a waking dream. His breath caught. When she reached out and touched his jaw, his control snapped. He pulled her against him, molding her body to his.

"Are you an enchantress?" He buried his hand in her auburn curls, forcing her head back until she gazed up at him.

Her lips twitched in amusement. "I have no such powers."

"Ah, but you must have bewitched me somehow." Her hair glided like silk between his fingers. "If you desire to be my queen, then you will surrender yourself to me. Be mine in every way. Do you understand?"

"Aye." Her eyes drifted closed at the contact of his fingertips against her throat.

"You. Are. Mine. Every fiber of your being belongs to me.

Do not avert your gaze." Her eyes opened wide. "Face your king, your master, your lover. Night after night, I shall treasure you until you shatter from the overwhelming pleasure only I can give you."

Ruby licked her lips and nodded. As if regaining command of her body, she slid her hands along the front of his doublet until they encircled his neck. Her fingers toyed with the curls along his collar. Without hesitation, he swept her up into his arms and carried her to the bed, tossing her onto the coverlet.

Crispin undressed quickly, leaving his clothes in a heap on the floor. He climbed onto the bed, prowling toward her, covering her body with his own. Ruby tangled her hands in his hair and pulled him down, kissing him with a hunger he had not expected.

"Mine," he murmured against her lips. His hand slid under her shift and cupped her soft mound. She whimpered when he slid against her swollen lips. He delved his fingers deeper. "You are so wet for me already." He slid her shift up and, with a little maneuvering, pulled it over her head tossing it aside. "Skin to skin, as it should be, my queen."

"Nothing between us," she whispered with reverence. He nodded before delving into the delicious cavern of her mouth, stealing whatever words remained on her tongue.

His palm ground against her swollen center while he nudged her legs apart with his knee and settled between her thighs. With a single thrust, he entered her. The kiss broke on her gasp. Her nails dug into his shoulders, pinching his flesh. He savored the pain, withdrawing and thrusting again and again. Crispin took her with an unrelenting fury of need. She wrapped her legs around his waist and drew him deeper. He laid claim to her body.

"My king." Her moans and cries echoed off the walls, punctuating the nibbled bites he placed on the soft curve of her shoulder. Her cries escalated and her body tightened around him. He pushed harder, faster. Wrapping his hand in her hair, he tugged her head back, exposing her throat. Crispin sucked on the tender column, and she bucked her hips against him as she came apart in his arms.

She looked so beautiful, enraptured in her release, her eyes closed, her mouth open, gasping for breath. His name like a prayer on her panting breaths. He ground his hips against her once more and came hard, spilling his seed inside of her. He collapsed against her, their bodies pressed close, their breaths mingling.

They clung to each other, shivering in the aftermath of stolen pleasure. Crispin gathered her to his chest and stroked his thumb across her nipple. Silence descended on the room, and he basked in it. A sense of peace drifted over him. *Perhaps this could work.*

There were still many unanswered questions. Where had she come from? How had she become the Lady of the Forest? What of her family? He held her tighter. A lifetime together would sort out the secrets plaguing both their pasts. He kissed her shoulder.

In the glow of their passionate fever, her past mattered little. As of this moment, Ruby was his queen, his lover, his mistress, and together they would bring the kingdom to its knees.

Chapter Eighteen

The bath water sluiced over her shoulders and soothed her aching limbs. After a long night in Crispin's arms, her body pulsed with awareness of every painful twinge. Even a long day in the saddle or training with her sword never caused her such pain or exhaustion. A warmth spread through her cheeks at the thought of the wicked things they had done. She grinned as the servant washed her hair, allowing the secret thought to linger.

"Would you like wine, my lady?" A young girl of barely ten approached holding a goblet.

"My thanks, lass." Ruby accepted the goblet from her trembling hands. The girl dipped into a low curtsey and avoided her gaze. "Pray tell, give me your name?"

"Mina." The girl kept her eyes downcast.

"Come closer. I promise not to bite."

Mina stepped up to the edge of the tub, her dark hair hiding her face. Her hands were clasped in front of her, fingers twisting together.

Ruby took a sip of the wine. The liquid warmed her. "Mina, how long have you worked in the castle?"

"Nigh on a fortnight, my lady," the girl replied, her voice soft. "After my father was killed, I had to find a way to earn my keep."

With a nod of understanding, Ruby handed her the cup. The girl took it and backed away as the maid poured warm water over her head, washing the soap from her locks. After soaping and scrubbing herself, she stood and stepped from the tub. Wrapping the robe around her body, she turned to Mina again.

"You shall be my personal attendant. I will need you to be sharp of wit."

The girl nodded, her stringy brown hair bouncing against her shoulders. "Many thanks, my lady."

Ruby turned to the maid. "See that Mina is properly washed and dressed, then have her brought to my chambers this evening. I shall take care of myself from here, I thank you."

The maid nodded as she moved toward the door. Mina set the goblet on the table and followed behind the retreating maid.

Ruby collapsed on the chair before the hearth and brushed her hair. The rhythmic motion and the flicker of the flames mesmerized her. Her mind replayed the events of the last fortnight. She never imagined she would be in the castle, or fucking the king. A giggle escaped her lips while the anxiety stirred inside her.

When they brought her into the throne room bound in chains and branded a traitor, the odds were stacked against her. There would be no escape from his wrath. He wanted to use her, punish her, show no mercy. She begged for death to be swift. Perhaps this explained her hasty demand. If he truly wished to kill her, then she gave him the perfect opportunity to do so.

But he did not. Instead, Crispin accepted her challenge and agreed to her terms of surrender. She nearly burst into hysterical laughter. The impulsive act changed everything. No longer was she free to be the Lady of the Forest coming to the aid of the weak and defenseless. On the contrary, it provided the opportunity to influence significant changes for the people. A grin lingered on her lips. Plus, she had the ear of the king. Even though she did not trust him, Ruby could use this new position to her advantage. As Marian had said, sex could be a powerful motivator.

"What wicked thoughts linger in that pretty head of yours? Are you plotting against me already?"

The tenor of Crispin's voice wrapped around her, and she turned to face him. "I always harbor wicked thoughts. 'Tis nothing new." She finished brushing her hair and then plaited it over her shoulder as she stood.

He leaned against the bedpost, watching her, his blue eyes glittering with dangerous mischief. "Mayhap you require another lesson in how to behave properly as my future queen should."

Ruby approached him, her body humming with the

unspoken promises and a hint of uncertainty. "You think I am a prized mare you must break."

"Tame, perhaps. Any man who tries to break you, well, he is a fool." Crispin's lopsided smile made her heart clench. *Handsome, bewitching devil.*

"So you do not want to break me?" She trailed her fingertips down his arm.

"Sweeting, I shall instruct you in every way you can please me. But to lose the spark in your eyes would be to lose the very essence of who you are."

"Who am I?" she whispered, leaning closer.

"Mine." He pulled her against him and kissed her.

Ruby melted into his solid warmth and sighed. She would never tire of his mouth upon hers or the feel of him pressed firmly against her. She whimpered when his hand closed over her breast beneath her robe, sliding over a tender nipple. He drew her lip between his teeth and slipped his hand lower, his fingers delving between her legs.

"Wet for me already are you, my sweet?" He urged her back until she collapsed onto the bed, then spread her legs and dropped to his knees. Before she could form a coherent thought, his mouth covered her hot center, his tongue flicking between the folds where his fingers had been.

"Aye." She moaned as he licked and suckled, drawing her pleasure to the surface. His hands grasped her thighs, massaging gently as he laved her pussy. She reveled in the sensation, the swirling heat building inside of her.

Crispin slid a finger inside of her and made slow circular motions. She ached, her hips rocking against his hand, wanting more, needing more. She groaned in frustration when his mouth left her.

"Something amiss?" he asked as though discussing the weather.

Ruby wanted to throw something at him, anything. She grabbed a pillow and threw it at his smirking face. "Stop torturing me."

He thrust a second finger inside of her. She whimpered as

he curled them, stroking a sensitive spot.

"I shall give you what you need. Close your eyes and relax. Let me bring you pleasure; let me see you bloom for me." His words were punctuated by a predatory smile.

While she did not trust his motives, Ruby's body screamed for release, the kind only Crispin could provide. She closed her eyes and focused all her attention on his hands, his heat infusing her, his mouth trailing over her stomach. Ruby bit her lip to keep from crying out.

"Let it go. I want to hear your cries echo off the walls. I want everyone to know I brought you pleasure. To know beyond a doubt you are mine." He withdrew a finger from her and slid it against her rear opening.

Her eyes flew open. "What are you doing?" She shifted away from his invasive touch.

He climbed onto the bed, stalking her like a mountain cat. She pulled the robe closed and crossed her legs. As he approached, her protests died in her throat. He pinned her beneath him with an arm on each side of her torso, staring down at her.

"What are you afraid of, Ruby?"

You. She swallowed hard and met his gaze. "Nothing."

"I see the fear in your eyes just as I can smell your desire." He leaned down and removed the robe from her breast with his teeth. "I promise, no harm will come to you." His breath whispered over her skin, causing her flesh to prickle with delightful anticipation. "Let me show you."

She gasped as he took a nipple in his mouth and rolled it between his teeth, suckling. He released it with a soft pop and trailed kisses up her neck, across her jaw, and then stopped, hovering over her lips. Ruby nodded offering her consent, and he kissed her, taking what she offered.

He tasted like sin and wine. As she shifted beneath him, he slid the robe from her shoulders and down her arms. She lay naked beneath him, her body aching, prepared for whatever pleasures he held in wait for her.

"Spread your legs." He knelt between her thighs. "Open for

me, let me see you swollen and wet for me."

Ruby's embarrassment rose, the telltale heat burning her across her cheeks. She met his bold gaze as it shifted to her face.

"Your body is flushed; your face, stained pink. Does it embarrass you, being thus?"

"Nay." She slid her hand across her stomach and down, barely brushing the curls covering her sex. Crispin's eyes followed her hand. He betrayed no emotion but followed her motions carefully. "Would you like me to..." She let the words trail off as her fingers slid along her cunt, delving between the folds.

"Wicked girl." A smirk played at the corners of his mouth.

Her finger slid inside. Her pussy wept for attention, pleading for his touch. Ruby let her head fall back as she stroked the same spot Crispin had touched moments before. A whimper escaped her lips.

His hand covered hers and his finger joined in the teasing exploration. "When you touch yourself, I want you to think of me inside of you." He withdrew his finger and once again slid it over her rear entrance using her own juices to ease their way.

Ruby tensed, but his gentle caress soon lulled her into a relaxing state. She quickened her strokes, her thumb sliding between the folds, finding the tender nub hidden there. A shock of pleasure washed over her, and she arched her hips in reaction.

After a few moments, the pressure of Crispin's finger against her arse made her gasp as he slid it into her slowly. She froze at the intrusion.

"Relax, my love. I promise you only pleasure."

With a nod, Ruby took a breath and resumed her erotic exploration. The sensation of Crispin's finger was not painful or uncomfortable, merely strange. He slowly stroked his finger in and out.

"Oh, sweet mercy!" The sensations crashed over her, pulling her into a vortex of pleasure. Her hips bucked against her hand and his as the tremors slowly ebbed. Her hand dropped limp at her side, while the other stayed buried in her, feeling the aftershocks of her climax. Ruby closed her eyes.

The soft pressure of Crispin's lips on hers renewed her ardor. Her fingers slipped into his hair and tangled in the curls. His naked body pressed close to hers. When had he removed his clothes? What did it matter? His cock replaced his fingers, demanding and insistent.

Ruby shifted her hips, and he slid inside, filling her. "Crispin," she murmured against his lips, momentarily breaking the kiss.

He smiled against her mouth, kissing her deeper as if wanting to consume her very essence. Then he rocked his hips. The rhythmic thrusts brought the swirling heat back to her center, making her body hum with pleasure. This man...this wicked man would be the death of her. Untouchable and unmovable, yet he moved her, body and soul when he made love to her. She pushed the thoughts away and focused on every tingling sensation he brought from somewhere deep inside.

His pace quickened as the kiss grew more frenzied. She met the motion of his hips with her own, searching for the balance that would bind them together. Grinding against him, she savored the flex of his muscles beneath his skin and his panting gasp as he came. She raked her nails across his shoulder as flickering sparks of her own climax flashed beneath her lids when she closed her eyes. When she opened them, Crispin lay half atop her, a strange look etched on his face as though he was consumed by conflicting thoughts.

"Why do you stare at me so?"

He shrugged. "Can I not admire your beauty?"

"I do not believe you would linger so long on my beauty when you have already seduced me."

Another shrug. "Mayhap you are correct." Crispin removed himself from the bed. "You should dress."

A shiver of disappointment racked her as she pulled the robe on. Ruby stood, trying to force herself not to think on the frustration and shame lingering too close to the surface. Brushing past him, she crossed the room to where her gown hung on the wall.

What is wrong with me? She shook her head. It was bed sport, a way to keep him close, nothing more. Crispin possessed not the capacity to love her, and she refused to bestow him her heart, not even a sliver of it. She glanced over her shoulder. He straightened his doublet and glanced up to meet her gaze. Turning back to her gown, she let the robe fall from her body into a heap on the floor. Ruby pulled a clean shift over her head. As she reached for her drawers, Crispin's voice stopped her.

"Leave them off."

She faced him again. "Why would I do that?"

"Because I want nothing in my way should I want to take you."

Ruby swallowed the retort hanging on the tip of her tongue. He crossed the room and took down the gown from the wall. He slid the fabric over her head, arranged it neatly, and tightened the laces. The man was truly an enigma. When he finished, he swept his hand across the nape of her neck and whispered in her ear.

"Make sure you are presentable, my dear." A glimmer of humor flickered in his eyes. "My mother would like to meet my future bride. We should not keep her waiting any longer."

Surprise gripped her, and she spun around to face him. "Your mother?" A nervous mixture of fear and apprehension bubbled up inside of her. "She requested...I mean..." Her words failed. She had faced Crispin, even challenged him. Why did the thought of meeting his mother terrify her?

He cupped her chin in his hand. "This is merely a formality. I informed my mother of my choice of bride, and she wishes to meet you." Crispin smoothed his thumb across her lower lip.

"The queen." Ruby swallowed the fear rising like bile in the back of her throat.

"The Queen Mother," Crispin corrected. "You will be queen soon." He stepped back and dropped his hand. "Tidy your hair. Something simple should suffice. Mother is probably wondering where we are."

Ruby sat before the mirror and quickly untangled and wove her hair into a more tidy plait. She pinned it up in a simple style and forewent the head covering for the sake of comfort. It was not her intention to make a bad impression, but she abhorred wearing the constricting headpieces noblewomen favored.

Crispin's reflection in the mirror caught her attention. He watched her with careful attention from where he leaned against the bedpost. His expression remained passive, but she could not ignore the hunger and possession in his eyes. A flutter of desire stirred in her again. *He has turned me into a wanton.*

She rose from the chair and walked past him. When she reached the door, Ruby glanced over her shoulder. "Shall we? I dislike the thought of keeping your mother waiting."

He approached and opened the door. When he offered his arm, Ruby placed her hand upon it and allowed him to lead her from the room. They meandered down a series of corridors and finally paused before a large, ornate door with magnificent scrollwork. The servant standing at attention outside the door knocked and then swung it open, permitting them entrance.

Ruby entered the most lavish room she had ever seen. The flowing curtains, feminine décor, and exotic colors wove a spell around her. The rich, dark woods of the furniture would have been expected in the king's chambers, but in the queen's sitting room it spoke of power and exquisite taste.

Then she noticed the woman sitting next to the hearth. She bore a similar coloring to Crispin, with her dark hair spun with threads of silver and vivid green eyes. The deep crimson velvet of her gown shimmered in the light as she stood. Her gaze reflected curiosity and kindness as it drifted over Ruby.

"Mother, may I introduce my future bride, Ruby." He released her arm, dropping his hands to his sides. Crispin's introduction startled her, but she recovered quickly and proffered a curtsey as the heat of a blush swept across her face.

"You failed to mention how lovely she is, Crispin." His mother smiled. "Sit down, both of you." When she resumed her seat, they followed suit.

Crispin's leg brushed her own, and she stole a glance at him. He maintained his cool demeanor, but Ruby sensed the turmoil beneath it. She rested her hand on his knee for a brief moment before clasping her hands together in her lap and turning her attention to the Queen Mother.

"My apologies, Mother, for our tardiness." Crispin reclined in the chair.

"I have come to expect it from you. My prayer is this charming girl will be able to soften your rough edges." She turned her attention to Ruby. "My son has told me next to nothing about you, but then again, persuading him to speak on anything relevant is a chore."

"You are gracious, Your Majesty." Ruby maintained a calm tone even though the nervous flutters in her stomach intensified. What if she said something to insult the queen mother? What if she did not like her or the opposite? Crispin's hand settled against the small of her back, suppressing the invasive thoughts.

"Please, call me Vivienne. I saw them lead you into the throne room in chains last eve." She picked up her goblet and took a sip of wine. "I must say, Crispin has an interesting method of choosing a bride."

The truth seemed the best course of action, considering the circumstances. Ruby took a deep breath. "I am an outlaw. They call me the Lady of the Forest. I saved Crispin's life outside of a brothel, killing the men who wanted to beat him to death. He did not reveal his identity until several days later once he assisted me in a small task."

His mother's mouth rounded in a small *o* before she cleared her throat and took another drink of wine. "Why does none of this surprise me?" She shook her head and set the goblet aside. "Do you have kin?"

"My family was killed in a raid near the borderlands when I was a child. I was the only survivor. A kind couple took me in and raised me as their own. I left them several years ago to pursue justice for the people of Meradin." Ruby prayed her story sounded plausible enough. She did not want to give details. It was not deception if some of the details were omitted, was it? The truth was not something she readily provided in an attempt to protect Marian and herself.

"May the Lord have mercy on their souls. It must have been difficult for you to grow up in such a manner. Who were your parents?"

Bloody hell. Surely telling part of her story would not endanger anyone. Ruby licked her dry lips. "Baron and Baroness Skye. My father earned his title serving as a knight in the previous court."

Vivienne's hand trembled, but she smoothed her skirts, masking the sudden tremor. "How old are you now, Ruby?"

"I shall mark my nineteenth year this summer." Ruby glanced at Crispin, perplexed by the sudden shift in the direction of the conversation.

"Do you desire to be queen?"

Her question startled Ruby. She turned to meet Vivienne's vibrant green eyes. "Aye, more than anything." Crispin's hand trailed along the base of her spine, the gentle caress a reminder and a distraction.

"I have no objections then. You shall be married and crowned in a fortnight. There is much to be done in a short amount of time. A royal wedding is no small event. It shall be a grand affair." Vivienne stood, and they took it as a signal of dismissal. "Forgive me, I must rest. Crispin, take good care of her. I know not how you found her, but you are a fool if you do not cherish this woman." Vivienne cupped her chin. "Ruby, you were born to be queen. I can see it in your eyes."

Crispin led Ruby from the room. Once the doors closed behind them, he looked at her, a lopsided smile playing on his lips. "Was it as terrible as you imagined?"

She returned his playful expression. "Nay, but you should not touch me so intimately while in your mother's presence."

He leaned close and whispered in her ear. "When I want to touch you, I will do so. You are mine now, my sweeting. Every inch of you is at my disposal should I desire to explore it. Do you not enjoy my touch?"

His words ignited the banked fire smoldering in the recesses of her soul. "Too much. I fear it may be the death of me."

Crispin's wicked grin met her words, and heat exploded inside her chest encircling her heart. Ruby bit her tongue, knowing any more confessions from her lips would betray the direction of her thoughts. Not even she was ready to face the truth yet. She belonged to him. If only there were a way to ensure his reliance on her, the forfeit of her heart and soul would be well worth the sacrifice.

Chapter Nineteen

Having returned Ruby to her chamber, Crispin strode toward his presence chamber with a determined gait. The events of the past day proved such a whirlwind, he had not considered the impending coronation being amplified by the marriage. He relished the power it provided him, even though it encouraged the simpering, groveling behavior he loathed. Nothing irritated him more than wasting his time with false, placating sycophants.

He reached his chamber and opened the door. A servant entered behind him, offering a goblet of wine as he sat in his favorite chair before the hearth. Taking a drink, he turned to the boy. "Fetch me the swordsmith and his apprentice, Matthew."

"At once, Sire." The servant bowed and left the room, closing the doors behind him.

Crispin sank into the chair, draping his leg over the arm. He drank deeply until the crimson liquid was gone. Letting the goblet dangle from his fingertips, he stared into the flames. The dark embers resembled her hair when it shone in the sunlight. He shook his head. She had bewitched him. It was the only logical explanation.

The woman, an orphan and an outlaw, had gone from being his prisoner to his betrothed in a matter of moments. 'Twas true he had no intention of imprisoning her, not after the passion they shared. Her fiery temper and impassioned will made her strong, much stronger than he believed any woman could be.

He tapped his finger against the rim of the cup. If she was to be his bride, his queen, then he would show the world her strength and beauty. This event would be the talk of the kingdom for years. He anticipated the wedding and coronation celebration would last nearly a sennight, including the tournament.

Where in damnation is Henry? When he returned after his father's sudden death, Crispin dispatched a summons for Henry to return from his duties as an emissary to Wales. A duty his father laid at Henry's feet upon learning of their mishap with the Duchess of Montrose. He and Henry had been careless in their dalliance with the lady, and in turn, his father separated them by force to punish them.

"Where are you when I need you, Henry?" He stood and crossed to the table holding the pitcher of wine. Pouring himself another drink, Crispin wondered how his friend would react to the news of his taking a bride. Henry, ever the stalwart and stable companion, teased him on countless occasions about his duty to his country in finding a suitable bride. While the thought terrified him at the time, as he pondered it, the institution became palatable with Ruby by his side and in his bed. The memory of her beneath him was enough to make his cock as hard as an oak. He groaned as he downed the contents of the goblet and poured another.

Henry would approve of Ruby. Crispin himself had never been a good judge of character, but his closest companion and friend proved, on more than one occasion, he held insights into others most could never grasp. As boyhood friends, they were raised side-by-side, training, playing, working, wenching, and even fighting. Henry's family sent him to train as a squire in Culver when he was eight years old. He and Crispin came to each other's aid quickly when tormented by the older boys, Francis and Simon, as well as others. The duo had been inseparable ever since. Both younger sons, they forged a bond that lasted through adulthood. Now as king, Crispin required his companion and confidant by his side.

A knock sounded, echoing through the chamber.

"Enter." Crispin turned to see the swordsmith and his apprentice in the doorway, their heads bowed.

"You summoned us, Your Majesty." The smith spoke as he twisted his cap in his hands.

"Aye, I have a commission for you." Crispin stepped closer. "I wish for you to make a poignard with certain specifications and decorations on the hilt and scabbard. Are you capable of making such a blade within a fortnight?" Crispin handed him a parchment with the details.

The smith unrolled the paper and scanned the drawing. "Between me and the apprentices, it should not be a problem. The design is simple enough. If you provide the gems and gold for the hilt and scabbard, we can begin this night, Sire."

With a nod, Crispin turned to Matthew. "How have you settled into life in the castle?"

Matthew met his gaze hesitantly. "Very well, Your Majesty. My thanks for granting me the opportunity to improve my craft."

"Has your father recovered?"

"Aye. He is well enough to work again. My family offers you thanks for your generous gift." Matthew dropped his gaze.

"I merely compensated your family for their hospitality and payment for the horse."

The lad nodded and clasped his hands before him. "Ghost is a fine beast. I am happy to serve you in all ways, my liege."

"My thanks for your service. I shall leave you both to work on the dagger."

The men retreated without a backward glance. Crispin turned his attention to the portrait of his parents, painted several years prior. The artist had not captured his father's harsh expression or his mother's regal bearing, yet the likeness was fair. He should have it delivered to his mother's chambers. Nothing irked him more than having his father hovering over his shoulder even in death.

Finishing the wine in his goblet, he focused his attention on some political matters. If he returned to his private chambers, he would be haunted by his desire for Ruby. Thinking of her alone in her chamber and the ways he could bring her pleasure nearly drove him mad with lust.

He sat down at the overlarge desk. Arranging a piece of parchment, quill, and ink before him, he pushed the image of her naked and draped across his lap from his mind. Focusing all his energy into the task before him, he wrote with intent, content in the knowledge she waited willingly for his return.

Chapter Twenty

Torches cast deep shadows along the walls of the castle lighting the way as Henry climbed the stairs leading to Crispin's chambers. He arrived later than he anticipated, providing no notice of his return. When the messenger delivered the summons, Henry packed his essentials and returned to Culver posthaste. News of the king's death reached him at the same time as Crispin's missive. His closest companion was now king of Meradin. After nearly a fortnight of travel, Henry pushed past exhaustion in the hopes of seeing his friend before he retired for the evening. Knowing Crispin, he was in his chambers, indulging in a bit of bedsport.

Henry shook his head. While he never overindulged in paying for the company of a whore, he rarely turned down a willing woman. The thought alone made him hard. It had been too long since he bedded a wench...warm and wet, with curves to make a man's head swim.

He strode past the entrance to the king's private gardens when a flash of movement brought him to a halt. A willowy silhouette slipped down the path next to the rose arbor. Henry paused, leaning against the archway. A woman in the king's gardens? He ventured closer.

Her dark hair shimmered like a flame in the torchlight, her white gown casting an ethereal glow around her as she strolled down the path. She seemed agitated, as though arguing with herself. Everything about her called to him, the sway of her hips, the swell of her breasts. She must be one of Crispin's latest conquests.

Henry crept up behind her as she neared the stone wall along the outskirts of the garden. Crispin and Henry shared wenches before. He bragged countless times about how little the women meant to him, and they never once fought over a woman.

Crispin gave him carte blanche, even though Henry rarely took advantage of it. Seeing such a beauty in the gardens, Henry could not refuse this time.

"My lady." He grasped her shoulder. When he touched her, she spun on him, her arm catching him in the chest, pushing him back against the wall.

"What do you want from me?" Her strong and steady grip lay firm against his torso.

"Does it matter?"

"Aye, state your intent." Her eyes glowed like honey in the firelight.

"I merely wish to inquire as to your purpose here. These are the king's private gardens. Only his most valued consorts are privy to his chambers."

"'Tis none of your concern who I am. Who, might I ask, are you to intrude on the king's private chambers?"

With one smooth movement, Henry reversed their positions. Pressing the lovely vixen against the stone wall, he stepped closer, leaning his body into hers. She struggled, but he held her steady, his hands on her shoulders.

"I am whomever you wish me to be." He pressed closer, savoring the feel of her against him.

Her breath came in short pants and her eyes flashed fire. She tilted her head back as if inspecting him. "Release me."

"I think not." Her scent wove around him, roses and mint mixed with her arousal. God, he could smell it on her, thick and cloying, tempting him to sin. She licked her lips, and he lost all control and sealed his mouth over hers.

She froze beneath him, but as he deepened the kiss, she softened slightly. Her body relaxed, and he slid his hand into her soft tresses. Her taste intoxicated him. Like a fine wine, she was heady and sweet. He groaned as she leaned against him, her hand shifting near his groin. His cock leaped in response, but the words echoing behind him gave him pause.

"Henry, I suggest you step away carefully. Do not do anything rash."

He glanced over his shoulder and saw Crispin standing a

few paces behind them, his arms crossed. Turning his attention back to the lady, he noticed it was not her hand pressed to his cock, but the blade of her dagger. Henry released her and stepped back slowly, realizing the second command had not been for him but her.

Crispin came up beside him as she sheathed her blade in the folds of her skirt. With a toss of her hair, she smoothed her gown over her hips.

"Allow me to introduce my betrothed, Henry." Crispin clapped a hand on Henry's shoulder. "This is Ruby."

"You...your..." Henry could not breathe. He kissed his best friend's, the king's betrothed. Soon-to-be Queen of Meradin. Henry closed his eyes and swallowed. When he opened them, her grin made his stomach twist with regret. He turned to Crispin, noting amusement and a hint of jealousy in his expression. "I need a drink."

Crispin laughed. "Come then, let us enjoy a pint together. There is much to discuss."

Henry glanced at Ruby one last time and followed Crispin into the castle. He would never live this down. Crispin never forgot nor forgave anything...ever.

Chapter Twenty-One

Returning to her chambers, Ruby slammed the door behind her and leaned against it. *Sweet merciful saints above.* She pressed her fingers to her lips. Another man kissed her. A stranger, who seemed to be on such terms with Crispin that finding him kissing his betrothed had done nothing but spark amusement. Would he turn this on her?

Many men, finding their wives with another man, would call her a whore and toss her into the street. 'Twas always the woman's fault for leading men astray. She nibbled on her fingernail. What would Crispin do to her? Would he punish her? Would he punish the man?

Her thoughts turned to the stranger in the garden. In faith, he was handsome, his eyes sparkling and bright, his lips shaped like a perfect bow. She whimpered. They were soft and warm, and he tasted like the summer breeze. While it was pleasant and made her warm inside, his kiss did not ignite an inferno inside of her like Crispin's.

Ruby pulled off the gown, leaving only the shift, and collapsed on the bed. How had she become entangled in such a mess? God must be punishing her for her wickedness. That was it. His wrath poured from the heavens in the form of temptation, and she could not resist it.

Sliding beneath the coverlet, she allowed her mind to race, wondering what the consequences would be for her indiscretion. Crispin would come. She knew beyond a doubt he would come. This time she feared his response. Pulling the blanket over her head, she lay surrounded by her shame and willed sleep to steal her away.

A soft knock at the door startled her. She popped her head from beneath the blankets. If it were Crispin, he would not stand on ceremony. He would enter without an invitation. She slid from the bed and stood, pulling on a robe and wondering who it might be. As the door opened, she held her breath.

"Good eve, my dear. I pray I am not intruding." Crispin's mother stepped into the room and closed the door behind her.

"Your Majesty." Ruby dipped into a curtsey. "What brings you to my chambers?"

Vivienne crossed the room to the chairs positioned by the hearth. "Come sit with me a while." She sat delicately and waited.

"If you insist, Your Majesty." Ruby hesitated for a moment before joining her next to the fire.

"Please, call me Vivienne. There is no need to stand on ceremony here when it is only the two of us."

Ruby smiled, relaxing at her kind words, but her heart fluttered in anticipation for the repercussions of her actions and the uncertainty before her.

Vivienne took Ruby's hand in her own. "Is something wrong, my child? You look as though you are about to shatter into a thousand pieces."

With a laugh ending on a sigh, Ruby nodded. "Aye, I believe I may be out of my element." She shook her head; perhaps she should not say anything should it make things worse for her. "'Tis no matter, truly."

"Come now, I have seen this expression before. I wore it myself a few times in the past. Has my son done something horrible to you?"

"Nay, he has not." Ruby fidgeted with the hem of her robe. "I was walking in the private garden when a man approached me. He kissed me, my lady, and your son happened upon us at the exact moment." She froze, unable to voice her fears.

"How many men have you kissed, my dear?" Vivienne rhythmically stroked the back of her hand. Her voice remained soft and sympathetic.

"Three." She turned her gaze to the fire, letting the heat hide her shame.

"My son and this stranger among them?"

"Aye, but I do not believe he is a stranger, not to Crispin. He addressed the man by name. Henry."

Vivienne laughed, her body shaking with mirth. "My dear, this is quite a state you find yourself in."

"What will he do to me?" Ruby trembled, confused by her response.

"Crispin?" She pondered a moment. "Probably nothing. He and Henry have been friends since childhood. They have been inseparable since the day they met. What did you do when Henry kissed you?"

"I put my blade to his ballocks." Ruby warmed at the memory of his lips on hers, and her body's hesitant reaction to his touch.

"And Crispin saw this exchange?"

"Aye," Ruby confessed.

"There is naught to be concerned with then. My son may be a possessive man, but he is not quick to lose his temper or react with violence." Vivienne released her hand and poured two goblets of wine from the decanter sitting on the table beside them. "Did you enjoy it?"

"Enjoy what?" Ruby arched her brow.

"Henry's attentions." Vivienne watched Ruby carefully as she handed her the goblet.

"I am faithful to your son." Ruby took a drink, letting the wine warm her throat and soothe her nerves.

"Of this, I have no doubt, but Henry is a fine man and chivalrous to a fault. I am sure had he known who you were and what you meant to Crispin, he would have never touched you. But you have not answered my question." A smile curved her lips before she took a sip of wine.

"'Tis always flattering to be desired." Ruby searched for the right words. "I had no time to consider enjoying his advances."

"Oh darling, I like your diplomacy, and you shall make a wonderful queen, of this I am certain." She leaned back in the chair and drank deeply from the cup.

"I fear Crispin will blame me for the incident." Ruby blurted her concern in a rush of words.

"Why? Did you throw yourself at Henry?" Vivienne regarded her closely.

"I have never thrown myself at anyone."

"Then you have no reason to worry, my dear." Vivienne soothed her with confidence. "I shall tell you a secret. In all his life, my son has never brought any of his women to my attention. Not one. Yet he brought you to my chambers and sat by your side during our little conversation. And do not think his hand resting on the small of your back escaped my notice. Such a possessive gesture should not be overlooked or underestimated."

Ruby gaped for a moment, then smoothed her expression into a semblance of decorum. "What are you trying to tell me?"

"My son is a master of control. He prides himself on ensuring his emotions are separate from everything else. When I watch him with you, I see glimpses of him I believed had been buried with his brother."

"I do not understand." Ruby finished the wine in her goblet.

"Several years ago, my oldest son, Francis, was killed in a fire. The stories maintain he died a hero, attempting to rescue a family trapped in the inferno. He rushed in, oblivious to the danger, and was trapped when the structure collapsed. His body buried in the rubble, burned to ash." Vivienne's gaze grew misty with unshed tears.

"I remember hearing the tale as it spread through the countryside." Ruby bowed her head. "My condolences on your loss."

Vivienne nodded, her expression clouded with the pain of loss and her obvious acceptance of the situation. "Francis and Crispin were close as children, but my husband favored Francis and his shining accomplishments. Crispin fell by the wayside, growing more resentful and rebelling at every opportunity. Crispin and Henry witnessed Francis's final act of bravery, and my husband blamed them both for not stopping Francis. For not saving his life."

"I am sure there was nothing that could be done to dissuade him. When a man sets his mind to something, little can change the course of his determination." Ruby remembered Guy's sacrifice but pushed the gnawing pain of the memory away.

Vivienne refilled their goblets and continued in her tale. "Crispin blames himself for his brother's death, although he will never admit it. My husband never forgave Crispin or Henry, and in retaliation, they both ran wild, causing mischief and wreaking havoc wherever they could. When they seduced a neighboring king's courtier, Crispin and Henry were separated and punished accordingly. My husband threatened them both with banishment should they refuse to comply with his commands."

"He was willing to disown his son?" Ruby stared at her, slowly absorbing the information.

"Aye, Crispin has potential to be a great ruler, but his soul is twisted, charred by the actions and betrayal of his father as well as by the guilt he feels over his brother's death." Vivienne sipped her wine and stared into the fire with an unfocused gaze. "I love my son. I fear for his soul. When his father tossed him out of the castle with no horse and no coin, my heart broke, but there was naught I could do. He made his choices and must suffer the consequences of his actions."

Ruby stared into the wine. Her heart ached to hear the tragic tale. Crispin was more than a spoiled and heartless noble. While she pitied him, Ruby knew life was filled with pain and suffering. She knew from experience how such emotions could warp one's soul or set them free. It seemed she and Crispin shared a common pain, yet chose different paths.

"Then you found him." Vivienne's words broke her reverie, and Ruby met her gaze. "You have restored my hope, and for that, I shall be eternally grateful."

"I did naught but follow my own heart." Ruby's cheeks bloomed with heat at the praise. "'Tis a miracle he has not locked me in the dungeons for some of the things I have said and done."

Vivienne smiled so brightly it reflected in her green eyes. "He would never hurt the woman he loves."

Loves? Ruby's mind raced. "You must be mistaken. I shall admit a great amount of lust exists between us, but love?" Ruby shook her head emphatically. "He does not love me."

"He may not say the words, but his actions speak clearly enough, my dear. If he is not in love with you, may the plague take me." She set her goblet aside and leaned forward, taking Ruby's hand in her own. "Trust me."

Ruby nodded, dumbfounded by her statement. "But everything has happened so quickly, how can you be so sure of his affection for me?"

"Perhaps it is a mother's intuition." Vivienne shrugged as she squeezed Ruby's hand. "You shall see it too in time."

"Why have you told me all this?" Ruby's heart overflowed with gratitude at her kindness.

"You have a very important role to play, my dear. Your destiny is far greater than you may have ever dreamed." Vivienne's expression softened and grew distant. "'Tis fate which has brought you here."

"I am nothing special," Ruby admitted. "I am an orphan who chose the life of an outlaw."

"It makes you even more special," Vivienne countered. "You have seen and experienced things that would have broken a weaker woman. It proves you are strong. The perfect balance for my son."

"I did what I needed to do in order to survive." Ruby stared at her in disbelief. No one had been this understanding of her past or her choices, ever. It entrenched Vivienne even deeper in her confidence.

"This is why I believe you should be queen." Crispin's mother met her gaze with an intensity that took her aback. "I have never been more proud of my son than when he brought you to me."

Ruby said nothing. She had no words to counter or validate Vivienne's statement. All she could do was nod.

"I shall take my leave now and allow you to rest. You have had quite an eventful day." Vivienne rose and crossed to the door. Ruby followed suit. "On the morrow, you shall join me, and we will discuss plans for your upcoming nuptials and the celebration."

"My thanks, Vivienne, for everything." Ruby curtsied out of respect.

"Ruby, my dear. We are to be family soon. It will be a

delight to have you as a daughter." She pulled Ruby into a hug, pressing a kiss to her temple. "Sleep well."

Ruby closed the door behind her and leaned against it. Her heart surged against her ribs. *Crispin.* Part of her longed to go to him, but the rest of her revolted, telling her this new information changed nothing about their relationship. At war with herself, she conceded defeat, tied the robe, and slipped into the darkened hallway.

Chapter Twenty-Two

Crispin closed the door to his presence chamber, tension humming between them. Henry stood with his gaze lost in the flames crackling in the hearth. Without a word, he crossed to the table where the wine sat and poured two goblets.

"My thanks." Henry took the proffered goblet without glancing away from the fire and downed the contents in one long draught. With a sigh, he turned to Crispin. "Had I known who she was, I never..."

Putting his hand up, Crispin nodded and pushed the pang of jealousy away. "I know, Henry. After all these years, it must come as a shock to see me brought to this point."

"I will admit, I never imagined..." He blew out a breath and refilled his goblet. "Where did you find her?" Henry's voice held a mixture of amazement and curiosity.

"She saved my arse," Crispin admitted without hesitation. "I was ambushed by four men intent on murder. She is quite talented with a blade, but give her a bow, and she transforms into an avenging angel."

"She saved your life?" Henry choked on his wine. "A woman saved you." He laughed, obviously unable to control himself.

"Ruby is known by another name, the Lady of the Forest." Crispin followed the swift change of Henry's expression from awe to shock as the implication of his words sank in.

"The outlaw!" Henry slammed the goblet down. "You chose a traitor for your bride? How could you even consider such a woman?"

"Contain yourself. You may be my closest companion, but do not think I will hesitate to run a blade through your heart if you exceed the boundaries of my tolerance." Crispin leaned against the large desk behind him. "I have weighed my decision to bind her to me and bear no qualms about making an outlaw my queen. If anything, her strength and fortitude will only add to her appeal as the Queen of Meradin. Besides, I have seen her passion and past actions were only to help the people of this land, not to further her station."

Henry nodded in silence as if weighing his words with care. "I see."

"Consider yourself fortunate I have decided to not take retribution alone for you indulging in a passionate kiss with my future queen."

"It will not happen again," Henry vowed with a solemn expression. "I swear on my honor."

"She is quite intoxicating," Crispin admitted. "I cannot fault you for desiring her." He glanced at Henry, who wore the telltale stain of regret high on his cheekbones.

"If what you say is true, then the woman is a rare treasure indeed. Her name suits her." Henry picked up the goblet and cradled it in his hand.

"Can I trust you to watch her without acting on the compulsion to touch her again?" Crispin arched his brow in question.

"Aye, Your Majesty." Henry bowed his head.

Crispin nodded with satisfaction. "Very well. I would choose no other to protect her. Do not give me a reason to regret my decision or end years of friendship with the tip of my sword."

Henry's head remained bowed. "You have my oath of service and fealty, Your Majesty."

Contented with Henry's response, Crispin turned the subject to other matters. "How fared your journey? I trust there were no complications."

The lines of worry on Henry's face softened. "None, Sire. I left as soon as I received word of your father's passing." He paused then added, "Rumor maintains he was murdered. Is there any truth to these claims?"

Crispin turned to his friend, his expression passive. "'Tis true, someone poisoned the king, and I believe I know who bears the burden of fault."

"Have you made your concerns known?" Henry asked.

"Not yet." Crispin took another drink. "But soon I shall have the proof I need to see the traitor brought to the block for his crimes."

"Is there something more I should know, Crispin?" Henry's voice remained low, the question almost a whisper.

He finished his wine and filled the goblet again. "You have been by my side for longer than any other. You hold all of my secrets in your breast. Had I something to share, Henry, you would be the first to know of it."

Henry crossed the distance between them and enclosed Crispin's arm with his hand. Crispin glanced into his friend's earnest face. "I know how much you despised your father and the agonizing torment he caused you over Francis' death. He never gave you the proper attention or credit you deserved. That slight has caused the bitterness inside of you to fester and rot. Tell me truly, did you have anything to do with his death?"

Ignoring the pressure of Henry's hand on his arm, Crispin drank from his cup before replying. "How do you expect me to answer such a question?" He shook free from his friend's grasp. "My father had enemies, as does every man. I shall confess the thought had taken root in my mind, slowly growing to the point of action." With a shrug, he leaned against the desk.

"You did not poison him then?" Henry persisted.

"In truth, I know not," Crispin replied in a cryptic but honest manner. 'Twas true, he had no notion if his plot had come to fruition without his assistance, or if someone else with much grander plans had acted with much more cunning and swiftness than he had.

"Even the king can be tried for treason." Henry crossed his arms.

"Would you have me drawn and quartered, my head liberated from my body for an act I cannot conclude with all certainty was directly related to the strained relationship between me and my father?"

"You know I will stand by your side until my final breath, Sire. I am only able to protect you if I am privy to everything."

Henry's tone softened. "I am neither your judge nor your executioner, merely your ally."

"While I appreciate your concern and your loyalty, I cannot share every burden with you." Crispin walked toward the hearth. "You may be loyal to me now, but should the tides turn, how am I to know you will not turn traitor, spill my blood, and steal my bride?"

"You wound me to even think me capable of such treason." Henry scowled, an edge of hurt lacing his words.

"All men are capable of treason, lust, murder, and revenge." Crispin sighed. "Perhaps trust is an illusion, as is love."

"You do not deserve her then."

Crispin turned and stared at Henry. "What did you say?"

"Ruby deserves better than you." He tilted his chin up as he spoke.

Of all the years they spent in each other's company, Henry never crossed the line more than he did with those words. Crispin came within a breath of Henry, whose gaze never wavered. They stood still, each taking the measure of the other. The tension in the room snapped tight with the ensuing silence.

"And what does she deserve then, Henry? I have offered her the world, a place by my side, pleasure unlike anything she has ever known, and the security of my name and protection. She will be my queen."

"You offer her everything but what a woman truly deserves," Henry replied. "Love, admiration, respect, and trust."

"You presume to insinuate I offer her none of these things by taking her to wife?"

"I have never seen you offer anyone these things. I do not believe it in your nature to even understand them."

Crispin fumed. How dare Henry assume to know the inner workings of his mind? As much as he wanted to rage against the man for such a blatant disregard for his station, Crispin reined in the anger thrashing inside of him. "You walk a fine line. Take care not to cross it further, or I shall not be held responsible for my actions."

"When have you ever been held responsible for any of your

actions, Crispin?"

The dam broke inside, releasing years of repressed rage. Crispin swung his fist, catching Henry's face. The crunch of flesh and bone echoed in the room as Henry stumbled backward, clutching for purchase to stop himself from collapsing on the floor. Henry straightened to his full height, his left cheek red and swelling.

"'Tis as I feared." Henry stepped back. "You have no heart to offer her. You will use her for your selfish amusement."

Crispin glared at his supposed friend. *Selfish amusement?* The barb stung even though it rang of truth the longer the thought lingered. He pushed it away. "I will not hesitate to run you through should you step between us. Friend or not, you will not take her from me and live." His hands clenched into fists.

Henry shook his head. "I shall not let you steal the light from her eyes as I have seen you do to scores of women before her."

"She chose me over certain death," Crispin growled. "'Twas her choice to be here."

"So you threatened her with death should she not marry you? How generous."

"Ruby was an outlaw. An outlaw does not fear death and neither does she." Crispin itched to strike him again, the impudent cur. He never saw Henry react in such a strong manner.

Henry sighed, pressing his hand to his face. "I beg of you, Crispin. She deserves more than physical trappings and titles. If she is as special as you say, then Ruby is a woman worthy of love."

"When did you become a scholar on love?" Crispin snapped, irritated by the unexpected divergence of the conversation.

"One needs only see the way she looks at you to know what is in her heart." Henry dropped his hands to his side. "I shall retire before one of us ends up bleeding in a heap on the floor. I shall attend you on the morrow." With a slight bow, Henry slipped from the chamber, leaving the door cracked in his wake.

Crispin collapsed in the chair next to the hearth. His hand ached, his head throbbed, and he wished he had stronger wine to dull the pain constricting his withered heart. As he stared into the flames, he realized Henry had the right of it.

Ruby deserved more than the superficial trimmings he offered. She deserved to be loved. Crispin scoffed at his cynicism. *Love.* How could a man trust an ideology in which he placed no faith?

Chapter Twenty-Three

Ruby glanced down the deserted hallway. She remembered the location of his presence chamber from the impromptu tour he gave her earlier in the day. Spotting the door, she crept along the wall and peered through the crack. Crispin sat in a chair next to the hearth, staring into the flames. Ruby stepped into the room and closed the door behind her with a solid *thunk*.

If he heard her, he made no acknowledgment of her presence, remaining firmly fixed in his chair. She approached him cautiously, unsure of the reception she would receive. His gaze never left the fire. Ruby stopped beside him, twisting her fingers together.

"You should be abed, Ruby." The timbre of Crispin's voice made her shiver, husky with an edge of resigned impatience.

"Sleep eludes me." She cleared her throat. "I had a hope we might speak."

"What would you have me say?" He met her gaze.

She stared at him, stunned for a moment, opening and closing her mouth. Ruby worried this might not be the best moment. Crispin seemed lost in a dark mood. Had her actions earlier caused him displeasure? The conversation with Vivienne flashed through her mind imbuing her with confidence. But in his presence, Ruby felt lost, consumed with guilt.

Crispin stood and circled her, brushing the wisps of hair at her nape with his fingertips. Her throat tightened at the contact, brief as it was. The heat of his body seeped into her as he crept closer. She swayed toward him but remained still, waiting.

"I would know your thoughts, my lord." Ruby's last remnant of strength seeped into the words.

"My thoughts..." Crispin began, his voice trailing off. He dropped his hands, but his body remained a hair's breadth from her. "Why have you come?"

"Am I unwelcome?" Her body brushed against his.

He groaned and wrapped an arm around her waist, pulling her flush against him. His whispered words brushed the delicate spot below her ear. "Is there not somewhere else you would rather be?"

Ruby shivered, confused by his words, yet aroused by his voice, his touch. "Nay, my lord."

"What of Henry? Would you rather find your pleasure in his embrace?" His grip tightened, his free hand grasping the tender skin of her throat tipping her head back.

"Nay, my lord." Her body trembled beneath his touch.

"Why are you here, Ruby?" He nipped at her neck, his teeth grazing the tender skin. "Would you like to confess? I can hear your penance and punish you accordingly."

A whimper escaped her lips. He slid his hand into her chemise, cupping her breast. She arched against him, unsure of the direction of their conversation. One thing was certain: He had complete control.

"Would you have me summon Henry? Let him take you here in my chambers." He pinched her nipple, and she gasped. "I saw the flush in your cheeks when he kissed you. The desire in your eyes, even as your lips said no."

He released her, and she stumbled, collapsing against the chair. Ruby glanced over her shoulder at him. "I cannot control my body's reaction." She straightened at the accusation.

"Take off your gown." Crispin crossed the room and picked up his leather whip.

The command shocked her. *Oh, sweet mercy, he is going to strike me.* She trembled as she pulled the robe free, letting it slide into a puddle at her feet.

"The shift as well."

Ruby pulled the thin cotton shift over her head and tossed it on the chair he occupied moments before. She stood before him naked and tilted her chin up in defiance. Her hands clenched in fists by her side. "If you desire blood, then take it, but I shall not suffer in silence. I would rather die than be a prized animal you beat for sport."

His gaze hardened as it combed over her bare skin. "You misunderstand my punishment." A smirk crept across his lips, lingering there. "'Tis not your blood I desire, merely your pleasure."

Her breath caught in her throat. He stalked closer, brushing the tip of the leather against her breast and trailing it down over her stomach. Ruby focused her attention on his eyes and not on the desire consuming her.

"Come here." He crossed to the large mahogany desk and motioned to the smooth expanse of wood. "Bend over."

Ruby stepped closer and leaned over the smooth top, pressing her breasts to the wood. She thrust her backside out, knowing he could see every intimate part of her. The heat of shame and arousal flooded her.

"Open for me." He touched the whip to her thigh. Following his command, she braced for the sting of the whip against her flesh, but instead, the soft leather slid across her bare skin. Her anxiety stretched thin as she anticipated the strike...but it never came.

When she glanced over her shoulder, his gaze burned into hers, his hand trailing the whip across her legs and backside. He stepped closer and pulled her to her feet. She gasped as his grip on her wrist tightened. Her body burned as he pressed her against the desk, his desire evident in his voice and his body's reaction to her.

"When we are wed, no man will know your touch, your taste, your scent...you will be mine and mine alone. Have I made myself clear?" He kissed her throat, sending her mind into oblivion.

She nodded as he licked her skin and teased the lobe of her ear with his teeth.

He kissed her lips softly. "Now, return to your bed and dream of none but me."

Her heart sank as he stepped away, but she held her chin high as she retrieved her clothes and donned them. What dark thoughts churned inside his mind? Why did he refrain from punishing her? Even more curious, why would he push her away when she was so obviously willing? She stood aching, naked, and wet before him, yet he denied his own desire. Her thoughts returned to Vivienne's earlier words. Perhaps this was how Crispin showed love? She glanced in his direction.

Crispin's silent, brooding gaze followed her as she crossed the room. Her hand hovered over the door handle, and she turned toward him.

"Will you be joining me?" She noted the way the firelight danced across his features, casting half of him in light and bathing the rest in deep shadows.

"When the inclination strikes me."

Something had shaken the calm façade he kept in place. His words might be cold and calloused, but Ruby sensed the powerful undercurrent beneath the river of indifference. He wanted her, even now, but fought against it. She offered him a smile and dipped a small courtesy.

Crispin dismissed her with a nod. On the journey to her room, her mind churned with images and emotions. This man never ceased to surprise her. He teased her with his words and actions, baiting her, drawing her out. While the bond between them had grown, Ruby hesitated to allow herself the indulgence of being seduced by the comforts surrounding her. Until he proved himself worthy of her trust, she refused to allow him even a glimpse of her heart, even if he held full possession of her body.

Chapter Twenty-Four

Henry wandered the keep until his feet led him back to the garden where he met Ruby. He shook his head as he sank onto the stone bench next to a trellis of roses. Their comforting scent wrapped around him. He sighed at the conflict raging inside him. Crispin went too far this time.

They were nearly brothers. Training together as knights had brought them closer than their blood-kin had ever been. Memories of them together flashed in his mind's eye. The two of them with swords clashing in combat. Crispin's roguish expression as they drank their fill at a tavern with whores hanging on both arms. Crispin buried deep in a willing wench while Henry indulged in a woman of his own. The images unfurled in his mind like a mummer's farce.

He hung his head and rubbed the crease between his eyes. Crispin's thirst for debauchery and games had only increased after Francis's death. He blamed himself for that fateful night. It tore at his heart since Francis had been like a brother to him as well.

Francis had taken them under his wing, as a good older brother and prince should do, but he never understood the close bond between Crispin and Henry. A bond forged from blood, steel, and misplaced honor. Then the night the golden prince had been stolen away by death, there had been nothing Crispin and Henry could do but watch the flames climb into the night sky.

Henry raked his hand through his hair and stood to pace the garden. Crispin held himself above everyone else, manipulating and seducing them for his amusement. It came as no surprise when the king sent Henry on a diplomatic mission and threatened Crispin with banishment. Even though he was the prince and heir to the throne, Crispin remained unpredictable and temperamental. No matter how hard he tried, Henry continued to be unsuccessful in his attempts to sway Crispin to the truth of his folly.

Ruby. As beautiful as her namesake, an image of her returned to him, bathed in moonlight, caught in his embrace, the soft press of her lips and the unforgiving steel blade. An outlaw with a heart of pure gold taken to wife by the sadistic Prince of Whispers. He kicked the rose bushes. His encounter with Ruby and the argument with Crispin left a bitter taste in his mouth. While his allegiance remained intact, Henry held no qualms when it came to confronting Crispin.

In their youth, Henry saw the trail of heartache Crispin left in his wake, bounding from wench to wench without a thought for anyone but himself. The Prince of Whispers, a teasing moniker bestowed by the ladies of the court, suited him to perfection. His silver tongue could charm the devil himself. Henry abandoned the garden and proceeded toward the kitchens, hunger consuming him even as the frustration lingered. At the late hour, he anticipated the kitchens to be vacant and thus easier to indulge in something savory to ease his stomach. He pushed open the door.

A comely maid smoothing dough on the table glanced up at his arrival. "My lord." She bowed, brushing her hands on her skirt. "How may I be of service?"

"Have you any meat and bread, something simple to ease my hunger?"

She gathered the requested items and placed them neatly on a tray. Henry admired her as she worked, her chestnut-tinted hair tucked beneath a cap. Soft tendrils of escaped curls bounced on her flour-dusted cheek as she moved. The soft curves hidden beneath a worn kirtle. At least Ruby's presence would save her the unwanted attention of the prince.

Henry winced at the unwarranted thought. When had he begun to think so ill of his friend? He pushed the painful topic from his mind and focused on the lovely woman gracing him with her smile. Tearing off a piece of bread, he popped it into his mouth.

She picked up the dough and placed it into a pan, making a

pie of some sort he assumed. He munched on the meat and cheese in silence while she worked. Her delicate fingers smoothed the crust and added decorative touches around the edge of the pan. His gaze followed along the length of her arm to her neck, over the swell of her breasts and down her hips. Henry licked his lips.

"How else may I serve you?" She gestured to his empty bowl. "Would you like something sweet?" Before he could reply, she appeared before him with a small fruit tart poised on the tips of her fingers.

"Taste this," she whispered, her voice husky and full of sensual promise. She dipped a finger into the filling and held it to his mouth.

Henry's cock ached when her finger slid between his parted lips. He groaned as the berry flavor melted on his tongue mingling with the taste of her sweet skin. Her touch lingered long after the fruit dissolved. Releasing her from his mouth, he slipped an arm around her waist and pulled her closer. She came willingly, her eyes darkened with need.

"Delicious. Did you make this yourself?" He smoothed his hands over her hips as he nodded to the tart on the table.

Her dark eyes flickered with amusement. "Aye."

Henry pulled her flush against him and grinned when her arms slipped around his neck. "You are a bold one." He pressed a kiss to her neck.

She clung to him, her soft moans echoing in his ear, making him harder than iron. "I have a confession, my lord."

He pulled back and stared into her lust-hazed eyes. "Do I look like a priest?"

"Nay." She bit her lip.

"I shall hear your confession and punish you for your wicked thoughts if that is your desire." He spun her in his arms and slid his hands along her bodice to cup her breasts. "What shall I call you?"

"Ivy." She moaned as he squeezed harder.

"Such a lovely name." He drew his teeth over her throat enjoying the gasps escaping her lips. "What is your confession then, sweet Ivy?" The maid whimpered with every touch, every kiss. She blossomed under his ministrations, and he reveled in her reactions.

"I have dreamt of this. Of you."

Her words slammed into him like a runaway carriage and made him harder than he ever imagined possible. "Have you been watching me? Imagining all the wicked things you want me to do to you?"

"Aye."

Henry grasped her chin and forced her to face him. "What do you wish of me?"

"I only wish to please you, my lord." Her face pinkened under his scrutiny like a rose unfurling in the summer sun.

The lovely girl before him softened in his embrace, and he trailed his hands over the coarse woolen gown she wore. "How have I not taken notice of you before?" He searched her wide green eyes.

"Mayhap I did not wish for you to see me, my lord." Her hips pressed against him, making him moan in appreciation. "I have seen too many servant girls seduced by the handsome knights. 'Tis wiser if I keep to the shadows."

"You have been hiding from the prin...I mean king." His eyes narrowed on her. "Clever wench."

She traced her fingertips along his jaw and brushed his lower lip. "Does that make me wicked too?"

Henry slipped his hands around her waist and hoisted her onto the counter. She squealed in surprise as he stepped between her legs, buried his hands in her hair beneath the cap, and dragged her close. His whispered reply brushed across her lips.

"Aye, strumpet. It does." He kissed her, claiming her lips, tasting the fruit juices on her tongue. So sweet and intoxicating like the finest wine.

She grasped handfuls of his hair and held him close. Her soft moans encouraged him, drawing him into her. Their bodies pressed together, curve to curve. When his hands slipped beneath her skirts to trail up her thighs, she gasped.

Henry pulled back. "Come with me." At her tentative nod,

he gripped her waist and pulled her into his arms. Crossing the room, he kicked open the door and stepped out into the night.

"Where are you taking me?" she whispered in his ear, drawing the lobe between her teeth.

"Somewhere I can ravish you without being interrupted."

She pulled back and arched her brow as if to question his decision, but silence followed. Leaning her head against his chest, she sighed.

Upon arriving at his modest chamber, Henry set her down and opened the door. As soon as they cleared the threshold, he pushed the door closed, grasped Ivy by the shoulders, and pinned her against the solid wood. He threw off the cap and wrapped his hand in her long hair, pulling her head back exposing her neck and shoulders. Kiss after kiss he lavished on her. The taste of flour and skin and spices assaulted him.

"H-Henry?" Her husky tone made it dangerously difficult for him to contain his desire.

"Aye, strumpet." He paused, allowing his nose to brush against the delicate skin beneath her jaw. His tongue darted out of its own accord, making her shiver.

"I have never been...well...I have never done this before."

Henry stopped and leaned back to gaze down upon her. Her mussed hair, kiss-bruised lips, and dazed expression did nothing to hide the truth he saw in her eyes. He sighed and ran his hand down over his face.

"Ivy, if what you say is true, I cannot in good conscience continue as I have been." He stepped back and dropped his hands, clenching them into fists.

Ivy closed the gap between them and wrapped her arms around his neck. "It was not my intention for you to stop." A blush stole across her cheeks. "Please, I do not wish for this moment to end."

He closed his eyes and took a deep, fortifying breath. If she kissed him again, he would surely lose all control. Unclasping her hands from his neck, he lowered their clasped hands between them, his thumb idly brushing the soft skin of her wrists. God's teeth, he wanted her with a desperation which startled him.

An image of Ruby flashed in his mind, the memory of her kiss nearly forgotten by the substitution of another's. He shook his head. Ruby was nothing to him. Ivy could be nothing to him, at least nothing more than an engaging romp. Henry had a responsibility, first to his king and second, to his family. Tears formed in her green eyes and he cursed himself for bearing a conscience.

"My dear, I may not be a saint, but I am certainly no scoundrel. I cannot do you harm, and I certainly have nothing more to offer than a solitary night of passion." He released her hands and raked his hair.

"So if someone else deflowers me, will you then have me?"

He stared at her, his mouth agape. "You would sell your body so cheaply?"

"If it allows me to partake in one night with you, aye, I would." She laced her fingers together and dropped her gaze.

Henry tipped her chin up and forced her to meet his gaze. "Why are you in earnest?"

"Do you not remember my confession, my lord?"

With a nod, he gathered her into his embrace once more. "I cannot promise you more than this night," he murmured into her soft tresses.

"One night is more than I could hope for." Ivy smiled up at him.

His heart thundered in response. Gently, he led her to his bed and sat on the edge, pulling her across his lap. She kissed him. Her hands cradled his head, her lips demanding and persistent as they plundered his.

He slowly tugged at the laces of her simple gown. Her fingertips brushed against his chest as she removed his doublet and tunic. With each article of clothing they dropped to the floor, another expanse of skin lay unveiled and ready to be explored. Henry pushed her to her feet and peeled the gown from her body along with her shift. She stood bare before him, highlighted by the glow of firelight, her arms crossed over her chest, gaze downcast.

Tipping up her chin, he kissed her and slid his hand over

her throat, pausing only to grasp her wrists and reveal that which she hid from his gaze. His lips traced over her jaw, blazing a path down to her breasts where he took a dark nipple into his mouth and suckled.

Ivy arched against him, a cry tearing from her lips. "My...I..." She moaned fully this time as he cupped her breasts in his hands and lavished attention on both. He spun her and laid her down on the bed.

Henry straightened and slid the rest of his clothes down over his hips. Climbing onto the bed, he leaned over her, skin brushing against skin. Her eyes flew wide, lip tucked between her teeth. He rested his hand on the curve of her hip and swept it across her stomach. She trembled beneath his touch. He smiled and kissed her softly on the lips, letting the touch linger and grow desperate. Ivy snaked her arms around his neck and pulled him against her. Her nipples brushed against his chest, and the last vestiges of his control snapped.

Settling between her thighs, he brushed his fingertips across her sex. "You are certain this is what you desire?" Through the haze of lust, he warred with his conscience.

"Aye." She writhed against him, pressing herself into his hand.

He kissed her again as he stroked her slick quim, toying with her, making her squirm. Every mewl, every moan and whimper drove him deeper into oblivion. Slipping his finger into her, he groaned. *Tight, wet, warm*...he kissed her again as he stretched her, knowing this would be uncomfortable for her. *Damn you for being so chivalrous.* The more he teased her, the closer he came to spending before he even entered her welcoming body.

"Take me, I beg you...I cannot..." She bucked beneath him, her cheeks flushed with pleasure.

Henry withdrew enough to fit himself and thrust into her as he captured her lips in a tender kiss. She stiffened, and he stilled, careful not to inflict more pain and allow her body to acclimate to him. Her nails bit into his back. Her lips trembled against his. Deepening the kiss, he sighed when she softened against him. Gently, he rocked against her. Her body played in harmony to his, the tender give and take of new lovers.

When she tilted her hips to meet his, Henry tugged her lip between his teeth and met the passion rising within her. Their bodies surged and retreated like waves crashing upon the shore. She gasped at the brush of his fingertips over her sensitive nipples. He ground his hips against hers, making her body arch against him again. The tension built between them until she shattered in ecstasy. He kissed her once more, allowing his release to claim him. He pulled from her heat and spilled on the bed.

He remained poised above her, their foreheads pressed together, their breaths mingling. Henry pulled back to take in the afterglow brightening her features.

Ivy kissed the tip of his nose. "'Twas better than I expected." She cocked her head and met his bold stare.

"Did you expect less of me?" He mock frowned. "Your strange words make me wonder if this was not a calculated seduction on your part. Strumpet."

"I am now, am I not?" She grinned.

Henry shook his head. "I tease you with the name, but you are no whore, Ivy." Her brow furrowed and her lips tugged into a frown. Henry smoothed the lines between her brows with his thumb. "Stay with me tonight." The words left his lips before he could stop them. *Why am I inviting her to stay?*

Her tender kiss silenced his inner conflict. She pushed him back to lie on the bed and straddled him. The sudden change in position made him wonder if the innocent façade hid a daring, sensual beast.

"Are you going to let me sleep at all this eve, strumpet?"

"Probably not." Ivy leaned down and captured his nipple in her mouth. He grasped her hips and gave her a light tap on her backside.

"Have a care. You may still want to walk on the morrow."

"Such confidence." She trailed her tongue over his nipple again, and her breath sent a delicious wave of lust straight to his hardening cock. She wiggled her arse against it and grinned. "'Tis why I chose you."

He barely had a moment to think on her comment before she slipped down over his cock, taking it deep. Henry decided all coherent thought could wait until the morrow.

Chapter Twenty-Five

Sitting at the large table, Crispin drummed his fingers on the wood as he listened to his Privy Council. He would have preferred to avoid a meeting like this, but their request demanded a reply. So he sat silently listening to their never-ending drivel. This opportunity proved adequate to determine the strength and cunning of his inherited council. It crossed his mind to remove them all and replace them with selections of his own, but there was only one he trusted enough to fill the highest of the vacant positions.

As if reading the direction of his thoughts, the Lord Privy Seal turned to him. "Have you decided on your Lord High Steward, Sire?"

Crispin turned to the gangly man and leaned forward in his seat. "We have decided to give the position to Sir Henry, soon to be invested as His Grace, Henry Balmont, Duke of Westdell."

"You are choosing the fourth son of a northern lord as your Right Hand, entrusting him with the safety of our country and its military might?" The Lord Chancellor posed the question with an air of disbelief. He bowed his head slightly under Crispin's narrowed gaze. "'Tis not my place to question your choices, Sire, but there have been whispers of his family dealing with the northern raiders from Ireland and Scotland. Can he be trusted?"

With a tilt of his head, Crispin allowed his gaze to trail across the expressions of the five men sitting around the table with him. "Henry has proven himself to be unwavering and loyal in all ways, and without reservation, he has proven himself worthy of this high office. He fought by my side since we were but children. We have no cause for concern when it comes to his fealty to our kingdom."

"Your father sent him away; perhaps he found a reason to distrust your friend." The Lord Privy Seal idly twisted the hem of his robes between his fingers.

Crispin defaulted to a less formal address. "My father sent me away as well, but merely to provide an experience he believed would strengthen my competence as the future king of Meradin. 'Tis my belief his orders for Henry were solely to strengthen him as a diplomat and a soldier." Crispin leaned forward and met the unwavering gaze of each man in the room. "Although my father and I did not agree on many matters, I hold my responsibility as the ruler of Meradin as sacred as he did."

"Your father was a generous and benevolent king," the Lord Chancellor added sagely.

Crispin nearly ground his teeth in frustration but forced a smile nonetheless. "I have only just begun my reign. There is no telling what the future holds for my country and my people."

"If your actions have proven anything, it reveals you are reckless and selfish." One of the quieter men spoke freely.

Mustering all the patience he possessed, Crispin nodded. "My actions have been foolhardy and more often than not vain and self-serving. I cannot deny that." He opened his hands, palms up, in a conciliatory gesture while controlling his desire to release the rage building inside of him. "However, I have seen the error of my ways and am willing to make a fresh start as the King of Meradin." Reverting to more formal speech sent a cautionary note to those seated at the long table.

"If only Francis…"

Crispin slammed his fist down on the table, effectively cutting the man off. The council members shrank back in obvious terror. He shook his head to clear the dark thoughts swirling around him and focused on the one thing remaining. He was King of Meradin. He rubbed his chin, the bristles of his beard biting into the skin of his palm.

"My brother would have made a far better ruler, I grant you. Alas, it was not in the stars for him to take our father's place on the throne." He heaved a sigh for emphasis. "No matter how much we wish it otherwise, Francis is dead. May God rest his soul." The men surrounding him nodded in solemn agreement. "And might I remind the council that to speak of anyone else as king—even in the hypothetical—is treason."

"What of this woman you have claimed as your queen?" The Lord Chancellor refocused the topic once again. "We know nothing of her history, her lineage, or her family. There are several women of noble birth from neighboring countries who would desire nothing more than the opportunity to be your wife and become the future queen. Why would you place a commoner upon the throne beside you?"

The frustration and rage boiling inside of him for the past several hours came to a pinnacle and threatened to consume his wits. Taking a deep, steadying breath, Crispin closed his eyes and envisioned Ruby in all her naked splendor. A smirk crossed his lips before he could stop it. She may not be of royal blood, her heritage be damned, but he would have no other. No woman would ever be enough for him since he claimed Ruby for his own.

"For the moment what we know of her past is sufficient. One day, we shall unlock the secrets of her upbringing and her blood, but these things do not bring a cause for concern. Lady Ruby has devoted her life to the service of the people, coming to the aid of those in need and foregoing her personal comfort to ensure those around her are well cared for. Will these qualities not endear her to the people? Will they see her as not only a fair and generous queen but a champion of the common folk?" The men nodded at his words. Crispin allowed his expression to brighten not at their slow acceptance of his statement, but at the thought of Ruby in a crown standing beside him.

"It would be prudent for you to postpone this marriage, Sire." The Lord Chancellor voiced his concern, unconvinced of Crispin's persuasive argument.

"Lady Ruby shall be our queen, and nothing short of the hand of God Himself will interfere with the marriage ceremony in ten days." Crispin's gaze narrowed on the Chancellor and then skimmed over the rest of the men who nodded in agreement, their eyes wide. "Very well, now the matter is settled, we shall continue the discussion about Henry serving as my Lord High Steward. Is there any just cause besides those discussed as to why

Henry should not be considered for the position?"

"Nay, Sire." The Lord Chancellor spoke for the men as they all shook their heads.

"Then it is settled. Sir Henry shall serve as my Right Hand as well as my Lord High Steward." Crispin nodded, finally pleased with the direction of the meeting. "Are there any other points of business you wish to bring to attention?" His gaze alighted on each of the men.

"There is nothing more, Sire," the Chancellor replied.

"Very well, my lords. I shall be in my presence chamber." Crispin rose, and with a nod, he left the council chamber adjoining the throne room. He closed the door behind him and made his way to his private chambers with haste. He would suffer fools gladly to see himself permanently ensconced on the throne. Unfortunately, his cousin seemed all too eager to have him attend a long-overdue meeting with the council. The same cousin who stood to inherit should Crispin die without issue. He felt the scowl bearing down on his expression and shook it away. 'Twould be no matter in a mere ten days. The crown would be his, and his cousin could go to the devil along with his father's council.

He pushed open the door to his presence chamber to find Henry sitting in his chair, his feet propped on the desk with a half-eaten apple in his hand.

"Sire, 'tis a pleasure to see you in so fine a mood this day." A sly grin tugged at the corner of Henry's lips.

Crispin wanted to punch him, ensuring his teeth would no longer be in his mouth but on the floor. He cocked his head and shut the door behind him. "Get your impertinent arse out of my chair."

Henry rose to his feet, walked around the desk, and plopped onto the small settee by the fireplace. He took a bite of the apple and chewed, watching Crispin thoughtfully.

"What?" Crispin practically growled at his friend's lopsided smile. "I swear by all the saints, if you do not cease your grinning, I shall have you banished to the farthest reaches known to mankind."

"I take it your meeting with the council did not go as well as you had hoped." Henry finished the apple and tossed the core into the fireplace.

"Nay." Crispin sat in his chair and placed his feet where Henry's had been moments before. "They did not reject my proposals, however, it will take more effort than I am willing to expend to ensure they do not change their minds."

"You are the king; there is nothing they can do about it."

"Aye, but I did make one change to the council that should please you."

"Sire?"

"You will be invested as His Grace, Henry Balmont, Duke of Westdell with all the lands and privileges attendant, after which you will take your seat on the council as my Right Hand and Lord High Steward."

Henry choked on his wine. A full minute passed before he found his voice again. "Your Majesty...Sire...Crispin...you cannot be serious. I am the youngest son of a minor Baron."

"And my most trusted friend. Who else could I choose to fill such an important post? I need your counsel, Henry. You are the only man who will tell me what I need to know rather than what you think I want to hear."

Henry paced, clearly agitated. He stopped and turned to his king...his friend. "Crispin, you know I would do anything for you without question, and not solely because you are my king. But this is..." Henry paused unable to find the words.

"My will and royal decree, my friend. 'Tis good to be King."

"Sire, in truth, I know not what to say."

Crispin extended his arm, and the men shared the clasped handshake of equals and embraced. "It is customary to thank your king for such a gift."

Henry laughed nervously and dropped down on one knee. "Thank you, Your Majesty. I am your loyal and most humble servant."

Crispin gave a nonchalant wave of his hand. "Get up. Now, when I came in here you were looking rather pleased with yourself. What could...wait...I have only seen you like this..." He fisted his hand in his friend's doublet and lifted him to his feet. "You were with a woman. God's bones if you touched Ruby, I will show you no mercy."

Henry laughed. "Nay, I have not laid a hand on your precious treasure, you lovesick fool."

Crispin released him and retreated a step. "Careful, Henry, you are treading dangerous territory as it is. Do not tempt me into rash action."

"As lovely and charming as Ruby may be, I have kept my distance and my vow to not touch her again." He turned his attention to the fire, losing himself in the flames.

"Who is she then?" Crispin crossed his arms and watched Henry's expression haze with the memory of lust and passion. "Must have been quite a fuck to get you in such a state."

Henry shrugged. "One of the serving maids offered me a night of pleasure. It would have been quite remiss of me to leave her in such a state of frustration."

"How chivalrous of you to show concern for her wellbeing." With a nod, Crispin returned to his desk and sat on the edge. "The council was not in favor of my taking Ruby to wife. While their concerns are valid, I cannot allow them to dictate my choice of bride. No matter how politically advantageous it may be."

"Ahh, the truth is apparent now. You chose Ruby so a bride would not be chosen for you by the council." Henry sat down again and laid his arm on the back of the settee, resting an ankle on his knee.

"I chose Ruby to be my mistress. She chose a much grander role."

"You offered her a place as your mistress or death?"

"I did." Crispin smirked. "However, she countered with queen or death. How could I refuse such an offer?" He shrugged and continued without waiting for Henry's reply. "She played into my hands, as I knew she would."

Henry shook his head. "You are taunting fire and steel, Crispin. Ruby is not the type to be played like a chess piece on a board. If she realizes you are using her to your own ends, she may very well kill you."

"It would not be the first time she has threatened to do so, and besides, what would you know of her temperament? You know less of her than you know of the kitchen wench you bedded."

Henry pointed a finger at Crispin. "Mark my words, that woman will be your undoing if you push her too hard."

Crispin waved him off with a flick of his wrist. "What I do with her is no concern of yours." He grinned and leaned forward. "Unless you would like to join us in the bedchamber one night and see how responsive she is to my touch."

Henry scoffed and rolled his eyes. "The handful of times we shared a woman, you barely left her coherent for any pleasure to last more than an hour."

He shrugged barely remembering the wench in question. The temptation to put Ruby in such a situation did not entice him as it once would have; however, he was not averse to teasing her in his own way, even if it was for one evening. He tapped his fingers on the desk. While the idea of sharing Ruby with Henry sent a pang of jealousy clawing at his chest, he would consider the matter further if it would work in his favor for his plans. He pushed the thought away and reached for the glass decanter of wine. After pouring a dram for himself and Henry, he handed a goblet to his friend.

"Have you sent the messenger to fetch your family for the wedding?" Crispin took a drink, letting the crisp flavors revive him.

"I have already dispatched one of my men to deliver the summons. That is what it is, is it not? A summons?"

"You would not welcome your family to celebrate my marriage and coronation?"

"I have not spoken to my family in nigh on four years; why would I waste the breath now?" Henry glowered at him over his cup as he brought it to his lips.

"They are your blood, the only family you will ever have...and all that rot." His sarcastic tone was not lost on Henry.

"After Francis...well, there was nothing but animosity

between us. They believed you led me down a path far from the destiny they had designed for me." Henry scoffed into the goblet and took a healthy swallow. "Who am I, but the fourth son and a disappointment?"

"They have pushed you away long enough. When they see your new position in my kingdom, they will eat their spiteful words." Crispin finished the wine in one swallow.

Henry shrugged and tapped his finger on the cup. A knock echoed in the chamber. Both men stood at the sound.

"Enter," Crispin commanded.

A knight slipped into the room panting and breathless, his red and gold doublet pristine, denoting his position as a palace guard. He snapped a courteous bow before addressing Crispin.

"Sire, Lady Ruby has left the palace."

All the rage he channeled and successfully slid beneath his careful façade slipped at the simple phrase.

"*What?*" He slammed the goblet down on his desk. "I gave explicit instructions to have her under your watch at all times. How in the hell did she manage to slip out of the gates?"

"Your orders were to watch her, Sire, not imprison her."

Crispin's teeth ground together making his jaw ache. "God's blood, teeth, and bones! Must I do everything myself?" He strode toward the door as the knight fled the room in haste. Henry's voice stopped him.

"Allow me, Sire. I shall return her to the safety of the keep before dark."

Charging off after Ruby would be worse than folly, it would show his desperation and concern. After denying himself the warmth of her bed last eve, he kept his distance in the hope she would seek him out. Never would he have assumed she would run from him, from the safety of the castle walls. He ran his hand over his face.

"Henry, bring her back. Take Matthew as your guide. He knows where she will go, where you will find her."

"The blacksmith's new apprentice?"

"Aye, the lad is sharp, so mind your tongue around him." Crispin's pointed look earned a solemn nod from Henry.

"As you wish, Sire."

"And Henry..."

"Aye."

"Watch her before you bring her back to me." His voice dropped in timbre. "I want to know who she was so desperate to run to when she should have come to me."

Chapter Twenty-Six

The wind whipped in her hair as she bent low over Ginger's neck. Ruby seized the opportunity when it presented itself. Her heart twisted in regret over her deception. But there was no possible way to get a reliable message to Marian without compromising her mother's safe haven.

She feared Marian's reaction to the news. The last time they had spoken, her situation was quite different. The last few days spun her into a whirlpool of conflicting emotions. She slowed the horse as they approached the small cottage tucked into the forest near the edge of the lake. As she slid from the saddle, Marian came around the back of the cottage with a wooden crate in her arms.

"Ruby! What are you doing here, child?" She set the crate down and approached Ruby with her arms outstretched. "Come and hug me. You look as though you are about to burst into tears."

As Marian wrapped her arms around her, Ruby clutched at her mother's clothing. Her heart burst and the tears fell in hot streaks down her cheeks.

"Oh, Mother, what am I to do?" she whispered between hiccupping sobs born of relief and uncertainty.

"Come inside, my gem. Tell me what has you so distraught." She led Ruby into the cottage and set her down on a chair by the hearth.

As Marian fixed some tea, Ruby rubbed her tear-stained face against the sleeves of her borrowed, plain woolen gown. "I have been a fool, Mother. A bloody, simple fool!" The tears came again, silently this time. She wiped them away with an angry swipe of her hand.

"The prince?"

"How did you...oh, well, I suppose that would be the

general assumption considering our last conversation." Ruby shrugged.

"What happened, my child?" Marian set the warm brew before her and sat across from her at the table.

"His soldiers captured me, brought me before him in chains, and left me at his mercy. He demanded I choose between death and becoming his whore."

Marian nodded as if anticipating more. "And what was your reply?"

"I told him to make me queen or take my life."

A toothy grin split Marian's lips. "Such fire in your spirit, my dear. When is the wedding?"

Ruby stared at her stunned. "How do you know I did not escape and return here in fear for my life?"

"While the boy may be manipulative, selfish, vain, and reckless, he is no fool. He met his match in you, even if neither one of you see it." Marian sipped her tea. "What then?"

"What?" Ruby stared at her mother in awe. How was she always so perceptive?

"What happened after this? 'Tis obvious he has not chained you up in a tower and thrown away the key. Tell me everything."

The tale spilled from her lips in a rushed jumble of words, and emotions poured from her in torrential waves. As she approached the end of her story, Marian's expression never changed. She listened to every word with attentive care. Once she concluded her tale, Ruby took a drink of her tea and waited for Marian to speak.

The older woman nodded and took a healthy gulp of her now chilled tea. "Well, this is quite an interesting quandary you have found yourself in. What does your heart tell you?"

Ruby shook her head. "I thought I wanted to be queen. Think of all the good I could do for the people in such a position of influence." Her heart sank. "But Crispin—'tis like he has no thought for anyone but himself and his own pleasure. How am I to understand a man such as him?"

Marian's laughter rang throughout the small cottage, startling Ruby. "One can never completely understand a man."

She wiped the tears from Ruby's cheek as the laughter continued.

"Why are you laughing?" Ruby asked, stunned by Marian's reaction.

"Guy was much like you described, once upon a time." Marian sighed as the laughter subsided. "He was vain, arrogant, and insufferable truly."

"Your husband...are you positive you are talking about the same man who instructed me to use a bow, taught me to hunt and track, and raised me like his daughter?" The image of Guy being anything but the caring father she leaned on in her childhood proved too much for her to comprehend.

Marian nodded. "Aye. It was your appearance in our lives that finally touched his heart. Since we could have no children of our own, he believed it to be punishment for the misadventures of his youth. When he found you amidst the burning wreckage of the raid, he realized you were a gift from God, his opportunity for redemption."

Ruby shook her head in disbelief. "How did I not know these things?"

With a shrug, Marian stood to refill their cups. "When Guy passed, I wanted you to remember the good things about him. There was no need to show the darkened shadows of a man's poisoned past. 'Twas not my wish to tarnish the memories you held of Guy."

"I see." Ruby chewed on her lower lip, her thoughts racing through her mind. There were so many questions, but she fought to contain the emotion threatening to bubble to the surface at the mention of her father. Marian compared Guy to Crispin; how were they similar? What would make someone choose such a man? She met her mother's gaze. "How...I mean why did you choose to be with him?"

"One cannot choose whom they love. It happens. A bolt of understanding through the heart or a slow warming of endearment toward the other, it does not matter how. Love chooses you, not the other way around." Marian sipped her tea, watching her carefully.

A rush of warmth spread up her neck and into her cheeks.

"What if it is not love but desire which draws you together?"

Marian nodded in understanding. "Ah yes, the prince has made his desire for you quite apparent, has he not?"

Ruby bowed her head, fearing the heat of her blush might spontaneously catch her aflame. "He speaks to me in ways I never imagined would affect me so. Every touch, every kiss, every whisper, and I am consumed by unexplainable need." She fidgeted with the mug in her hands. "Although his mother claims to see love in his gaze and his actions, I fear she may be mistaken."

"You have spoken to the queen?" Marian's brow arched, her eyes wide.

"Aye, on several occasions. She has accepted the fact I have no money, no connections, and no royal blood." With a tilt of her head, Ruby pondered the few occasions she spoke with Vivienne. "She believes in me. Is that not strange?"

"Did you tell her everything of your history?"

"I told her of the raid and of my time as an outlaw." Ruby met Marian's concerned gaze. "I told her of a couple who raised me, but not your names or location."

"The monarchy has long been at odds with what Guy and I spent most of our lives trying to achieve." She rested her hand on Ruby's. "It will turn out in the end. This is where you are meant to be."

"Sometimes I feel he does things, says things to merely exhibit his control over me."

"He knows no different. The man was raised to believe he is above everyone else. He was the prince and is now king. In his mind, everyone is beholden to him and his wishes. 'Tis the way of all royal bloodlines." Marian's words and warm touch did little to allay her fears of Crispin and his demanding, possessive ways.

"I cannot live under such oppression, Mother."

"Do you truly fear he will quell your spirit, silence the independent soul deep inside you?" Marian asked.

"Aye." She bit her lip before continuing. "I fear he will manipulate me, break my spirit, and then leave me for his harem."

"You think so little of him."

Ruby shrugged. "I fear he will tire of me when I am no longer of use to him as he has done a hundred times before."

"Ah, I understand." Marian stood, crossed the room, and knelt before a small trunk in the corner. She pulled a key from a chain around her neck and unlocked the trunk. "I once held the same fears as you. As I said before, Guy was not always the man you remember." Marian removed a small cloth-wrapped parcel and returned to the table.

"What is that?" Ruby asked leaning closer.

Marian opened the cloth and revealed a metal contraption. "Perhaps this may gain you the answers you seek."

"Is it a chastity belt?" Ruby's jaw dropped open at the sight of the contraption she had only ever heard rumors about. Her eyes drifted up to study the older woman's expression. "What is this supposed to achieve besides adding to my discomfort?"

"You say he will tire of your company and replace you. If you have concerns about his fidelity and his feelings for you, then you must challenge him." Marian handed her a small key on a delicate chain. "When is the wedding?"

"In ten days." Ruby placed the chain around her neck. "This will only anger him."

A grin split Marian's lips. Her dark eyes twinkled in the ambient light. "Do you trust me?"

"With all my heart." Ruby glanced at the metal garment. "I am convinced this will only infuriate him if I choose to deprive him and withhold the key until our wedding night."

"Then let him hold the key. Make it clear he can use it as he sees fit, but if he does not wait until you grant him permission, then he will suffer a consequence."

"You want me to manipulate him?"

"Fire with fire, my dear."

Ruby narrowed her gaze on Marian. "Are you sure about this?"

"Take control of your situation, Ruby. You do not have to surrender yourself completely to him until you are ready. Do not give him your heart until you are certain he is worthy of it."

"How will I know when that is?"

Marian pressed her hand to her chest above her heart. "Trust your instincts. They will never fail you."

With a nod, Ruby stood and took the bundle with the chastity belt out to where her horse grazed near the forest. She led Ginger back to the cottage and tucked the parcel into the bag tied behind her saddle.

Marian followed behind with a satchel and handed it to Ruby who slung it across her shoulders. "Deliver these to the monastery on your journey back to Culver."

"I will." Ruby pulled herself into the saddle and adjusted the straps on the satchel to ensure none of the bottles broke. "Thank you for everything, Mother."

"I will see you again soon. Take care, my gem." Marian waved as Ruby turned Ginger in the direction of the monastery and nudged the horse into a walk.

Emboldened by her conversation with Marian, Ruby focused on her task. The monks of the monastery relied on Marian's healing elixirs and salves. They were the last refuge of the broken and downcast. Ruby remembered the last visit to see the monks. Brother James offered his assistance, but what could a monk truly do to aid an outlaw about to marry a wicked prince?

A branch snapped in the distance, and she pulled Ginger to a stop. Scanning the trees, she searched for the source of the noise. A stag darted from the thick brush and bound in the direction she had just come. Ruby sighed and patted her horse's neck.

"Let us away, Ginger, the monastery awaits."

The rest of the journey remained uneventful. She slid from the saddle as a hooded monk appeared at the gate leading to the herb garden. He lifted his hand in greeting and motioned for her to follow him.

"Brother James, I have come to deliver the medicines from Marian." She pulled the bag from her shoulders and offered it to the lone monk as she entered the small garden.

He inclined his head and accepted the satchel. "May the Lord grant you mercy, my child." The rough timbre of his voice juxtaposed the gentle words and graceful movements. He tugged the hood farther down to cover his face. He always kept it hidden from her view.

Curiosity tugged at the back of her mind. "Is there anything else I can do for the monastery?"

He slung the bag over his shoulder. "These provisions should last us for several months. May you be blessed for your kindness."

Ruby waved her hand. "'Tis nothing. The work you do is truly a blessing." She held her breath for a moment then pushed forward. "I doubt you shall see much of me from this moment hence."

Brother James paused mid-stride. "Why is that, my child?"

"I am to be married in less than a fortnight." Ruby twisted her fingers inside the sleeve of her gown. Why was she telling the monk this? Was it because the last time they had spoken he gave her advice? How could she expect him to listen to her childish problems when he had a much larger mission to fulfill? "I did not want to cause you concern when I did not return. Marian will be delivering the medicines from this day forth."

"You do not sound overjoyed at the prospect of marriage." His raspy words gave her a sense of comfort. It seemed he understood.

"You should not concern yourself with my welfare." She turned to leave. "I thank you for your kindness."

"Wait."

The tender tone of his request stopped her. Ruby turned and faced him. He set the satchel aside and slipped his hood back, revealing his face. Scars and puckered flesh crisscrossed his skin. A small part of his left jaw lay untouched, but even so, the sight proved more than she expected. Ruby gasped and pressed a hand to her lips.

"What happened?" She stepped closer.

"A fire." His brusque reply caught her off guard. "Now, tell me. Why does this marriage have you so forlorn? Has your betrothed done something to harm you in any way?"

"Nay." Her heart ached at the mention of Crispin. Why did

he cause such a riot of emotion within her?

"I dislike seeing you in such turmoil."

"You are quite perceptive, Brother James." She bowed her head and inhaled a deep breath. When she glanced up, his concern-laden blue eyes met her own. "But as I said, there is no need to fret over my simple problems."

"'Tis my concern when one of the Lord's children is in obvious distress. Come, let me get you something refreshing to drink." He retrieved the bag from the ground and entered the building.

With a sigh, Ruby glanced at the horizon. The sun would set soon. She should not linger longer than necessary lest Crispin discover her absence and send his army in search of his errant bride. As she glanced around, the serenity of the small garden soothed her. Finding a small bench, she sat and waited for Brother James to return.

He stepped from the building with a goblet in his hands. "Here is some wine from our vineyard. Drink."

She accepted the proffered cup and sipped from it. The flavors mingled together bursting in her mouth, refreshing and delightful. "My thanks, 'tis quite delicious."

Brother James sat next to her on the bench. Ruby could not help but study his profile as he gazed toward heaven. Beneath the scars, she noted a strong jaw and handsome profile. She knew the fire had stolen what the world perceived as beauty, but Ruby saw the tender spirit and the generous soul beneath the pinched and pinkened, fire-kissed flesh.

"You are a woman unlike any I have ever met. Knowing you are entering into a union that brings you apprehension pains me. I do not wish to see anyone's spirit broken by an institution which should bring joy."

Ruby scoffed. "Since when has marriage brought anyone joy?"

A smile tugged at the corners of his mouth. His fair hair fell in waves against his forehead. Pushing the hair back from his face, he turned toward her. "Are you being forced to marry a wealthy man to safeguard yourself?"

"I am to marry Prince Crispin." Ruby handed him the empty goblet.

Brother James's eyes grew wide. "The prince?" He fumbled with the goblet and set it aside. Taking a deep breath, he turned back to her. "A woman of common birth marrying into a royal family."

"Aye, an outlaw and an orphan as well." She teased him with her words, but his reaction worried her. "Does this concern you even more, Brother?"

The man shook his head, but she noted his expression shifted momentarily. Was that pain she glimpsed in his eyes? He stared toward the setting sun for a moment and turned back to her.

"The prince is a difficult man to please. Has he forced you into this arrangement?" His eyes narrowed, and she caught sight of a man deep within, a man with secrets and skill.

"Nay, he holds no power over me," she lied. The twinge in her heart told her otherwise. Could she truly feel something other than desire for Crispin? "And you are correct, he is an extremely difficult man to please."

Brother James laid his hand over hers, taking her by surprise. "If you find yourself in need of a safe haven, our door is always open to those who seek sanctuary." His blue eyes twinkled in the twilight. "You should go, the hour grows late and the prince will be concerned at your absence." He led her from the small garden.

Ruby picked up the reins and mounted her horse. "Gramercy, Brother James, and my thanks for your kind words."

"May the Lord be with you, my child." He offered a wave and a smile as she turned Ginger in the direction of the palace.

She did not need to turn to know he followed her progress until she vanished into the darkening forest. As she wove down the worn path, the encroaching night closed in around her. The insects began their evening serenade, and the breeze whispered through the trees, making the leaves dance in the dying light. When Ruby approached the castle walls, the crunching thud of horses behind her made her stop. Turning in the saddle, she spied two riders approaching her.

"My lady, you should not be traveling without an armed guard or, at the very least, an escort." Henry leaned against the pommel of the saddle as his horse slowed beside hers.

Ruby glanced at Henry then at the young man beside him. "Matthew, Sir Henry, there is no need for concern. I am more than capable of taking care of myself."

"Aye, my lady; however, the king is quite protective of what belongs to him." Henry's pointed remark stung.

"What belongs to him?" She choked on the words. The idea of being owned made her stomach churn.

"As his betrothed, you are a valuable asset to someone should they decide to inflict harm upon His Majesty." Henry clarified, his words soft but his gaze sharpened like a falcon's centering on a hare. "'Tis my responsibility to ensure no harm comes to you."

Ruby snapped her jaw shut before she said something inconceivably rude. "Far be it from me to keep you from performing your duties." She ground out the words between clenched teeth.

"From this moment hence, I, or one of my men, will serve as an escort when you leave the castle." Henry leaned closer. "We are concerned only for your wellbeing, my lady. Should something happen to you, the king would be quite distressed." His words were meant to be a comfort but they only served to enrage her further.

"Then I shall have to make it clear to His Majesty that I do not require a nursemaid to stalk my every movement. If he wishes to know my whereabouts, then he can lock me in the tower. I will not be a treasure for him to hide away and flaunt for his own amusement." Her gaze pinned Henry and his jaw twitched...in amusement or frustration, she could not tell. Ruby held her ground and pressed on in her rebuke. "Tell him he may clip my wings, but I will not be his pet."

"You were misnamed, my lady." Henry's comment was so soft she nearly missed it.

"Pardon me?" Ruby rested her hand on her hip.

"Your name. Ruby does not suit you at all." He grinned. Henry's entire countenance shifted with the simple action.

"And why would that be, sir?"

"Because a ruby is a valued rarity, a talisman, a possession. But you see yourself as none of these things." Henry tilted his head to the side.

"I shudder to think what name you feel would suit me. Shrew, harpy, crow..."

"You are none of those things. Strong and dangerous, perhaps, but a woman such as you could shine a light in the darkest reaches of a blackened heart." With a nod, Henry reined his horse toward the postern gate, Matthew following close behind.

Ruby shook her head. Did Henry compliment her? "Come, Ginger." She kicked the horse's flanks and retreated into the safety of the palace walls.

Henry and Matthew had already disappeared by the time she entered the bailey. She tossed her reins to the stable boy and slid from the horse's back. Quickly untying the bag behind the saddle, she slung it over her shoulder. Her borrowed dress itched where it rubbed against her skin, and she longed to soothe her aching limbs in a warm bath. As she ambled toward her chamber, she spotted her maid, Mina.

"Have a bath drawn for me in my chambers." Ruby smiled as the girl curtseyed and ran toward the kitchens to have the hot water brought to her room. Slowly she climbed the stairs, praying Crispin would not be waiting around every corner. By the time she reached her chamber, the sight of her soft bed tempted her. Her stomach grumbled in protest.

When she glanced around the room, her maid stood by the bath preparing it with rosehip oil. "My thanks, Mina." The girl added one last bucket of hot water and followed the other servants from the room.

"Can I fetch you anything else, my lady?" The young girl bowed low.

"A tray of food would be nice. Whatever you can find."

The girl nodded and left the room, closing the door behind

her. Ruby stretched her arms over her head. Within moments she unlaced her gown and slipped it over her head, then divested herself of her drawers, chemise, and boots. She stepped into the hot water. The soothing aroma of roses encircled her as she sank into the water. Dipping beneath the surface, she allowed the anxiety that plagued her all day to melt into the languid waters.

After washing, she lounged in the bath and the heat absorbed the ache from her muscles. A knock echoed in her chamber.

"Enter." She turned toward the door, expecting her maid with her evening meal.

Vivienne entered carrying a tray laden with food and latched the door behind her. "Good evening, my dear. I hope you do not mind my company."

Ruby sat up, crossing her hands across her bare chest. "Not at all." She grabbed the drying cloth and stood, wrapping it around herself quickly. After wrapping the other around her hair, she crossed the room to slip on her shift.

Vivienne set the tray down on the table, knocking Ruby's bag to the floor. The clatter of metal on wood drew her attention downward. "What is this?"

"Nay!" Ruby shouted reaching for the bag, but Vivienne had already opened it and withdrew the chastity belt.

The chamber echoed with laughter. Vivienne sat on the edge of the bed, clutching her sides as tears slid down her cheeks. Ruby felt the heat rising in her own.

"My dear." Vivienne wiped the tears away as the laughter subsided. "Has my son seen this?"

"He has not." Ruby sat on the bed and picked up her brush. She turned her attention to her hair instead of her betrothed's mother and her questions.

"Where did you get this?"

Ruby turned to Vivienne ignoring the burning heat in her face. "A friend."

"Is that where you went, to visit a friend?"

She nodded and ran the brush through the wet, tangled knots in her hair. Never had she felt so mortified in all her life.

Ruby braced herself for a lecture. When it did not come, she glanced at Vivienne.

"My dear, I am available should you require anything. I promise not to judge you; 'tis not my responsibility to pass judgment. But I can offer guidance." She set the chastity belt aside. "Tell me of this friend. They must have great importance to you for you to risk Crispin's wrath by leaving the castle without an escort."

"My mother." Ruby sighed. "The woman who adopted me. I needed to see her, to let her know I was safe."

Vivienne nodded in understanding. "Could you not have sent a message or summoned her to the palace?"

"Nay." Ruby feared volunteering any more information about Marian would put her in danger. "I shall not venture out on my own again. She is aware of my situation."

"Did she give you this?" Vivienne tapped the chastity belt with her fingertip.

With a nod, Ruby resumed untangling her hair.

"Allow me." Vivienne approached her, taking the brush from her hand. "Turn around, my dear."

Ruby turned, and as Vivienne untangled her hair, her mind drifted. The gentle touch lulled her, and she found herself relaxing into a companionable moment of peace.

"What results are you hoping to elicit from using such a contraption?" Vivienne murmured as she tugged on a knotted lock of hair.

"A test." Ruby chewed on her lower lip. What if Marian was wrong, what if it only drove a wedge between them?

"You are certainly his match. Attempting to outwit him at his own game." Vivienne chuckled. "Do you believe it will stop him from seducing you?"

"Nay. I intend to give him the key."

"Then what is the point of the belt?"

"I want him to know he can take me if he wishes. But I want to see if he can refrain until our wedding night." Her hand drifted to the key around her neck.

"And if he cannot?"

Ruby shrugged. "Will he run to the bed of another if I deny him? Will he seduce me with his wicked whispers, tempting me with promises of pleasure and use the key? Or will he respect my wishes and wait until our wedding night?"

"You are concerned about my son's fidelity and whether or not he wants you for more than sex?"

With a nod, she glanced over her shoulder at Vivienne who was braiding her hair in a long plait. "Am I a fool to test him in such a manner?"

"A challenge may be good for you both. But do not be surprised if he fails. My son is no saint. While I do not think he would hurt you deliberately, he can be selfish and determined. If he senses a challenge, he may retaliate." Vivienne turned her by the shoulders, forcing them to face one another. "One day he will see the error of his ways, but until he does, be patient with him. Love does not come easily to some."

Before Ruby could ponder the cryptic words, Vivienne bent and kissed her forehead.

"Sleep well, my dear. You know where I shall be if you require a confidant."

As the door closed behind Vivienne, Ruby collapsed on the bed, her tray of food and aching bones forgotten. A riot of emotions and questions assailed her. She drew the blanket over her and stared into the hearth.

Fire with fire.

Chapter Twenty-Seven

Crispin paced before the magnificent stone hearth in the throne room, a goblet of wine in his hand. He downed it in one swallow and threw the cup, eliciting a satisfying clatter against the far wall.

"Am I interrupting your tantrum?" Henry retrieved the cup from the floor and placed it on the nearest table.

"Have you found her? Where is she?" Crispin ran his hand through his hair nearly pulling it from his scalp. "Damn her! Where did she go?" The fury built inside of him as he waited for Henry's reply.

"She is safely returned, ensconced in her room according to the servants." Henry poured himself a cup of wine and took a drink.

Without thought, Crispin strode to the door.

"Are you not curious as to where she went?"

Crispin paused, his hand resting on the latch, and turned to glare at Henry. There was no need for a reply. He leaned against the door and folded his arms across his chest.

Henry sat near the hearth. "She traveled to a cottage, tucked in the forest near Skye Lake. An older woman lives there, her mother perhaps."

"Her parents were killed near the border when she was a child." Crispin stroked his chin in thought. "Proceed."

"Then she rode to the monastery hidden in the forest not far from Culver."

"A monastery?" Crispin strode to the hearth stared into the flames. His mind churned with the possibilities. "What reason would she have for visiting a monastery?"

"The older woman gave her a satchel. Lady Ruby presented it to one of the monks."

"What was in it?"

Henry shook his head. "I do not know. She entered the monastery garden and vacated it soon after the sun began to set."

Crispin nodded. "Did she notice you following her?"

"Nay, Sire." Henry set the cup aside. "I confronted her outside of the postern gate. But she gave no indication she realized we had been following her."

"Very well." Crispin pondered the information presented to him unsure of what to make of it. "What are your thoughts?"

Startled, Henry glanced up, his brow arched. "You wish for me to speak my mind?" At Crispin's nod, he cleared his throat. "I do not believe your bride is meeting with a lover, nor is she conspiring against you."

"What makes you say that?" Curiosity burned deep in his gut.

Henry held his gaze steadily. "I saw nothing in her actions belying any ill intentions toward you. She hides her relationship with the woman in the cottage. However, given her past as an outlaw, her intentions could merely be to defend the woman's identity and ensure her safety. Having connections to an outlaw would make her a target for those who wished to arrest Ruby or remove her as a threat."

With a nod, Crispin strode toward the door.

"Do not do anything rash." Henry's words trailed behind him into the hallway.

His hands flexed repeatedly as he stalked down the empty corridor. The hour proved later than he anticipated but it did nothing to deter him. Crispin paused outside of the door to Ruby's chamber, resting his head upon the oak. He turned at the soft echo of footfalls behind him.

"Mother." He inclined his head and backed away from the door.

Vivienne stood with a heavy tray in her hands. "Crispin."

He knocked on the door and opened it when he heard Ruby's reply. His mother entered the room. Crispin closed it softly behind her, ensuring he remained hidden, and retreated to his chamber.

After pouring himself a goblet of wine, Crispin sank into

his chair and loosened the top buttons of his doublet. He took a drink and set the cup aside. The warmth consuming him came not from the fire nor the wine but from the aching need to hold Ruby.

"Bloody hell." He divested his doublet, tossing it to the ground, and raked his hand through his hair. "What am I to do with you, woman?" He pulled the linen tunic from his overheated body.

With a glance at his bed, images of himself and Ruby assailed him. He craved her more than ever. Crispin leaned his head back and closed his eyes. A vision of her soaking wet in the bath made him groan.

"Can I not escape your enchantment?" Finishing the wine, he stripped completely and climbed into his oversized bed. Would his dreams grant him a respite? He drifted into a fitful slumber plagued with haunting memories and temptations he could not ignore.

The next morning, Crispin woke to the sound of the maid shuffling around the room. He waited until she retreated and climbed from the bed. Once he dressed and splashed water on his face, he glanced out the window. The sun had barely risen over the horizon. He groaned. Even in his dreams, he was not immune to her charm and grace. His cock strained for release.

He slipped into the hall, making a direct path for Ruby's chamber. Without knocking, he entered the room, closing the door without a sound. The room was tidy, a small sack sat on the table, but the tray of food his mother had brought was gone. It seemed the maids took their duty seriously. As they should.

When he approached the bed, his heart softened at the sight of her curled beneath the blankets asleep. Her lips parted, eyelashes lying against her cheek like butterflies on a flower petal. Her plaited auburn hair trailed beneath the blankets. He climbed onto the bed and lay beside her, watching her sleep. He tucked a strand of her hair back from her face, and she moaned, shifting beneath the blankets.

Crispin froze, stunned by his tender inclinations. She looked like an innocent, but the feelings she roused inside of him were far from pure. He desired her more than any woman. Was it too much to demand her loyalty to him?

"Yours," she whispered against the pillow as if reading his thoughts. Was he becoming too soft, allowing a woman to touch him in such a way? Hardening his heart, he frowned at the direction of his thoughts. The woman confounded him at every turn. He refused to allow her wiles to affect him, to manipulate him in any way. She belonged to him, not the reverse.

Her eyes fluttered open and met his. With a gasp, she arched away from him, her limbs flailing beneath the covers. "What are you doing in my bed?" She sat up, clutching the blankets against her chest.

He grinned at her futile attempt at modesty and propped his head upon his hand. "It will soon be our bed. Would you have me keep myself from you until our wedding night?"

The telltale stain of pink crept from her neck up into her face. Her eyes widened then narrowed as she pondered his question. Her brow arched in defiance.

"Aye."

Crispin stared at her, his amusement turning feral. "Do you intend to keep me from enjoying what is mine?"

Ruby nodded.

Without hesitation, Crispin moved swiftly and pinned her beneath him before she could draw a breath. He gazed down into her enchanting amber-colored eyes, filled with desire and trepidation, and ground his hips against hers. Even with the blankets between them, he savored the curves of her body as she fought to free herself.

"Release me!" Her frantic cry gave him pause.

He stilled. Her chest heaved with each breath she took. Crispin leaned down, running his lips across her bare shoulder.

"Please, stop."

Her broken request touched his cold heart. Even though he hungered for her, he was not a man to take a woman against her will. Crispin leaned his head against her chest, feeling the pulse of her heart thundering against his cheek.

"Would you deny me your touch, your sweet embrace, the

haven of your kiss for so long?" He released her hands and raised his head.

She laughed. "Oh, my king. Your whispers could woo even the coldest maiden to your bed."

"But not you."

Ruby regarded him thoughtfully. "Nay."

"Then tell me, have you tired of me already?"

She rested her hand on his cheek, forcing him to meet her gaze. "Nay."

"Then why did you leave the castle yesterday?"

She dropped her hand. "I had to visit someone."

"A man?" Crispin searched her gaze for some sign of deceit.

"My mother." Ruby glanced away. "I have an obligation to tell the woman who raised me about my impending marriage."

"I would have sent a messenger and had her summoned if you asked."

She shook her head, panic swimming in her eyes. "Nay, I had to tell her myself. I could not invite her here."

Crispin nodded in understanding. "She raised you, and I can only assume she bears the monarchy no affection, as you once confessed yourself."

Ruby blushed again. He adored the color as it tinted her skin. It spoke with unbridled honesty when she could not.

He traced a finger along her jaw and down her neck. "A visit to your mother. Was this your only reason for leaving? Did you meet with anyone else?"

"I delivered some salves and herbal tinctures to the monastery. Mar—My mother makes them specifically for the monks as they specialize in the comfort of the sick and dying." She frowned. "Do you think me untrue to my word? I have given myself to you, and only you."

An ache tugged in the vicinity of his heart. "Yet you deny me." His hand slid over her breast, across her stomach, and settled on her hip. He cursed the fabric between them. Crispin longed to feel her flesh beneath his fingertips, the pull of her body as he claimed her. "Why?"

"My request is not enough?"

Crispin rolled away and sat on the edge of the bed. "I will not take you by force."

She sat with her hair tousled, her full lips parted, shift hanging from her shoulder. He bit his lip until he tasted blood, easing the ache in his groin.

"But know this. I desire to have you writhing beneath me, screaming my name. I crave the taste of your skin. I want nothing more at this moment than to be buried in your sweet cunt and have you begging for release."

Ruby gasped, her fingers tightening in the blanket she gripped to her chest. Her lips parted with a gasp as he spoke.

"Telling me I cannot have what I desire most...well, sweeting, 'tis a challenge I accept without hesitation for I always obtain that which I set my sights upon." He grinned, allowing the implication of his words to register. "Until then, I shall leave you to your own devices."

Crispin retreated from her chamber without a backward glance. If he turned, if he caught a glimpse of her bare skin and hazed expression, he would not be able to contain himself. He tugged on the material stretched tight over his aching cock. He could find a willing wench and let her take care of him. But Ruby...*God's blood, teeth, and bones!* She consumed him so completely he wanted no other woman save her.

Upon returning to his chambers, Crispin took himself in hand, imagining the last time he had Ruby on his cock. Within seconds, the warmth of his seed coated his hand. *The bloody woman has ruined me.*

Chapter Twenty-Eight

The light of dawn crested the treetops, illuminating the bailey as Henry stepped from the building housing his quarters. After reporting to Crispin the night before, he retired, exhausted from a day of riding. His concern for Lady Ruby and Crispin's reaction to her adventure kept him awake for most of the night and nagged at his conscience upon waking. There was naught he could do to mitigate his friend's temper. He stretched his arms overhead and ambled toward the kitchens in search of something to fill his stomach.

Lady Ruby possessed strength far superior to any woman he had ever met. She deserved a man who understood her worth. Henry prayed Crispin would realize this before he lost her forever.

Stepping into the kitchen, he scanned the servants. The room seemed more full than it normally would. The necessity to hire more servants in preparation for the upcoming wedding and coronation proved cumbersome, making his duties quite frustrating. How was he to protect the royal family amid the chaos of such an event? He groaned in anticipation of the upcoming challenges.

Damn and blast. Where was she? Henry searched the flour and soot smudged faces of the servants, hoping to catch a glimpse of Ivy. But her glowing face was not among them. He caught the attention of a passing maid.

"Where is Ivy?" He ensured the question held enough disinterest as not to make him seem desperate.

"There are no servants by that name, Sir." She cast her gaze down when he frowned. "But there are so many new servants, it may be you seek one of them." The maid scurried away lost in the bustle of the kitchen.

Henry returned to the bailey, deciding to make his rounds

to secure the castle and the grounds. He could also utilize the time to search for Ivy. Beginning at the stables, he took the morning to methodically check every building, every parapet, and every chamber. As the sun climbed higher in the sky, Henry became frustrated by her absence. Even though his duties were completed with efficiency, it bothered him she disappeared without a trace of evidence of her existence.

He leaned against the entrance to the stables and watched the knights training in the bailey. Where could she have gone? Henry scanned the people milling around the courtyard. Part of him longed to go into the village and search for her there. He frowned, his mood growing darker.

"Henry!"

A shout brought him back from his absent thoughts. He glanced up as Crispin approached him. The prince wore a simple combination of black hose and tunic with a dark brown jerkin buttoned over top. The cloak around his shoulders hid the quiver of arrows and he gripped a bow in his fist. His sword lay tucked back on his hip, keeping it out of the way. But it was the set of his jaw which betrayed his agitation. Crispin's ill humor would not be avoided.

"Have you intentions to leave the palace, Sire?" Henry asked as Crispin pushed past him and entered the stables.

"Fetch my horse," he ordered a young squire and turned back to Henry. "Aye, I intend to hunt. Will you join me?" Crispin ran a hand over his face.

Henry leaned close so no one would hear. "Does something ail you?"

"Why do you ask?" Crispin snapped.

"You seem a bit agitated." Henry regarded his friend carefully. Never had he seen Crispin this discomposed. It worried him more than his friend's occasional rage.

"'Tis nothing a good hunt or a fuck would not cure." Crispin leaned against the wall and stared out at the knights practicing their swordsmanship. "What news have you? Are your men prepared for the upcoming festivities?"

"Aye, they are willing to serve in any capacity they are

required." Something set a thistle in Crispin's codpiece. He grinned. *Ruby.*

"Wipe that damned smirk off your face, Henry. Are you coming or not?" Crispin snatched the reins from the squire and led Ghost from the stable.

Henry sent the boy to fetch his mount. He waited where Crispin stood stroking the horse's muzzle. "'Tis a fine beast you have there."

"Aye, while Jack is a fine warhorse, Ghost makes up for his looks with speed and agility." He moved around the side to mount. Once he settled in the saddle, he glanced down at Henry. "Come. I intend to kill something today."

Henry swallowed the hint of fear rising like bile in the back of his throat. *As long as you do not kill me.* Not that Crispin had any reason to do so, but one could never be too careful when their lord possessed a temperament to match his passion for inflicting pain.

The squire approached, leading a sleek chestnut mare. The horse nudged him in greeting, and he patted her neck before pulling himself into the saddle. "Come, Frigga, let us away before the prince decides to banish us both for slowing his progress."

As they exited the front gate, a messenger arrived on horseback. He slowed as he approached Henry and Crispin. "Your Majesty, my Lord High Steward. I have a message from James Balmont, Baron Norrington."

"My father?" He glanced at Crispin. "What is the message?"

"He and your brothers are en route to the palace to join in the celebration of the coronation and marriage ceremony." The rider took a breath. "They will arrive within four days."

"My thanks." Henry nodded. "Please see yourself to the kitchens and partake in some refreshments for your service."

The young man nodded to Henry, then offered a haphazard bow to Crispin while still astride his horse. At Crispin's acknowledgment, the lad slipped into the bailey and dismounted.

Crispin urged his steed forward. Henry caught up to him within moments. As they rode side by side, Henry studied his friend's countenance. Crispin seemed lost in thought. Distracted perhaps by the fiery vixen who would soon be the queen. Crispin caught him staring.

"Out with it," Crispin growled.

"Why the sudden urge to hunt?" Henry treated carefully, unsure of how to engage the prince in conversation without starting an argument. Even after nigh on fifteen years of friendship, he hesitated before broaching certain subjects with Crispin.

"Can I not want to kill something without having a reason?"

"Aye, 'tis your right as the ruler of the land." Henry swallowed. "But I fear in the mood you are in you may slaughter the entire population of woodland creatures."

The corners of his friend's lips quirked up in a smirk. "Have you no faith in my restraint?"

"Your restraint is legendary, Sire, in most things."

"You doubt me in this?" Crispin narrowed his gaze.

"I have complete faith in you, my liege." Henry bowed his head, hoping it would supplicate his temper.

Crispin tutted. "I did nothing to harm her. She was hale and hearty, if not a bit wet before I left her."

The prince wore the devastating smile he often boasted when a conquest concluded with success. Henry pinched the bridge of his nose. "There is no reason to give me details such as these."

"Can a man not jest with his friend? Come now and tell me you are not curious as to the taste of her pretty cunt."

"This is not a matter in which to jest. She is your betrothed and the future Queen of Meradin."

"Aye, she will be mine in all ways under the sight of God. But she is still a woman...and one you mistook for a whore."

Henry's face heated at the memory. "I beg you, Crispin, do not remind me of my misdeeds."

"Let us run the devil out of these horses and find us some prey." Crispin drove his heels into his horse's flanks, driving him forward with a shout.

Henry shook his head. *Saints preserve us now that he is king.*

Chapter Twenty-Nine

Despite the ache deep in her chest, Ruby vacated her chamber in search of Vivienne. There were plans to be made for the coronation and the wedding. She could not sit aside and allow everyone else to do the work. Her gaze fell upon the chastity belt lying on the table.

"You will have to wait." She shook her finger at the contraption and stepped from the room. Ruby strode toward the small garden where Henry had...no, she refused to think about his kiss. Strolling along the small stone pathway, she picked some roses for Vivienne and tucked them into a small bouquet. Then she wandered down the halls in search of Vivienne's chamber.

It had been three days since Crispin had confronted her in her chambers. She remained there, half in agony, half in hope of a summons from the king. But it seemed he respected her wishes enough to keep his distance which unraveled concerns of a different sort. How long would the silence last? She sighed, deciding to push aside the questions for the moment, and paused outside the chamber door. Before she could knock, the door swung open.

"Her Majesty is expecting you." The servant bowed as she entered the room.

"Ah, Ruby, join me." Vivienne motioned toward the expanse of open space beside her on the settee. "I require your advice on some of these details for the ceremony."

Ruby sat next to the older woman, admiring the way the sunlight caught the fine silver strands in her dark hair. Vivienne glanced up and caught her staring. Her kind smile chased away any lingering doubts.

"Since the coronation and the wedding will take place on the same day, I believe the best course of action would be to combine both into one ceremony. First the marriage, then the coronation of both Crispin and yourself as king and queen." Vivienne explained.

A sudden wave of worry swept over her, and Ruby swayed. She pressed her hand to her stomach and braced herself with the other.

"Are you well, my dear?" Vivienne's concern reflected in her words and expression.

Ruby nodded. "I am perfectly fine. Just a bit nervous."

Vivienne took her hand between her own. "There is nothing to worry about, my dear." The warm, soothing touch calmed Ruby. A maternal caress designed to calm even the most fretful child.

"You are too kind, Your Majesty."

"Tut, tut, I have told you before to address me as Vivienne." The older woman grinned, and Ruby caught a glimpse of Crispin in her smile. "There is no formality when we are behind closed doors. Now, tell me, how progresses your little experiment?"

"The...belt?" Ruby whispered.

Vivienne nodded.

"I have not worn it yet." The confession sounded weak and uncertain.

"Are you telling me my son has not come to you since that night?" Vivienne's eyes widened in surprise. At Ruby's nod, she shook her head. "My, my, this gets more interesting by the day. The wedding shall take place in sennight, do you think he will respect your request?"

"I do not know." Ruby's heart sank. "He has avoided me since. I fear I have angered him."

"Well, I am sure it has not pleased him." A smile brightened her expression. "But there can be no doubt now, my son is madly in love with you."

"How can you be so sure? What if he has another woman hidden away?"

Vivienne shook her head. "He has been in meetings with the council and opened the court to take petitions from the people."

Ruby's jaw dropped. "This...that...well..."

"I am as stunned by his sudden dedication as you are. Perhaps the distance between you two is what he needed to take charge of his responsibilities." Vivienne cupped Ruby's cheek in her hand. "I could not have chosen a better wife for him." Her eyes shone with unshed tears.

Ruby covered Vivienne's hand with her own. "'Tis truly an honor to be chosen, even if our union is unconventional."

"You are the woman who was destined for him. God works in mysterious ways, I have faith in His plan." She patted Ruby's cheek and returned her attention to the parchment on the table before them. "Now then, would you prefer the red and gold garland with or without flowers?"

After several hours, Ruby excused herself from Vivienne's chambers. She needed to take a walk outside, breathe in the late summer air. Her heart did not ache with crushing pressure as it had earlier. A smile broke upon her lips as she stepped into the bailey, the sun kissing her skin.

"Good morrow, my lady."

The familiar and reverent voice made her turn. "Sir Henry, how fare you this day?"

He tipped his head, the soft wisps of dark hair falling across his forehead. "I am well. Would you care to stroll outside the palace walls?" He proffered his arm.

"I would be delighted." Ruby slipped her arm through his and walked beside him toward the postern gate. As they stepped through to the other side, the forest rose up to greet them. She closed her eyes and savored the freedom of being outside the stone walls.

"Are you well, my lady?" Henry's question broke her reverie.

"Aye." She turned her face up to his. "I lived in the forest for so long it became my sanctuary, my home. I had not realized how much I missed it until this moment."

"You were an outlaw." His words sounded more like a statement than a question. No judgment rested in his peaceful blue eyes, merely curiosity.

"I was." She tilted her head back to the sky, letting the

warmth of the sun hide the blush on her face.

"There is nothing to be ashamed of, my lady." He tugged her arm, leading her deeper into the forest. The sound of a stream running over rocks in the distance reminded her of home. "I understand and admire your passion to serve the people." He hung his head, a hint of pink staining his cheeks. "I have heard many tales of the exploits of the Lady of the Forest."

"There are tales of me?" Ruby turned to him, her eyes wide. "Truly?"

His genuine smile enhanced his charm. "Aye, they say you can shoot an apple off a man's head at half a league, and you can kill with only a kiss." Henry chuckled.

"Well, that may be stretching the truth." She choked back a laugh. "Although, my kiss did nearly kill you." Ruby could not hold back the laughter when his grin widened. She doubled over as it consumed and shook her whole body.

Henry stared at her, shaking his head.

"Do not look at me thus, Sir Henry. Surely we can laugh about the misunderstanding now, can we not?"

He strode ahead and leaned against a tree. When she approached him and rested her hand on his shoulder, he spun around to face her, his eyes wide. She drew her hand back as though the touch burned her.

"My lady, you should not jest about such things." Henry ran a hand through his hair. "My actions that night were unforgivable. Had I known the truth—who you were—I never would have committed such a trespass." He bowed his head.

"It was a kiss, Sir Henry. Nothing more." Their prior conversations never came this easily before, and to be perfectly honest, seeing a man blushing and uncomfortable made him more sincere. She took pleasure in teasing him, although her conscience warned her against trying his patience. "Perhaps you did not enjoy it?"

"This conversation serves no purpose. It matters not if I enjoyed this kiss or loathed it. You are betrothed to Crispin and—" He snapped his mouth shut upon seeing her reaction.

Ruby trembled with laughter. It burst from her, the sound

echoing through the trees.

"You make sport of me, fetching me out thus?" Henry nodded in understanding, his face stained crimson.

"My apologies. 'Tis not ladylike to tease you so, but you make such a fine target." Ruby grinned.

He turned away and folded his arms against his chest, staring off into the forest. The silence between them grew. She knelt by the stream and plucked some smooth stones from the water. When she stood, Ruby stole a glance at Henry. Was he truly angered by her words? A pang of guilt settled in her chest, and she searched the distant trees while gathering her thoughts.

"I harbor no ill will toward you. Although your future husband may not find your teasing me an adequate pastime."

Ruby's conscience eased as he continued the conversation. "You have known Crispin since childhood, have you not?"

Henry shifted his feet. "Aye, we trained together. I have spent more time with him than I have my own family." He clenched his teeth, pressing his lips into a thin line.

"Are you not on good terms with your family?" Curiosity begged her to ask the question.

"After they sent me to the palace, I rarely heard from them. The only occasion they visited was when they required a favor from the king." He rested his hand on the hilt of his sword. "My brothers refused to even speak with me, claiming I was naught but a weakling."

Ruby stepped closer and rested her hand on his arm. "They must be proud of you now, being Right Hand of the king."

"I shall find out soon I suspect. They journey to the palace even now. Several days ago I received a message to expect them for the celebration."

"What wonderful news." Her grip tightened on his arm, making him glance at where her hand lay upon him. She removed it in haste. "My apologies. I was never one for propriety."

"'Tis an honor to receive your kind words and tender concern." Henry motioned toward the stone walls of the palace in the distance. "Shall we return?"

"Aye, I do not wish to keep you from your duties." Ruby

began walking in the direction of the castle.

"My duty is to protect you." Henry's statement brought her to a halt and she turned to meet his sincere gaze. Ruby knew in that moment Henry would lay down his life to ensure her safety. The gesture unnerved her as much as it solidified her trust in him.

"My thanks, Sir Henry." She gestured to the forest in an attempt to ease the seriousness of the moment. "I enjoyed our walk." The thoughtful gesture of inviting her to stroll through the forest she loved so dearly touched her heart.

He inclined his head, and together they returned to the keep with a new bond forged between them.

If only Crispin were such easy company to keep and as simple to understand.

Chapter Thirty

Crispin slipped behind the tree as they passed. He leaned his head against the rough bark and closed his eyes. God's teeth! Why was he eavesdropping on them? He was king. Could he not command them to remain at least a league from each other? He beat his fist against the tree. *Fool. There is nothing between them. She belongs to you alone.* His mind battled with his heart. There was no cure for this madness.

Truth be told, it pained him to see Ruby conversing so easily with Henry. The banter flowed between them as if they had been friends for years. Crispin scowled. Henry remained an honest friend and loyal servant. There was nothing for him to fear. Jealousy, an old, familiar adversary, wrapped its clawed hands around his heart.

He pushed away from the tree and shoved a hand through his hair. It had been years since he last allowed jealousy to sneak its tendrils into his mind. Crispin beat it down into the deep recesses of his soul. As he approached the main gate of the castle through the village, he pulled his hood up and slipped through the crowd. They ignored him, not expecting their king to be walking freely amongst them. He tipped the hood back as he stepped up to the inner bailey where the guards stood. When they recognized Crispin, they bowed allowing him to enter the courtyard.

The knights set targets along the far wall, and archers took turns perfecting their skill. The satisfying thwack of arrows piercing cloth sacks full of hay made him itch to pick up a bow. Nothing would tamp the emotion and desire raging through him. Killing a stag had not quelled it. Throwing all of his concentration into the council and planning the tournament to take place after the ceremony barely diverted his attention from her.

Ruby. She plagued his every breath. He stepped into the great hall and wove around the tables. He took to relieving the tension in his aching bollocks both morning and night since the last time they spoke. His hand was no substitute for her cunt, and no other woman could fill her void. He climbed the staircase leading to the royal chambers. Would she deny him again?

A grin split his lips. Did it matter? He was the king and her future husband. Surely she craved his touch as much as he hungered for hers. Could they not sate the other's burning lust? The wedding was only seven days hence.

He strode past the garden when he noticed movement beyond the hedgerow. Pausing in the doorway, he glanced into the quiet sanctuary Ruby claimed as her own. She stood near the roses, gently pulling the flowers from the bush. As he approached, her voice echoed a sweet melody.

"But long ago, my love's but lost his wandering sanity."

Crispin paused behind her, listening to her song. When the words faded into a gentle humming, he spoke. "Your voice is quite lovely."

Ruby jumped and spun around. The emerald gown she wore enhanced the amber color of her eyes and embellished her deep auburn hair. He admired the style of it, noting the pearl netting. She pressed a hand to her chest and took a deep breath.

"You gave me a fright." Ruby smiled.

Crispin licked his lips. He had been a fool to keep his distance. "I beg your pardon. I did not wish to interrupt your moment of solitude." He watched the recognition of his words alight in her eyes.

"You are far too generous." She turned to retrieve her basket of roses from the stone bench. "If you will excuse me, I want to give these to your mother." She pushed past him, and he wrapped his hand around her arm, pulling her to a halt. Ruby gasped as he held her against him, the basket dropping to the ground, the roses spilling from their nest. She sank into him and braced her hands against his chest. "Release me."

"I will do no such thing." He slid his hand around her waist, holding her firmly against him. "I have kept my distance. Have you not reconsidered your request?"

"I have not." Ruby met his gaze and held it steady as she fisted her hands against his body. "Crispin—"

He leaned down and kissed her, funneling all of his frustration into the action. She moaned as he tasted her. God help him, he missed her. The way she fit against him, the taste of her mouth, the wanton sounds she made when he brought her pleasure. Ruby pushed against his chest as he suckled her lip. They broke apart panting and gasping for breath.

"Tell me you have not longed for this?" He tightened his grip on her.

"I cannot." She cupped his face with her hand.

His hand drifted lower, over her hip. He snatched a handful of her skirts and drew the material up until his fingertips brushed her bare thigh. "You can, and you will—" The words died on his tongue when the unforgiving touch of steel halted his wandering exploration of her flesh. His hand slid between her legs, and he tugged on the chastity belt. "What is this?"

Ruby gasped. Her face flushed the same deep crimson of her flowers. "I—"

He dropped his hand, releasing her skirts. "You have so little faith in me."

"Should I? You attempted to seduce me even after I requested you refrain until the wedding night." She arched her brow, eyes blazing in challenge.

Shame cornered him, but he beat it into submission, allowing the hurt and rage to rise to the surface. "You are mine! I will not be denied what belongs to me."

Ruby cocked her head, her expression undaunted. She reached between her breasts and pulled a chain holding a key into view. After slipping it off her neck, she placed the chain around his own.

He stared at her. "What is this?"

"The key to the belt. Do with it what you will, but know this: If you use it before our wedding night, you will lose both my respect and my trust."

Blood pounded in his ears. He had every intention to keep

his distance, to grant her request. But seeing her, smelling her, even being near her drove him into madness. Chaos churned inside of him at the turmoil of emotions battling for dominance.

Crispin dropped his hands to his sides and took a step back. "Go, now," he commanded through gritted teeth.

Ruby stared at him a moment. She ignored the tumbled basket and spilled roses as she walked around him. He turned to watch her leave, but instead of taking the hall to his mother's chambers, she retreated into the safety of her own.

Raking his hand through his hair, Crispin dropped to the bench. His heart pounded in his chest. When he held up his hand, it trembled of its own volition. Try as he might, he could not contain his body's reaction. A long, hard ride through the forest or a bout of swordplay might ease the ache. Even a quick fuck with one of the more than willing wenches in the village would remedy the incessant pain temporarily.

"God's blood, teeth, and bones!" He stood and darted down the hall. Stopping before his mother's door, he paused for half a second before entering without knocking.

Vivienne glanced up from her writing desk. "Crispin, to what do I owe this pleasure?"

Crispin scoffed. "Pleasure. Pleasure," he mumbled and clenched his hands into fists. "Was it you then who gave her such ideas, Mother?" Crispin put his hand up when she stood and moved closer.

She paused and clasped her hands before her, watching him with a maternal eye. "Has something happened?"

"Do not play games with me." He studied her carefully. The fine lines bracketing her mouth, the kind glint in her eyes, the gentle arch of her neck as she leaned her head to the side and met his gaze.

"I must confess, I am surprised. It took you longer than I had anticipated."

"Then you knew of the damned belt." Crispin snarled. "Tell me, did you plant the idea in her mind? Did you give her the contraption?"

Vivienne stood firm. "I did neither."

"Then who did?"

"Does it matter?"

Crispin dropped his gaze. He flinched at the touch of her hand on his shoulder and jerked out of her reach.

"Is it so difficult to respect her wishes in this one small request?" Vivienne sat and poured a cup of tea.

"I have claimed her. She is mine!" Blood pounded in Crispin's ears.

"Treat her thus, and you will never have her heart."

He laughed, hollow and mirthless. "Why should I care if the rest of her belongs to me?"

"Can you truly be so selfish and blind?" Vivienne tsked with a shake of her head. "Foolish boy."

"I am king—"

"Aye, you are the king." His mother scoffed, ignoring Crispin's glare. "And your cousin sits patiently waiting for you to fail. Do not give him the satisfaction."

"I sit on the throne, and what I do with my future queen is no concern of yours." He crossed the room, his hand pausing on the door latch when she spoke.

"Ruby has more value than you can possibly imagine. She will stand beside you and be your strength...if you allow it. Do not underestimate her."

The tempest inside him raged. Crispin met his mother's knowing gaze. "She is only a woman." He opened the door and strode from the room, his mother's parting words ringing in his ears.

Ruby was far more valuable than they knew, and the thought of losing her terrified him.

Chapter Thirty-One

"**W**atch for the downward swing, Arthur!" Henry shouted to the men training in the bailey. He walked around the circle and propped his foot on the wooden railing. "Bring it across your body, careful to keep it under control." He watched the two men in the ring as they battled. A flash of movement out of the corner of his eye drew his attention to his right.

"Sire." He nodded in acknowledgment, keeping his gaze fixed on the bout in the ring.

Crispin came up beside him and gripped the top railing with both hands. Henry's attention remained fixed on the men in the ring when his friend did not respond.

Try as he might, Henry could not focus on the fight. Crispin's presence grew overbearing in its silence. He hazarded a glance at his king.

A scowl marred his face, intimidating and disconcerting at the same time. Something had happened. The oppressive angst consuming Crispin became a physical presence. Henry opened his mouth to speak but snapped it shut when their eyes met. The last time he saw that look was when Crispin's father blamed him for Francis' death. It had taken Henry weeks to work all the aggression out of him.

"Henry, step into the ring." Crispin's voice rumbled, a low menacing growl.

Taking a step back, Henry glanced around them. The bailey bustled with activity, knights at practice, servants and squires preparing for the coming festivities.

"Sire, do you think this wise?" Henry swallowed the fear lodged in his throat. To see the king in such a state would only aggravate what had become a tenuous, guarded peace.

Without a word, Crispin climbed over the rail and landed in the ring. He unsheathed his sword and motioned for Henry to join him.

Henry reluctantly jumped into the ring. "Out," he shouted to the two men who had been fighting. They scurried from the pit as he drew his sword and faced his friend.

Without a word, Crispin lunged, bringing their swords together with a clash of steel against steel. Henry pushed him away with a shove and they circled each other. Crispin's gaze narrowed as his lip curled in a snarl. Henry gripped the hilt with both hands and braced himself for the oncoming assault.

They parried back and forth. More of an animalistic attack than a predetermined fighting stance. Henry worked hard to fight off the blows. He never swung at his friend and focused on defending himself from the bold and vicious attack. Crispin spun and swung the sword in an arc across Henry's chest, nicking the inside of his arm.

"I am not your enemy!" Henry backed away with quick shuffling steps.

Crispin charged, his sword braced for a blow from the hilt. Henry ducked beneath the blow and punched him in the stomach. Crispin doubled over but regained his wits quickly and turned toward Henry, his eyes glowing.

"Fighting thus will not improve your mood," Henry spoke low so only Crispin could hear his plea.

"I will fight any damn way I please." Crispin snarled and charged forward.

They locked swords again. Henry attempted to keep some order to the bout, but Crispin fought as if in a blind rage. He knew this was Crispin's way of venting his anger and the pain he held inside. The subsequent exhaustion never helped uncover a solution, only delayed its resolution.

Henry stepped into a thrust. Crispin knocked the blade from his hand and pushed him to the ground. His gaze followed blade pressed to his throat, settling on Crispin's expression, and he raised his open hand. "I yield, Sire."

Crispin stepped away, withdrawing the weapon. He sheathed it and turned to Henry. When he offered his hand, Henry hesitated. "Come."

He slipped his hand in Crispin's and stood. "We have garnered an audience," Henry whispered.

With a shrug, Crispin walked to the railing and leaned against it. "I care not."

"You should take more caution in your actions, especially in view of your people." Henry motioned for two knights to enter the ring. As they began their bout, Henry turned back to Crispin. "Do not doubt the power they wield."

Crispin scowled at him. "I am in no mood for your lectures."

Henry shook his head. The king seemed to be in a right foul humor. Before he could wonder at the cause, a shout drew his attention to the main gate.

A group of men rode through the gate, their horses decorated in blue and white, his family's colors. The standard bearer at the head of the procession carried the banner with his family's coat of arms. He groaned. *From bad to worse.* His father's timing has always been horrible.

"Seems as though your father and brothers have arrived at last." The tone of Crispin's voice showed his equal lack of enthusiasm for their presence.

"Aye, shall we greet them together?"

Crispin motioned for Henry to go first. With a sigh, Henry exited the ring and walked toward his father who rode at the head of the procession.

"Father, I bid you welcome." He proffered a bow and a smile.

"Henry!" His father slid from the saddle and clasped his son in a warm embrace. He grimaced at the overemphatic action. His father released him suddenly, and Henry righted himself, tugging at his doublet.

"Sire." Henry's father knelt before Crispin and bowed his head. "My condolences on the loss of your father. He was an honorable king."

"You may rise." Crispin nodded. "I trust your journey was uneventful."

"Not a bandit in sight." Henry's father boomed with a

laugh. He had aged. The once dark blond hair had turned white, his eyes seemed tired and world weary.

Henry turned to his brothers as they bowed to Crispin. The three older brothers he had once envied had grown old. His gaze traveled over each of their rotund bellies. And fat, it would seem. His eldest brother, Richard, tossed his reins to the stable boy. The other two followed suit. Henry gritted his teeth. He would give anything to be sent on an errand, or into battle, rather than listen to his brothers and father speak. Any respect he had for them died years ago.

"Please make yourselves comfortable. Our Chamberlain will attend to you. The Lord High Steward and I have some matters to attend," Crispin interjected, sparing Henry the agony of interacting with his family.

"Lord High Steward?" Baron Norrington's gaze rested on Henry for a moment before returning to Crispin.

"Did I not mention your son has been elevated to the position of Lord High Steward? He will also be invested as His Grace, Henry Balmont, Duke of Westdell."

The baron's face blanched as he glanced at his other sons, whose faces took on a lovely hue of greenish-yellow. He turned back to Crispin and bowed. "I am grateful to have you bestow such an honor on my son."

"I could not have chosen a more loyal or stalwart knight to stand by my side and protect my kingdom." Crispin's gaze narrowed on the baron.

"You have chosen wisely, Sire." The baron bowed and glanced at Henry as he rose.

Henry buried the knotted turmoil churning in his chest. "We shall see you at the evening meal. As His Majesty said, we have some important business to attend before the festivities begin." He turned to walk away when a vision of loveliness in a midnight blue gown came toward them. Henry swore under his breath. Would he find no escape?

Ruby strode across the bailey. Her eyes were bright and her hair caught up in a delicate pearl-studded netting. Henry caught the heavy sigh before it left his lips and glanced at Crispin who tensed beside him.

"Sire, Sir Henry." She curtseyed and glanced beyond them. "Have we guests?"

"Aye, my family," Henry replied when Crispin made no move to answer because his gaze remained fixed on her; the intensity of it made Henry take a step back involuntarily. Ruby, however, seemed unconcerned with his rude behavior. "By your leave, Sire...Lady Ruby, allow me to introduce you to my kin."

Her smile brightened as Crispin and Henry led her back to where his brothers and father were speaking with a steward. Crispin hovered close, but never touched her. Henry arched his brow. They must have been fighting...again. He turned his attention back to his family.

"James Balmont, Baron Norrington, allow me to introduce Lady Ruby of Dorringbroke, my betrothed." Crispin found his voice it seemed. He pasted a smile on his lips as he introduced her. The perfect illusion of happiness and pride.

Henry held his breath.

The baron bowed. "My lady, you are an angel, a light in the darkness." His infamous charm bubbled to the surface as he greeted her.

Her smile faltered for the space of a heartbeat, but she maintained her composure. "You flatter me, my lord. 'Tis a pleasure to make your acquaintance." She turned to his brothers, who bowed low as each was introduced.

"We are at your command, my lady." Richard met her gaze with a bold smile.

Ruby's sharp intake of breath did not escape notice. Her cheeks paled and her delicate fingers clenched into fists. She bowed her head in response, but could not bring herself to meet their gazes again. *What in the devil?*

"Are you well, my lady?" Henry's concern overrode propriety.

Even Crispin watched, uncertainty evident in his expression.

She waved her hand. "I am well. By your leave, Sire, my lords, will you excuse me?" With those words, she dashed toward the postern gate.

They watched her disappear, and Crispin spoke to fill the awkward moment. "I look forward to seeing you again this evening." Crispin gave a slight incline of his head and walked calmly out the postern gate after her.

"What a peculiar woman." His father's assessment interrupted the awkward silence. "Quite lovely though. From where does she hail? Dorringbroke?"

"I believe so," Henry responded honestly, unsure of what to tell his father. Too much of the truth would lead to more questions, and Henry would not trust his family with a cart of horse shite.

"Interesting." His father stroked his chin as if suddenly consumed in thought. "We shall see ourselves settled then."

With a slight bow, Henry stole one last glance at his brothers, who murmured among themselves and then left them. He followed Crispin and Ruby out the postern gate, hoping to discover what made her react in such an odd manner. He had never seen her shrink from anything let alone run away.

He found them near the stream. Ruby stood with her back to Crispin, her arms folded across her chest. As he neared them, he noted her body trembled.

"My lady." Henry approached slowly.

She jumped, turning toward both of them. Tear stains marred her cheeks. Her lower lip trembled. He took a step closer, and she held a hand out to stop him.

"I pray you, do not come closer." She backed away, her eyes wide.

"What happened?" Henry asked, glancing at Crispin.

"I know not. I found her trembling and in tears." Crispin turned to Ruby. "You have nothing to fear, sweeting. What has you so frightened?"

Henry stared open-mouthed at Crispin's tender words. Ruby shook her head, backing away until she collided with a large elm tree. He longed to offer his aid. Anything within his power, he would do it. The fear in her eyes drove him to panic. Something was not right.

"They—" Her mouth trembled, stumbling over every word. "They did it."

Crispin approached her as one would a frightened colt. He reached his hand out, inviting her into his embrace. She dove into his arms, burying her face against his chest. As the king held her tight, Henry met his gaze.

"Who, sweeting?" Crispin asked, his voice velvet soft.

"Henry's brothers...his father..." The sound of her muffled words mixed with sobs hit Henry in the chest like a stone.

"What did they do, my lady?" Henry swallowed the apprehension clawing at his gut.

"They—" Her tear-filled amber eyes met his. "Killed my parents!"

Chapter Thirty-Two

"My lady." A muffled voice drifted through the door. "You cannot keep yourself locked away until the wedding." When she received no response, Mina retreated, her footsteps fading into the distance.

Ruby turned to stare out the window once more. Five days had passed since she saw the shock on both Henry and Crispin's faces. Her reaction had been childish, but the overwhelming torrent of emotion pulled her under and she reacted without thought.

The memory of Richard, Henry's eldest brother, staring down at her, a scar bisecting his otherwise handsome face made her shiver. A face she would never forget. She saw the same visage covered with streaks of paint hovering over her, smoke billowing behind him, a demon straight from the bowels of hell. Ruby clutched the shawl tighter around her shoulders.

Crispin had held her until the trembling subsided. When she finally looked up, Henry had gone, leaving them alone in the woods. Crispin brushed the tears from her eyes with his fingertips.

"Tell me what you remember." The low tone of his voice soothed her.

"I remember the carriage being overturned. The screaming. The bandits chasing down my family and the servants." Her gaze met Crispin's. "I remember his scar. Even beneath the streaks of blue and brown across his face, I remember wondering if a dragon had attacked him." She offered a shaky smile and turned to stare into the forest. "Silly delusions of a child."

"Are you certain beyond any doubt it was him?" Crispin scowled, darkness falling across his features.

"I remember hearing a voice asking if I was dead." Ruby shook as the memory manifested. "When Henry's father spoke—it was him. I would stake my life on it."

Crispin drew her close. "Come, you should rest."

He led her back to the castle, careful to keep their paths from crossing any of their guests. Once he reached the door to her chamber, Crispin pressed a kiss to her forehead. "I shall tell everyone you are ill. Keep to your room. I shall send your maid to your chamber straight away."

When he turned to leave, Ruby caught him by the sleeve. "Crispin." He turned, his gaze soft in contrast to his stern expression. "What will you do?"

"Nothing, yet." He smirked. "Rest." She watched him walk down the hall and had not seen him since that day.

Pulled to the present, Ruby searched the forest treetops through the window. She longed to run to Marian and tell her what had happened. But Crispin placed a guard outside her chamber, and her maids were the only company she had in days. Vivienne came once, but Ruby feigned a headache and was left in peace.

A knock echoed through the chamber. As if summoned from her thoughts, Vivienne stepped into the room. Her silver and red gown complimented the silver and red ribbons interwoven in her hair. She looked more regal than Ruby had ever seen her.

As she approached, Ruby slid from her seat by the window. "Vivienne."

Vivienne sat on the bench and patted the vacant seat next to her. "Come, sit with me."

Ruby heaved a sigh and sat down. She met the Queen Mother's concerned gaze.

"My son tells me nothing. You have shut yourself away. The wedding is in two days." Vivienne frowned. "I cannot help if I am kept at an arm's length. Tell me what ails you."

With a heavy sigh, Ruby turned to stare out the window again. "Several days ago, I remembered details from the raid which took my parents and left me an orphan." She chewed on her lip, worried her confession would cause Vivienne to think her insane. "The memories dealt quite a blow." Ruby pressed her hand to her head then dropped it to her lap. "I hoped some rest would ease the ache."

"Being confined to your chamber has done nothing to help you, has it?" Vivienne nodded in understanding and covered Ruby's hand with her own. "I may not be your mother, but I care for you as I would my own daughter." Ruby's sincere smile brought a hint of joy into Vivienne's eyes. "Would you like to take a ride outside the keep?"

Ruby nodded fervently. "More than anything."

"Meet me in the kitchens as soon as you have changed." Vivienne stood and shared a conspiratorial smile before she left the room.

Excitement thrummed through her. *Finally*. Ruby changed into a simple dark green gown and secured her short sword at her waist. She donned her brown cloak, tucked her thick braid into the hood, and pulled on her sturdy boots.

"Marian will know what to do," she whispered beneath her breath as she stepped into the hall.

The guards who had taken residence outside her chamber were gone. Ruby grinned. Vivienne made a wonderful ally. When she reached the kitchens, the servants paid her no mind. She caught sight of Vivienne near the door leading to the bailey.

"Come, the men are training. I have had your horse brought around, tied in the forest beyond the gate."

"You are not coming?"

Vivienne shook her head. "Not today, my dear. I must entertain our guests." She handed a small bag of coins to Ruby. "Take this. Give it to your mother." With a wave of her hand, Vivienne urged Ruby out into the bailey. "Return before sunset."

"I will. My thanks, Vivienne." She hurried out of the palace walls and darted into the forest. Ruby caught a glimpse of Ginger's rump. When she reached the mare's side, she froze.

A man on horseback with a dark hood sat astride a blood bay gelding. Ruby took a step back, her hand resting on the sword at her hip.

"Rest easy, my lady." The stranger tipped back his hood.

"Henry, what are you doing here?" She braced her hand on

Ginger. He held her reins in his hand.

"The Queen Mother requested I escort you." He wore a mask of indifference, but Ruby caught the concern in his voice. "I promised no harm would come to you while you are under my care." He held the reins out to her.

Ruby took them and mounted her horse. The indescribable joy of being in the saddle overwhelmed her. She ignored the man watching her. Clearing her throat, Ruby turned her attention to Ginger and gave her a pat.

"Shall we?" Henry gestured for her to lead.

She nudged her horse into a walk and found the trail. Henry came up beside her, and they rode in silence. The late summer forest came alive with birds and insects. Ruby nearly forgot her companion until he spoke.

"My lady, I hope you realize my loyalty lays with the king and with you." He rubbed his palm against his thigh. "I cannot bear to see you hold me in disdain."

With a glance, she noted his sharp profile, his hair hanging across his forehead, curling over his collar. He turned to face her, his eyes sharp and pleading.

"I hold no ill feelings toward you." She worried her lip between her teeth. "I fear my past has returned to haunt me." As they continued down the trail, silence descended again. The rhythm of the horses' hooves pounding the ground mixed with the sway of Ginger's gait lulled Ruby into contentment. She sighed.

"Where is your destination?" Henry asked, his voice breaking through her daze.

"Well..." She drifted off, unsure of herself. Should she allow him to know so much about her? Could he be trusted? Ruby studied him closely.

"I understand if you do not fully trust me, my lady." His serious expression offered her a bit of comfort. "Crispin told me of the raid. We were both in training as squires at the time it happened. Some whispered of the raiders being Northmen, barbaric tribes who live on the seas. Others assumed the raid had been in response to King Edgar's close ties to England. Only heaven knows if it was the Scots, Irish, or the French who took insult to our bond." He glanced at her. "Are you willing to swear on the bones of the Lord my family was the one to cause you such an injustice?"

"Aye," she replied, her voice strong. Ruby's hands tightened on the reins. "I remember only fragments from that day, but your father's voice and your eldest brother's face, they have been seared into my mind like a brand on a hide." She gritted her teeth and pushed down the bitterness rising inside of her.

Henry nodded solemnly. "Then I will take your words as truth, my lady. You have nothing to gain by implicating their involvement." He held his hand over his heart. "I swear by the saints, I will uncover the reason behind this treachery."

Ruby's heart clenched at his words. *A true knight of honor and chivalry.* "May God grant you mercy, Sir Henry."

"My sword is yours to command, my lady. Know that I am your most humble and loyal servant." His hand remained fisted over his heart as he spoke.

She inclined her head toward him, acknowledging his pledge. "I am honored to have you by my side."

"Will you now tell me where our travels take us this day?" His smile caught her off guard.

"Aye." She beamed. "To speak to my mother."

Henry looked puzzled for a moment as if trying to sort the details in his mind. "I believed your parents to be dead."

"They are." Her cryptic reply frustrated him.

He raked his hand through his hair. "God's teeth."

"The couple who found me took me in and raised me in a cottage near Skye Lake." Ruby pointed to the lake through the trees.

"They live there still?" Henry searched the area she indicated.

"My mother does, but my father was killed by bandits three years ago." Ruby hung her head to hide the pain of the memory of her father's death.

"The memory of his loss pains you even though you are not of his blood?"

"It does." Ruby brushed the quiet tears away. "My father taught me the skills to survive while my mother taught me the knowledge to heal."

"A woman of many talents." Henry grinned.

Heat rose in her cheeks at his words. "Aye, and where has it gotten me?"

"A throne."

Ruby's gaze snapped to Henry.

His smile never faded. "Are you sure you are not a witch or an enchantress?"

"Nay!" Ruby bristled. Such an insinuation would condemn her to death. "Do not even jest about such things! Why would you even—" Her cheeks burned hot as she let the words evaporate between them.

"You have bewitched us," Henry replied as if he was commenting on the weather.

"Us?" His sudden thoughts bewildered her.

"The king and I. You have us under your control, you realize this, do you not?"

"I...I do not know what to say in response to such an absurd statement."

"You know it to be true, my lady. There is no denying it. Should you give either of us the order, we would cast ourselves into the fire." He chuckled. "A pair of fools at the command of the queen."

Ruby waved her hand. "Enough of this nonsense. Come, I see the cottage through the trees." Kicking Ginger into a trot, she approached the small wooden building.

No smoke billowed from the chimney. Ruby frowned as she dismounted. Henry took the reins and waited as she approached the door. She knocked several times, but no one answered.

"Strange," Ruby mused. "Perhaps she delivered medicines to the monastery or traveled to the village."

"What would you have us do?"

Ruby picked up a branch and placed it on the door handle, leaning precariously against the wood. She returned to her horse and swung up into the saddle.

Henry motioned to the door. "What is the stick for?"

"'Tis an old trick my father once taught me. It will let my mother know I have been here." Sadness tugged at her heart. She hoped to see Marian before the wedding, to speak to her about Henry's family and invite her to the ceremony. There was naught that could be helped. Perhaps she could send Henry back with a message later.

"Shall we return to the castle, my lady? I would rather not cause the king any concern."

"Aye, we would not want to put Crispin in a foul mood." With a smirk, she kicked her horse's flanks and set off at a gallop with Henry close at her heels. As they raced through the trees, she glimpsed movement in the deep shadows lining the edge of the forest. Probably a stag spooked by their presence.

Ruby pushed Ginger faster, savoring this last taste of freedom before her marriage imprisoned her forever.

Chapter Thirty-Three

Crispin rode through the gate, his horse lathered and slick with sweat. He dismounted and tossed the reins at the gaping stable boy. "Be sure you cool him down before you put him away."

The lad fell into a quick bow. "At once, Sire." He led Ghost around the bailey.

The servants went about their chores, and the knights busied themselves with their armor and weapons. None of them turned their gaze in his direction. His frustration radiated in waves, setting everyone on edge. He raked his hand through his hair.

They did nothing to invite his ire, but fury raged inside of him driving him to the point of madness. Had he not done all he could to bring her comfort? Was he not enough of a man to meet her needs? *Henry, damn your hide.* There were marked differences between them, but seeing Ruby with his friend drove a dagger through his heart.

He cut a direct path for his presence chamber. A stiff drink would calm the uncertainty bubbling beneath his frustration. The servants gave him wide berth as he strode down the halls. When he reached his room, he swung open the door to find Henry lounging in his chair, his feet propped on the desk. Crispin entered and closed the door behind him.

"I trust you enjoyed your venture into the wood?" He poured himself a dram of brandy.

Henry eyed him. "Escorting your betrothed on an errand did not prove to be a tiresome way to spend my morning."

"You enjoy her company then?" Crispin took a long drink, ignoring the sting of jealousy.

"Aye, as I also enjoy your company when you are not behaving like a selfish bastard."

"Have you forgotten to whom you speak?" Crispin swirled

the liquid in the goblet, his gaze narrowing on Henry. "Perhaps I should remove your tongue for your insolence."

Henry exhaled in exasperation. "'Tis not as if you have not threatened to do so a hundred times before."

"I should follow through this time. Shall I have you castrated as well?"

"Do you take me for a man who would fuck another's bride two days before their vows?" Henry stood, slamming his fist down on the desk. "I have stood by your side when you were drunk, surly, and longing to meet death. But I refuse to stand before you and have you hurl slander in my face for a crime I have not committed!"

Crispin tapped his fingers against the goblet in his hand. Henry leaned against the desk, his hair disheveled and his eyes lit by the fire burning within. A smile crept across Crispin's lips as he watched his friend take several deep breaths, calming himself. Pushing Henry into the corner to watch him fight always proved far too simple and quite enjoyable. The jealousy hanging over his head disintegrated into the shadows once more. He downed the brandy remaining in the cup.

"Calm yourself before you say something you will regret on the morrow." Crispin stood and set the goblet down on the desk. "I need to be sure you are willing to do what is necessary to protect her. Have you gleaned anything from your father, your brothers?"

"You conniving arse." Henry shook his head and exhaled heavily. "I have spent the last several days listening to my brothers boast of their homes and their lands. My father speaks of nothing but his aches and pains. Oh, and his desire to remarry." He smoothed his hair away from his face. "I wish them far from here."

"You have not asked them about the raid then?" Crispin rubbed his hand across his jaw.

"I cannot very well ask them directly." Henry scoffed. "Even if I could get a word or two into the discussion. They talk incessantly about nothing of consequence." He hung his head. "I fear I may never learn anything about that day."

"Perhaps you should get them drunk and then ask them."

Henry glanced up. "Do you know how much ale it would take to get them drunk enough to expose themselves as traitors?"

Crispin shrugged. "Whatever truths can be bought with a few kegs of ale, a half dozen barrels of wine, or even my private reserve of brandy, I consider it well worth the cost."

"Shall we celebrate tomorrow eve then? In honor of Lady Ruby's recovery." Henry grinned as he followed the direction of Crispin's thoughts. "It would be the perfect cover."

With a nod, Crispin strode toward the door. "Send word to the kitchens to make tomorrow's evening meal special. Have my best casks brought up from the cellars. And Henry—" Crispin pointed at him. "Be sure to remain sober enough to get the information we need. Once you have it, come directly to me, I do not care the hour or the situation. I wish to be informed immediately."

"As you wish, Sire." Henry bowed as Crispin left the room.

As he traversed the halls, his thoughts strayed to the following evening's festivities. While Henry worked to gain the confessions of his bloodstained family, Crispin would attempt to obtain some confessions of his own. He had given Ruby enough time. She would fall beneath his seduction. His cock hardened at the thought of her squirming against him.

By the end of the night, he would be buried deep within her as he whispered his darkest desires against her silky skin. He grasped the key around his neck. She would beg for him to set her free.

Chapter Thirty-Four

The bright red banners strewn throughout the great hall added an air of celebration to the evening meal. Preparations for the wedding and coronation were gaining momentum, the servants working harder than ever to keep up with the demands of the royal family. Henry took his seat to Crispin's right while his father and brothers took up the space beside him.

"Problems?" Crispin asked, keeping his voice low.

"Nay, Sire. Everything is as it should be." Henry took a sip of wine, careful to consume it slowly. Too much would leave him muddled and forgetful.

"Excellent." Crispin turned his attention to the woman beside him.

Henry stole a glance at Lady Ruby. Her hair was swept up in an elegant style with twin braids encircling the sides of her head. The dark sapphire of her gown brought out the delicate hue of her skin and highlighted the vibrant color of her hair. She caught Henry's gaze and smiled. Her countenance beamed like sunlight through the treetops on a summer day.

He turned away with a nod and shoved a bite of meat in his mouth. Henry kept a careful eye on the room, taking in the servants, searching for Ivy. It had been a sennight since he had last seen her. His cock hardened at the image of her riding him. He promised her only one night, but he longed for more. Where could she have gone? Not one person in the castle remembered her.

Tearing a piece of bread from the trencher, he dipped it in the gravy. Bite after bite, he ate, the food tasteless in his mouth. His brothers and father laughed over their ribald stories. Henry turned toward them, attempting to take an interest in their conversation. He prayed Crispin's idea would take root.

After the next course, Crispin stood and the guests

occupying the great hall fell silent, every eye turned to him. "My loyal subjects, in honor of my lovely bride, I have decided to celebrate early. Bring in the wine!"

The servants rolled in large casks of wine and set them in the corners of the room. The guests cheered at his announcement while the musicians struck up a lively tune. Soon the feast took on an air of levity and celebration.

Henry called for one of the servants to deliver more wine. He kept his attention on the story his brother told, aware of Crispin behind him. After a few more rounds, the stories grew bolder and the laughter more raucous. Henry glanced over his shoulder to see Crispin leading Ruby from the table, his hand on her waist. They disappeared around the corner leaving Henry alone at the head table with his family. *Bloody fortunate bastard.*

"Have you not yet found an appropriate bride, Henry?" His father clapped his hand on his shoulder, bringing him back to the moment. "Pity you have not yet found a wench suitable enough for your position. All your brothers are wed and have grown quite adept at providing me with grandchildren."

His brothers winked and jabbed each other in the ribs. Henry shook his head. "The king has tasked me with an important duty. Besides, my brothers seem more than able to keep your pride near bursting."

"Aye, 'tis quite a comfortable seat you have acquired. Having a brother sitting as the Right Hand of the king will prove useful." Richard interjected taking another drink of wine. He swayed as he motioned for more from a passing servant.

She refilled their cups, and his brother, Donnal, grabbed her arse with his free hand. The girl shook from his grasp and hurried away. The brothers laughed as did his father. Henry stomped on the anger bubbling inside of him like a cauldron boiling over a flame. *They will mind their manners soon enough, just get on with it.*

The deeper they drank, the freer their conversation became. Most of the guests took their celebration away from the great hall. Henry heard the revelry in the bailey through the open door as it spilled into the village outside the gates. They were alone now; all Henry had to do was wait for his opportunity.

"I remember the one wench, traveling with family through the north—" Donnal slurred.

Richard jabbed him in the ribs. "Shut it, you yammering codpiece!"

"I do not recall that." Henry pressed gently pretending to be more intoxicated than he truly was. "Was this after I left for the palace to begin my training?"

Richard took another healthy swallow and turned to his father whose eyes held the glassy sheen of intoxication. At his father's nod, Richard turned back to Henry. "Aye. A man approached us on behalf of his master with a golden opportunity, it would have been unwise to ignore it." The other brothers nodded.

"We dressed as raiders from the north and caught them unaware." His father smiled. "That bloody day made me an extremely wealthy man."

Henry swallowed the bile in his throat but played the interested, bloodthirsty son they all expected. "They wanted the whole family dead?" He licked his lips, hoping to fool them into believing he was truly enjoying this tale of carnage.

"Nay, they cared not if the rest lived or died. 'Twas only the wee lass they wanted dead." Richard smirked.

The wee lass. It took every bit of self-control not to empty the contents of his stomach then and there. *Ruby.* He forced a vicious smile, pushing the revulsion deep into the pit of his stomach. "You killed them all for one small child?"

"Aye, they protected her as if she was the most precious possession they held," Donnal added. "Had to cut through all of them to get to her. Knocked her down when she was running away."

"They must have wanted her dead for a reason." Henry hoped to draw out the name of the man who paid them to murder an innocent family.

"I did not ask questions; I merely did as requested and got paid." His father chuckled, rubbing his rounded stomach as he leaned back in the chair. "'Tis a shame you could not have joined us in the raid. Although it does me proud to see you have weaseled your way into the king's good graces." He grinned, and Henry imagined running him through with a sword.

"However I may best serve my family," Henry lied, wondering if the good Lord would strike him dead for playing his family false. They were murderers and thieves who deserved to die for their crimes. Bound by his honor, Henry did as his king bade.

"There will come a time when I will call on you to help us. Be ready." His father winked as he indulged in another cup of wine.

Henry nodded taking another drink. His family was well and truly in their cups. Their words slurred together, and they waved their arms in animated discussion.

"Pardon me, I must relieve myself." Henry stood at his father's nod and gripped the edge of the table as the room began to sway. Righting himself, he straightened his doublet and carefully walked along the wall toward the corridor leading to the kitchens. Once out of sight, he leaned against the cool stone and took several deep breaths. His vision steadied, but the warmth infusing him warned of the strong effect of the wine. It had been months since he had been well and truly drunk.

"I must tell Crispin." He pushed away from the wall and carefully climbed up the staircase leading to the wing containing Crispin's chamber. Not a soul passed him. He approached the door to Crispin's bedchamber and knocked. Grasping the handle, he pushed it open and stumbled into the room.

"Crispin, I did as you asked. I—" Henry's mouth ceased moving, in fact, it refused to even close. A woman stood in the center of the room with nothing but a piece of cloth tied across her eyes. His heart pounded and his cock leaped.

"I hope you have a damned good reason for interrupting me." Crispin's voice echoed behind him.

Sweet merciful saints, what have I done?

Chapter Thirty-Five

The feast proved a welcomed diversion. Ruby indulged in the sweet and savory dishes laid upon the table, but her gaze drifted to the men beside her. Crispin and Henry both sat to her right, making it impossible not to look at one without catching a glimpse of the other. Her face heated when both of them caught her watching them. She stuffed a small fruit pastry into her mouth and savored the exquisite flavors.

"I trust you are enjoying the meal." Crispin's breath on her neck made her shift in her seat. He leaned close, speaking in hushed tones. "My only wish is to bring you pleasure."

A tiny shiver rippled through her. Ruby swallowed the food and turned toward him. "The feast is truly remarkable."

"The celebration tomorrow will be far more elaborate." He stroked a fingertip along the edge of her hand where it rested on the table.

Her breath stuttered at his touch. She picked up her goblet of wine and took a long drink in an attempt to drown the desire, but instead, the drink warmed her enhancing the sensations his touch elicited. When she set the goblet down, he summoned a servant to refill it.

"Are you trying to intoxicate me, my lord?" She fidgeted with the stem of the goblet afraid to turn and meet his gaze.

"I have every intention of plying you with wine and then seducing you." His breath caressed the nape of her neck with each word. He dropped his hand to her thigh and dug his fingers into the soft flesh. Even through the material of her dress, his touch burned her. "Will you come willingly? Or would you rather I command you?"

Her eyes drifted shut at his words. He held up his end of the bargain this long. But if she conceded to his demands, would he not consider her weak for giving him what he craved? The slow, rhythmic circles his fingertips made on her thigh drove the argument from her mind. He watched her with a steady gaze. Ruby licked her lips and picked up the cup, draining it in one swallow.

"Slow and steady, my dear. We would not want you to drink too much and fall asleep before the seduction could begin, would we?" He leaned down and pressed a kiss to her throat without so much as a pretense.

"Crispin." She meant it as a reprimand, but his name spilled from her lips dripping with need.

He pulled away to sit properly in his seat. Picking at his food, he drank more wine and watched the room. Crispin ignored her, purposely avoiding her gaze, keeping from even the slightest contact with her.

Ruby's body thrummed with desire. A pulse of longing pounded in the pit of her stomach. She pushed the food away and sipped her wine. She instructed him to stop, and he did. Her body revolted against her. *Take what he offers!* Her mind screamed. *You will be wed on the morrow, what does one night matter in the light of all eternity? 'Tis not as if you have never shared his bed.* Ruby groaned.

The moments passed and each one contained a multitude of tortures. The desire which began as a gentle hum now made her hands tremble. Ruby hungered for him, and she could no longer deny it.

"Crispin." She kept her voice low and eyes downcast.

"Aye." He leaned close once more.

Her hand shook as she laid it on his. Ruby met his gaze. "May we take our leave?"

"As you wish, sweeting." His handsome face transformed as a triumphant smile broke upon his lips. He stood and, keeping hold of her hand, helped her rise from her seat. "One moment."

Crispin turned his attention to Henry, who was deep in conversation with his brothers and father. With a nod, he turned back to her, pressing a possessive hand to the small of her back. Ruby tipped her chin up and walked from the great hall with Crispin by her side. The warmth of the wine spread through her limbs.

As they rounded the corner, Crispin tugged her into an alcove behind the staircase and pressed her against the stone wall. His lips crushed against hers, stealing her breath. She moaned as he tasted her. He pinned her hands to the wall as he kissed her repeatedly, plundering her mouth, stealing her breath. He ravaged her mercilessly only to pull back, freeing her hands.

The sound of servants passing by pulled her from the haze. "Take me to your chamber." She toyed with the chain around his neck.

"Are you giving me permission?"

"Aye." She kissed him tenderly lest she wake the beast inside him again.

Crispin swung her into his arms and carried her up the stairs. Moving swiftly down the hall, he kicked the door open to his chambers. He set her down on the bed and returned to close the door.

"Perhaps you should lock the door." Ruby melted into the coverlet as he stalked toward her.

"Who would dare disturb me in my chamber?" His hungry smile grew as he pulled the doublet from his body and tossed it onto the floor. The loose tunic he wore beneath it billowed as he stopped at the foot of the bed. "Stand, Ruby."

Holding his gaze, she stood and began to unlace her gown. He helped her until it slid from her body into a puddle on the floor. She pulled off her shift and laid it on the chair beside the bed. Crispin's eyes widened in appreciation as his gaze roamed over her naked form from head to foot. Taking the key from around his neck, he unlocked the chastity belt and removed it gently before tossing it into the fire.

"There will be no more of that." He smirked confidence radiating with every step. "Come, bathe." He led her to an oversized tub near the fire. Steam billowed from the surface of the water.

"How did you—"

"I had the servants prepare a bath while we ate," he replied. "Step into the water. I shall return." With those words, Crispin left her alone in his chamber.

Why was he always so confident? She eased herself into the hot water and sighed as it soothed the ache in her body. The belt had been uncomfortable. It proved a cumbersome hindrance for daily activity, but the reaction she garnered from Crispin made any frustration she encountered worth it. She reached for the oils sitting on the small table beside the tub. Taking her time, she washed her entire body with the sweet-smelling oil and settled back into the water.

Crispin returned as she laid her head back. Coming close, he sat in a chair next to the tub, his focus on her breasts bobbing in the water.

"Have you brought me something?" She gestured to the cloth draped over his arm.

"I brought a silk shift made specifically for you. However, I intend to keep you naked for the remainder of the evening." His grin boasted of wicked intentions and sensual promises.

Although she remained enveloped in the heat of the water, Ruby shivered. A memory flashed before her of Crispin dragging her from the bathtub and carrying her into the barn. Had they only known each other for such a short time? The connection between them felt like a lifetime bond forged in childhood.

"Get out of the bath." He draped the shift over the back of the chair. "Or do I need to drag you from that tub?" He remembered it as well it seemed.

With slow, deliberate movements, she stood and stepped from the bath. Taking the drying cloth from the table, she made slow work of drying her skin aware of Crispin's gaze following her movements. Her body tingled and her breath came in short pants, anticipating his reaction. Would he grab her, pull her into his lap, kiss her, or more?

"I would say my patience over the past sennight has brought me as close to sainthood as I could hope to achieve." He stood and pulled her against him, making her drop the cloth. He brushed his fingertips across her jaw and down her neck, longing burning in their wake. "But I am no saint, Ruby, as you can well attest. And the things I have planned for you would make even the most hardened sinner blush with shame."

She slid her hands beneath his tunic, smoothing her palms against the hard warm skin of his back. He hissed in a breath and bit his lip, his eyes drifting closed. Ruby enjoyed the power her touch wielded. A sprite of mischief took residence upon her shoulder. Dare she tease the man who held the fate of a kingdom in his hands? She dipped her hands into the back of his hose and squeezed his arse.

"You push me too far, woman." His eyes flew open, flashing deep blue and stormy with a hunger all too familiar to her.

"Perhaps *I* should make *you* beg." She teased him with a grin, raking her fingernails across his skin.

He growled, the sound rumbling in his throat, making him sound more beast than man. Crispin caught her up in his arms, and she squirmed against him as he carried her to the bed and tossed her down onto the covers. Stepping back, he tore the tunic over his head and threw it to the floor. He leaned over her, a wolf stalking its prey.

"You shall be the one begging, my dear." His fierce expression mixed with the feral grin made her breath catch.

Ruby placed her hand on his chest, and he halted. The heat from his body warmed her as the wine had, making her drunk with desire. Licking her lips, she smirked. "Is that a challenge?"

"There is no challenge." He bent and took a nipple in his mouth, suckling hard.

Ruby moaned and arched against him, gripping his arms and digging her nails into his skin. His teeth raked the sensitive peak. Her mouth fell open as the sensitive nub rolled against his tongue. When he released it, she clung to him as her panting breaths slowed.

"Are you so confident in your seduction?"

"I am." He licked the other nipple and blew on it.

The touch drove her mind blank. After denying herself, every single dram of attention he lavished on her sent her spiraling into a haven of pleasure. She wanted more, but his confidence gave her pause.

"If you make me beg, I shall grant you three requests." Ruby buried her hands in his hair, forcing their eyes to meet.

"Any request my twisted mind might devise?" The firelight flickered across his features, deepening the sharp contours of his face. His eyes flashed with amusement at the thought.

"Aye." She fisted her hands in his hair and pulled his head back. His moan sent heat straight to her cunt. "Anything."

When she released his hair, he kissed her, punishing and exhilarating. He pressed his body against her, grinding his hips against her stomach. She craved his touch lower, but he purposely denied her. With each move she made, he countered it until finally pinning her hands to the bed beside her head. Crispin tugged on her lower lip with his teeth as he broke the kiss.

"Shall we begin?" His hair fell in waves across his eyes.

Ruby bore the distinct impression she made a deal with the devil. There would be no surrender. She nodded.

He climbed off the bed completely. She lay against the soft blankets, her lips bruised from his kisses, her body screaming for his touch. Crispin stood at the edge of the bed and looked down at her.

"Stand up," he commanded. The deep tone of his voice made her body weep.

Ruby rolled over onto her hands and knees and climbed across the bed, giving Crispin an eyeful of her bare arse with a passing glimpse of what lay between her thighs. When she reached the other side, she climbed from the bed and waited for his next instruction.

Crispin walked to the foot of the bed and motioned for her. "Come here."

She approached him but refrained from reaching for him even as every part of her screamed to be in his embrace. With barely a breath between them, she stopped, and his bold gaze bore into her.

"Turn around."

She turned her back to him, closing her eyes. What would he do? Anticipation built inside of her like a bird climbing high into the sky. She feared she would expire from the torment. *Touch me, damn you.* She refrained from speaking, lest he interpret any verbal reply as her begging. Ruby refused to allow him best her. He would concede to his desires before she did. A flicker of doubt crossed her mind. *Dance with the devil, and you may lose more than your soul.*

His fingers pulled the pins from her hair, and it fell lock by lock around her bare shoulders. He plucked the ornaments from her tresses and unbound her heavy braids until she stood trembling, the long curls trailing over her breasts and down her back. The caress of silk drifted across her skin as he reached around her, covering her eyes with the soft fabric. The room sank into complete darkness as she closed her eyes. Crispin secured the blindfold with deft fingers.

"Can you see?" he whispered in her ear.

Ruby shivered and shook her head.

"Good." A brush of air drifted around her as he moved. His firm grip remained on her arms as he positioned her in the room. "Do not move until I tell you."

She heard his footsteps retreat, then silence descended. Her breaths came quicker, her hearing sharpened. Ruby clenched her hands firmly by her sides, willing herself to remain calm. Knowing he watched her made her slick between her thighs. Could he sense her arousal and sought to heighten it by depriving her of his touch and her sight?

Ruby focused her thoughts on Marian, on Vivienne, on the monastery, and the people she served. Anything to remove her thoughts from this moment and the pounding of her heart. It would do no good. Crispin initiated this game, and she strove to outwit him once more.

The creak of the door opening snapped her to attention. "Crispin, I did as you asked. I—" Silence fell.

Ruby gasped. *Henry.*

"I hope you have a damned good reason for interrupting me." Crispin's tone reflected his irritation.

"A thousand pardons, Sire. I only wanted to..." Henry stuttered, his words slurred.

"Shhh, look upon her," Crispin commanded. "Is she not

perfection?"

Was Henry drunk? Ruby's body burned from embarrassment and arousal. Knowing the two of them looked upon her nudity made her pulse quicken like the thundering hoofbeats of an army going into battle. She licked her lips.

"Aye, Sire." Henry seemed uncertain in his response.

"Would you help me win a wager?" Crispin asked his friend.

Ruby gasped in outrage but clamped her lips together. He would not...would he?

"A wager?" Henry queried.

"My lady has promised me three boons if I can make her beg."

She could hold her tongue no longer. "I never agreed to this." The sound of footsteps approaching made her tremble from both fear and longing.

"Tell me you want me. Confess your desire. Beg for me." Crispin's low voice cascaded over her, causing her desire to burn even hotter.

She shook her head.

"Henry?"

"Sire..." his faithful servant replied.

"Come here."

The footsteps echoed again. Heat radiated from both men as they surrounded her. Could she endure this? Did she want to? Her curiosity consumed her as her mind raged against the absurdity of it all.

"Remove your doublet and tunic. Do not touch the blindfold." Crispin instructed. "I am granting you the freedom to touch her, kiss her, and do whatever necessary to make her beg for me."

Ruby did not hear Henry answer, but she assumed he nodded his understanding. She braced herself as two pairs of hands settled on her naked body. One hand on her hip, one on her stomach, another on her side, and the last on her breast. She moaned. *Which hands belonged to whom?* As they explored her, she sighed. It made no difference, the sensations of their fingers dancing on her skin pushed her higher into ecstasy.

The hand on her stomach slipped lower as the one on her side drifted higher to cup her other breast. Fingertips toyed with her nipples as the hand straying down slid between her thighs and cupped her dripping sex. Ruby whimpered as a finger slid into her.

"Wet and willing, are you?" Crispin whispered against her ear.

Was he punishing her nipples or were those his fingers sliding into her cunt? She shook her head. The sensations blended as Ruby fought to tell them apart. A warm body pressed against her back as another came closer to her front.

The soft brush of her hair against her skin and the warmth of lips on her neck shocked her. She moaned as his fingers moved inside her and his hands kneaded her breasts. The kisses trailed along her jaw moving toward her ear. A nip of the sensitive skin below her lobe caused her to shudder and lean against the man behind her.

The man in front kissed her, his soft lips tasting of wine and hesitation. *Henry.* She kissed him in return and fell headfirst into abandon. The pressure on her breasts increased. *Crispin.* Breaking the kiss, she leaned into Henry trailing her tongue across his neck.

Crispin pulled her back, turning her in his arms and kissing her hard. "Shall I make it harder for you to tell us apart?"

Ruby whimpered as both of them released her and stepped away. Bereft and shaking, she cursed herself for being wanton, for enjoying their game. Henry and Crispin, friends as close as brothers, and she their plaything. Shame consumed her. She lifted her hand to remove the blindfold to speak when a voice halted her.

"Do you concede? Have you given up so easily?" Crispin's voice echoed off the walls surrounding her.

"Nay." She swallowed the shame and temptation.

"We shall lead you," Crispin informed her before a hand cupped each of her elbows, guiding her until her thighs bumped the bed.

Ruby climbed onto the covers and waited. She noted the

movement of the bed and the heat of their bodies as the men joined her. Neither spoke, and both of them carried the same build, the same physique. She had no way of telling them apart without exploring their faces with her hands. Although Crispin was shorter, it was impossible to tell from this position. *Damn him.* It would take only a simple phrase, and the game would be lost. Her pride refused to allow him to gain victory without a battle.

One of the men slipped behind her while the other pushed her back against the first. He settled between her legs and ran his hands along the inside of her thighs, spreading them. Exposed to him, she tried to bury her face against the man holding her. His arms locked around her and held her tight. The brush of breath against her cunt made her arch her hips off the bed. *Closer. More.* When his lips descended upon her weeping center, she cried out. He devoured her mercilessly.

She whimpered as he kissed and licked every fold, centering on the sensitive places hidden to all but him. She writhed beneath him until she feared she could no longer take the overwhelming pleasure. Then he stopped. His mouth poised over her, waiting. Ruby's heart pounded in her ears. His breath caressed her inner thigh. The man behind her wrapped his arms around her, his hands gently caressing her breasts. He leaned back, pulling her against his chest, his cock hard against her lower back.

The lover between her thighs came closer, his heat causing her breath to quicken. *Caught between two men.* She licked her lips in anticipation. But which one was Henry and which was Crispin? Her heart pounded as she felt the unmistakable press of one lover's cock against her tender folds.

"Cr—" Ruby bit her lip to keep from blurting out his name. Was it Crispin? Surely he would never allow Henry to take such liberties. Would he?

He paused as if waiting for her confession, begging for him to continue. She trembled between the two men. When he slid inside her, she gasped. The grip of the lover behind her tightened his grip while the one atop moved, thrusting in and out. The cock pressed against her back slid against her arse with each movement. Both men groaned.

Denying her vision enhanced her other senses. Every brush of skin against skin heightened her pleasure. The sound of their breathing increased her awareness of the two men caressing her, loving her. Her breath hitched as he quickened his pace. The hand caressing her breast slipped down to caress the tiny nub tucked between her folds. Ruby gasped and her body tensed as her climax built. Both men quickened their pace, and she tumbled from the precipice, gasping, arching against them both. Her lover tensed and followed with his own release. He slipped from her and pulled away. The man holding her from behind released her and moved from the bed.

Shame flooded Ruby. She sat naked on the bed trembling. What had she done? Before she could dwell on the implications of her actions a pair of hands covered her own. They drew her from the bed.

"Do you think you have won, sweeting?" Crispin murmured against her ear he drew her into a warm embrace.

She nodded, her pride still intact. The warmth of another body behind her made her tense.

"Your body spoke louder than words." Crispin's hands rested on her hips.

"My...what?" Ruby asked suddenly indignant.

"Your release was a confession in itself," Henry whispered in her ear.

Ruby resisted the urge to lash out for deceiving her. "You dare toy with me. I am no common harlot for you to seduce and manipulate for your selfish amusement." She struggled to escape their grasp, but they held her even tighter.

"Can you tell the difference between us?" Crispin teased her, his lips brushing against her jaw.

Another pair of lips caressed the side of her neck. Both of them caressed and licked her skin. She twisted in their grasp desperate to break free.

"Release me," she growled.

"Only if you can tell the difference." Crispin murmured, amusement dancing in his tone.

"Kiss me then."

They both released her. Ruby reached for the cloth covering her eyes when a pair of firm hands pinned her arms to her side.

"For that, you shall pay a penalty." Henry rubbed his cock against her hip before releasing her.

A pair of warm lips covered hers. They tasted of wine and spice and heat. Ruby sighed as his tongue delved into her mouth. As quickly as it started, the kiss stopped. Then a second assault against her lips stole her breath. The same taste assailed her. He punished her with his kiss, then released her. Ruby swayed and a strong pair of arms caught her. Could she truly not tell the difference between the two men?

"I—" Ruby stammered and fell silent.

"You cannot tell who kissed you first?" Henry asked.

She shook her head, her senses overloaded.

"Then we shall have our fill of you." Crispin's response startled her. "Bend over the bed, palms flat against the mattress." She stood still, and he continued. "Unless you would rather acquiesce my earlier request?"

Ruby shook her head. *I will not beg. I cannot let him hold those boons. Granting him even one request will leave me at his mercy. Am I not at his mercy now?* She pushed the thought away.

A gentle hand on the small of her back guided her toward the edge of the bed. She followed his lead and braced herself against the soft counterpane. Her face heated knowing she lay bared to them.

Ruby gasped as questing fingers caressed her exposed flesh. They slid into her, and she moaned.

"So wet." Henry's words made her bury her face in the fabric. He teased her, fucking her with his fingers, his thumb rubbing her swollen pearl with each stroke.

Ruby gripped the covers, her panting moans echoing off the walls. When she feared she could take no more, he pulled away. Before she could moan her disappointment, the head of his cock pressed against her opening. He slipped into her cunt, filling her. She cried out as he moved, fucking her with abandon. His fingers dug into her hips as he drove into her.

"Touch yourself." Crispin's voice echoed behind her as if he watched Henry's cock sliding into her body.

She slid her hand down to her slick folds and made urgent circles over her pearl. The pressure built until she could no longer control her body's reaction and shattered beneath the onslaught of sensations. Her cunt pulsed around his cock, and he growled as he fucked her harder. When he came, his fingers dug into her hips, and he drove into her until he slid, completely spent, from her trembling body.

Ruby laid there, their mingled juices dripping down her thighs. Warm hands slipped around her waist and drew her up. She blinked rapidly as the cloth was pulled from her head. Regaining her sight, she glanced up into Henry's face. He kissed her softly. Crispin stepped next to them and slid his hand around her waist. He captured her lips in a possessive kiss.

"Will you relent?" He buried his fingers in her hair, searching her face with earnest.

Refusing to answer, Ruby bit her lip.

"Henry." Crispin turned to his friend. "You may go. Methinks the lady enjoyed our little game."

With a nod and a smile directed solely at her, Henry released her and gathered his clothing. Once he left the room, Crispin wrapped his hand in her hair and pulled her head back, drawing his teeth across her neck.

"Come the morrow, you become my wife. I would see you well-rested." He released her and climbed into the bed. Ruby followed his lead and settled beneath the covers. Crispin pulled her against him and kissed her shoulder. They lay in the flickering firelight until the rhythm of his breathing changed as exhaustion claimed him.

Ruby pinched her eyes closed, her conscience at war with her actions. *What have I done?* Sleep refused to come until her exhaustion overwhelmed her and the blue light of dawn shone through the window.

Chapter Thirty-Six

A knock woke Crispin from his slumber. He blinked down at the woman nestled in his embrace. Her soft, even breathing revealed her peaceful state of repose. Crispin slid from the bed, careful not to wake her and crossed to the door as a second knock sounded. He opened it and glared at the servant who seemed unperturbed by his unclothed state.

The servant bowed. "The Queen Mother wishes to see you in her chamber at once."

With a nod, Crispin closed the door and ran his hand through his hair. What in the devil could she possibly need at this hour? He dressed quickly in a simple combination of hose and a loose tunic. Crispin glanced at the bed where Ruby lay asleep. The events of their evening remained vivid in his mind, making his cock hard. Without pursuing his wicked thoughts, he pulled on his boots and left the room, closing the door softly behind him. When he reached his mother's chambers, he entered without pretense.

"Mother, what reason do you have for waking me at this ungodly hour?" He collapsed in the seat across from her.

She studied him, her eyes bright. "Today is your wedding and your coronation. You should already be up and finalizing the plans for the day's festivities." Her gaze narrowed on him. "But after your revelries last evening, I can understand your desire to remain abed."

Crispin smirked and waved his hand. "I am certain you have taken care of all the important details."

"I will not always be here to care for you, my son." Her voice remained calm, but he sensed the underlying tension.

"Out with it." Crispin leaned back against the chair, bracing for her lecture.

"Will you treat your wife with such disrespect?" Vivienne narrowed her gaze.

"I have not treated her thus." Crispin folded his arms across his chest.

"Did you or did you not have both your betrothed and your best friend in your chambers last night?"

"I do not see what concern it is of yours, Mother."

She leaned closer, her words as sharp as her gaze. "I did my best to raise you in a Godly manner. Saints help me, but you are a stubborn, selfish young man." Her gaze dropped for a heartbeat. "Especially after Francis—"

"Do not bring him into this. Not on this day. Not ever." He jabbed his finger in her direction. The expression of hurt on her face made him drop his hand and glance away. Silence descended on the room, enveloping them both.

Vivienne poured him a cup of tea and set it on the table before him. "I have only ever wanted what was best for my sons and my country." She wiped a tear from her eye. "I will not sit idly by and allow you to treat your wife as you have treated every other woman in your past." His mother sniffed and straightened in her seat. "She has more value than you can possibly imagine."

"Do you think I do not know this?" Crispin clenched his teeth so hard his jaw ached.

"Do you love her?"

Her question gave him pause. *Do I love her?* His mind repeated the question over and over. He shrugged. "What difference would love make?"

His mother opened her mouth to speak when a soft knock echoed. "You may enter."

The door opened, and Crispin turned to see who had joined them. Ruby entered, her eyes bright and her cheeks still flushed from their night together. The red and blue damask gown accentuated her curves, inviting him to explore what lay beneath. Crispin licked his lips as she approached them.

"My dear, would you join us for tea?" Vivienne gestured to the tray before Crispin.

"You asked to see me?" Ruby's fingers twisted together as

her gaze drifted between him and his mother.

Vivienne nodded and motioned to the chair beside Crispin. "Please sit, my dear." When Ruby sat, she continued. "I called you both here for an important reason."

Crispin braced himself, expecting her to continue the lecture concerning his abhorrent actions and the importance of love. He shifted in his seat and glanced at Ruby. *Love?* His heart stirred at the thought, thundering in his chest. Ruby looked at him, her face flushing crimson before she turned her attention back to his mother.

"Ruby. Do you possess any memories of your life before the raid?" His mother's question made them glance at each other.

"Nay." Ruby shook her head, her eyes narrowed in thought. "Why do you ask?"

Vivienne poured a cup of tea and presented it to her. Ruby took the cup and sipped the warm liquid as his mother settled in her seat once more. "Because I know who you are, my dear."

The teacup clattered to the floor. "Who I am?" Ruby repeated, her voice wavering.

His mother nodded. "Aye, I told you before, you severely undervalue yourself."

"My parents were Baron and Baroness Skye." Ruby's hand trembled as her expression flickered with doubt.

"Nay." Vivienne's sharp gaze brightened.

"What is my true given name?"

"Eleanor."

She looked as though she would dissolve into a puddle of tears. Crispin grasped her hand in his and stroked her palm with his thumb.

"I do not understand. How do you know this? How do you know me?" Ruby tightened her grip on his hand.

Vivienne cleared her throat. "You were brought to our kingdom as an infant. A betrothal contract was made between you and my eldest son since the announcement of your birth. We had you fostered in the care of our trusted servant, Baron Skye, and his wife. When their caravan was attacked during their travels in the north, we feared you lost."

Crispin soured at the thought of her being betrothed to Francis, but his mouth remained sealed ensuring his loathing remained buried in the dark reaches of his soul. Ruby trembled as the truth of her past was unveiled before her.

"Where—who are my true parents?" Ruby's voice broke with emotion.

Vivienne offered a kind smile. "You are the daughter of the late King Henry V of England. Twin to the current reigning monarch of our neighboring ally."

Chapter Thirty-Seven

Crispin's hand tightened on hers. Ruby stared openmouthed at Vivienne. Her gaze flickered between Crispin and his mother as the implication of the truth sank into her mind. *That makes me a princess.* The surprise on Crispin's face dissolved quickly, masked with calm as he met her gaze.

"How can you be sure?" Ruby attempted to keep her voice steady, refusing to allow even a tear to fall in their presence.

"I harbored my suspicions since the first moment I met you, my dear." Vivienne's expression remained tender and compassionate. "The locket your mother brought to me removed all doubt."

"Locket?" Ruby shook her head, bewildered. "My mother?"

"Aye. Marian brought the small bauble to me a few days ago. I checked the engraving and the crest. 'Tis the seal of Henry the V. Marian claims you were wearing it the day her husband found you in the aftermath of the raid." She reached into her gown pocket and retrieved a small round pendant on a fine chain. Vivienne handed it to Ruby.

Crispin released her hand as she took the gift. Turning it over in her palm, she searched the locket for something familiar. The gold shone beneath the light, the engraving of Henry's seal clear on the front of it. Not a single memory bubbled to the surface. She sighed and closed her fist around the necklace, securing it in her palm. *How...why?* Her mind drowned with questions she knew would forever remain unanswered.

"Fate, my dear." Vivienne nodded as if sensing the direction of her thoughts. "You were meant to be queen." A solemn nod punctuated her words.

Ruby met her gaze, choking back the tears threatening to spill unchecked like a dam breaking. She turned to Crispin who seemed completely composed, but his fists clenched in his lap betrayed the inner turmoil she also experienced. Ruby laid her hand on his. His blue eyes flashed with surprise.

"I pray you will excuse me." She forced the words from her lips when all she wanted was to flee from the room and bolt herself in her chamber to sob into her pillow. "I must prepare for the ceremony." Ruby stood in a daze. When she reached the door, she glanced over her shoulder, nodding at Crispin and Vivienne who watched her expectantly. Without a word, she left them.

Ruby ventured toward her chamber with her head high and measured regal steps. Once she reached the safety of her room, she closed the door and slid into a heap against it. Heaving sobs wracked her body as emotion poured from the depths of her soul.

Princess Eleanor, daughter of the infamous King Henry the Fifth. The revelation shook the foundation of everything Ruby believed about herself. She had known her parents were of noble birth, but the daughter of a king surpassed even her wildest imagination. As the tears subsided, she wiped her face with her hands.

A familiar pair of faces watched her from across the room. Marian, and Ruby's faithful maid, Mina, stood waiting near a tub of hot water. Straightening quickly, Ruby ran to the only mother she had ever known and fell into her embrace.

The tears claimed her again. Her mother's tender rocking and gentle touch lulled her and the tears slowed. She leaned back and stared at her mother's careworn face.

"Why are you here?"

"I would not miss such an important day. My daughter is to be wed and crowned." Marian brushed the tears from Ruby's cheeks.

"But—" She hung her head, unsure what to say.

Marian tipped her chin up and her green eyes narrowed bright with pride. "You may not be my blood, but you will always be my precious gem."

"You knew who I was then?" Ruby asked.

"Guy and I knew you to be of noble blood. Why else would

a child wear such a token around her neck?" She smiled but it faltered as she continued. "We were wrong to keep the knowledge from you. 'Twas a selfish act on our part."

Ruby hugged her mother again. "You may have kept the truth from me, but you rescued me, raised me, loved me, and taught me to survive. For that, I cannot remain angry. But who am I now?"

"You are the same person you were before." Marian grinned. "Any remaining doubt of your assuming the throne should be laid to rest with this new information."

Ruby's heartache eased. "I am glad you are here."

"Come, my gem, we must prepare you for the ceremony." Marian pulled at Ruby's laces. Her maid stepped forward and drew the garments from her body.

As Ruby settled into the hot water, she groaned with relief. The ache in her body reminded her of the night shared in wanton pleasure with Crispin and Henry. Her face heated, but she blamed it on the steaming bath and pushed the memory aside.

Knowing she had been destined for this role since birth gave her little comfort. Vivienne mentioned her original betrothal had been to Francis, Crispin's older brother. She vaguely remembered the country in mourning over the loss of the eldest son and heir. Whispered stories of the fateful night had made their way through the villages. Some insisted Crispin had somehow been involved in his brother's death. Surely they were rumors enhanced by Crispin's already tarnished reputation.

"Mother." Ruby scrubbed her skin with a piece of cloth. "Vivienne mentioned I had been betrothed to her eldest son, Francis, from birth."

Marian nodded as she laid out the gold silk and crimson velvet wedding gown. "Aye."

"What was he like? Francis."

Her mother stopped and turned toward her. "What makes you ask such a question?"

Ruby shrugged. "Was he similar to his brother?"

Sitting on the chair beside the tub, Marian sighed. "Crispin and Francis were quite different. Francis was fair and charming, heroic to a fault. A generous and honest man, much like his father before him. He would have made a wonderful king." She offered her hand, aiding Ruby as she stepped from the tub.

Ruby dried herself with a cloth as they spoke. "Do you not think Crispin will make a good king?"

Marian arched a brow. "I believe with the right woman by his side he will make a fine king."

Ruby smiled, catching the underhanded compliment. "He is not a wicked man, Mother, merely misunderstood." She finished drying herself and stepped forward.

"Aye. The same was said of Guy, once upon a time." Marian pulled Ruby's hair free of the shift as she pulled it over her head.

Her maid handed her the locket she dropped by the door and turned to fetch the undergarments. Ruby glanced down at the gold pendant in her hand. She placed the delicate chain around her neck and fastened it. The cool metal rested between her breasts.

After Marian and Mina successfully dressed Ruby in her fine gown and coiffed her hair in an intricate braid wrapping around her head decorated with pearls and rubies, they placed the robe on her shoulders and stepped back to admire her. Ruby glanced in the mirror in the corner. No longer the Lady of the Forest, outlaw and orphan. A queen stared back at her. She smoothed her hand across her bodice, confidence infusing her.

"I am ready."

Marian walked her down the corridors toward the throne room. As they approached, Ruby caught sight of Crispin standing outside the large wooden doors leading inside. He glanced up as she approached, his eyes glinting with the reflection of the sunlight through the windows. *The King of Meradin...my husband...my fate.*

Standing proud and tall, she closed the distance between them. When he offered his arm, Ruby rested her hand upon it. The touch sent warmth through her, chasing away any remaining uncertainty and replacing it with courage.

"You look ravishing." Crispin's compliment caught her off guard.

With a glance from the corner of her eye, she noted the wolfish grin on his lips. A blush suffused heat across her cheeks. The man knew his effect on her. Ruby pursed her lips and turned to press her finger to the embroidered eagle on his doublet. "Careful, Crispin. Eagles take mates for life."

Without hesitation, he leaned close and whispered in her ear. "Binding you to me will only be the beginning. Taming you will be nothing less than a pleasure."

Ruby inhaled sharply, and his scent surrounded her, making her eyes drift closed.

"Fate, it seems, has plans for both of us." He kissed her jaw. "This day we both will fulfill our destinies."

Chapter Thirty-Eight

The guests lined both sides of the carpeted aisle leading to the platform where the thrones stood tall beneath the royal coat of arms. Henry glanced around at the guests as they admired the details of the transformed throne room. Heavy green garland interwoven with flowers crisscrossed overhead. Red and gold banners lined the walls accented with garland. Large vases of flowers and greenery stood sentry beside the doors leading into the hall. Garland hung sporadically throughout the room to give the illusion of trees sprouting from the stone.

Henry nodded in appreciation, flinching at the motion. His head ached from consuming too much wine the night before. He remembered leaving the feast to deliver the information to Crispin in his chamber. Unfortunately, he recalled very little after that. He searched for Crispin upon waking only to find his chamber empty. Had he delivered the information? The drunken tale his brothers regaled him with made no logical sense. Who would want a helpless child dead?

A choir sang traditional Latin hymns, the sweet, melodic strains filling the impromptu forest. The doors swung open, and a chorus of gasps and sighs filled the throne room.

Ruby and Crispin stood beneath the arch, her hand resting on his arm. The prince wore a fine red doublet with his family crest of a lion and an eagle in the center, the trim a matching gold. His black tunic, breeches, and boots placed all emphasis on his stern expression. He wore his father's sword and a long robe to complete the regal portrait. Lady Ruby beamed, radiant in her complimentary red and gold gown. A golden belt with a single ruby fastened high around her waist. Together, they proceeded down the aisle toward the throne dais where the priest, garbed in his finest robes, stood waiting.

The whispers hushed as they stopped before the dais. As

the priest spoke, Henry felt a tug on his sleeve. His brothers surrounded him, followed by his father, who stopped at his side. Henry exhaled in irritation.

"Where did you disappear to last eve?" His father leaned close.

"I had duties to attend," Henry snapped, attempting to focus on the ceremony.

They listened in silence as the priest requested Ruby and Henry repeat their vows.

"I receive you as mine, that you become my wife and I, your husband. I bind you to me forevermore." Crispin's voice resonated clearly through the room as he recited his vows.

"I receive you as mine, that you become my husband and I, your wife. I bind you to me forevermore," Ruby repeated, her gaze fixed on Crispin, her chin held high.

"Please kneel," the priest instructed. A servant in livery stepped forward, holding a pillow upon which sat two crowns. Crispin and Ruby knelt facing the priest. He held the first crown aloft. "By the grace of God, I hereby anoint and crown you, Prince Crispin Saville, son of King Edgar of Meradin, the title of King by right of birth." He placed the crown on Crispin's bowed head.

Picking up the second crown, he turned to Ruby. "By the grace of God, I hereby bestow upon you, Princess Eleanor Lancaster, daughter of King Henry V of England, the title of Queen by right of marriage." The priest laid the matching crown upon Ruby's head.

A collective murmur rippled through the crowd at the priest's words. Had he truly said Ruby was Princess Eleanor of England? The daughter of Henry the Fifth? He glanced at his father, whose hand grasped the pommel of his sword squeezing it tight. His father's expression tightened as his eyes narrowed, his jaw clenched firmly.

"In the sight of God and the church, I hereby authenticate the union and do name them the rightful rulers of Meradin. Rise, King Crispin and Queen Eleanor. All hail the king and queen!" The priest announced the royal couple who turned toward their subjects.

Henry regarded his father carefully. Everything fell into place. They wanted Ruby dead because she was of royal blood and a union of such magnitude would solidify Meradin's alliance with England. He must speak with Crispin. Pushing his way through the crowd, he approached them as they descended. Cheers and music rang throughout the room. Crispin met his gaze, and Henry nodded twice. At the slight incline of Crispin's head, he turned and left the room.

Waiting in the shadows near the head table in the great hall, Henry observed the bride and groom as they entered first, followed by their guests. When Crispin and Ruby approached the table, Henry stepped forward and pulled out Ruby's chair. She glanced at him, her face deepening to a lovely crimson before she quickly glanced away.

Before Henry could speak, Crispin came up beside him, pulling him into the shadows. Their hushed tones rose to drown out the guests' animated chatter.

"Did I inform you of my discovery?" Henry fidgeted with the pommel of his sword.

Crispin grinned. "Have you no memory of what transpired last evening?"

Crispin's mischievous expression made Henry shift uncomfortably. "Nay, I remember speaking to my brothers and father, learning of their part in the raid. When I rose to find you, I—well, I remember nothing after that."

"What did you learn?" Crispin leaned close as the noise grew louder around them.

"They were dispatched to kill Ruby. Unfortunately, they did not tell me who hired them, but they are guilty of the murder of Baron Skye and his wife as well as their servants. Would you have me arrest them, Sire?"

Crispin stroked his hand along his jaw. "Nay, leave them. We shall find a way to draw them out."

"During the ceremony, the identity of your bride was revealed. My father knows of his failure. He knows Ruby was the little girl from the raid. The one he was sent to kill. I fear for her safety and yours, Sire."

Crispin turned to Henry, his lips curled in a sinister grin. "Then we have the bait, now we shall set the trap." He clapped a hand on Henry's shoulder. "Come, let us join the revelry."

Henry disliked Crispin's easy dismissal of the severity of the traitorous actions they uncovered. Upon returning to the table, Henry took his place on Crispin's right. He glanced at the couple, attempting to ascertain the best method to protect them and bring his family to justice for their crimes.

The king rested his hand on his wife's thigh. When he glanced up, Ruby met his gaze, her face blossoming like a red rose. She shifted her attention away, flustered. Henry turned to the servants carrying in the first course of the feast. *Why does she blush like a virgin maid when she meets my eye?*

Henry sipped his wine and nearly spit it out when an image flashed in his mind. Ruby standing in Crispin's chambers wearing nothing but a cloth across her eyes. He wiped his mouth and glanced at her again then at Crispin.

A knowing smile unfurled upon Crispin's lips. Surely he had not—

Crispin leaned close. "Have your memories of last evening returned?"

Henry shook his head. "Only images."

"Do not worry, my friend. Your role was at my direction and played to perfection." He slapped his hand on Henry's back.

Ruby glanced at them both, her cheeks aflame.

Did I bed the queen? Henry downed his goblet of wine and poured another. How could Crispin use him thus? He never regretted taking an order from his king, until that moment.

Chapter Thirty-Nine

Crispin glanced up at the night sky as he led Ruby across the battlements. The moon hung full in the heavens surrounded by twinkling stars. He paused when they reached a small platform encircling the tip of the turret's peak. They leaned against the stone, taking in the magnificent view. From this vantage point, they could see the lights of the village flickering below and hear the revelers enjoying the celebration. The forest stretched far into the distance over rolling hills.

"'Tis quite lovely." Ruby glanced at him. "My apologies for earlier today." Her hands twisted in the folds of her skirt. "With the wedding and the feast, I—"

"There is no reason for you to apologize." Crispin covered her hand with his. "This day must have been overwhelming."

"Aye, but I finally know who I am and where I belong." Ruby interlaced her fingers with his. "What happens now?"

Crispin pulled her into his embrace. "I can think of one thing specifically."

She glanced at him, her expression wry. The moonlight cast a pallid glow on her skin, making her appear almost ethereal. Saints, she enchanted him.

"Have you no restraint? Can you think of nothing else?" Ruby pressed her hand against his chest in a vain attempt to put distance between them.

"You wound me." He pouted but refused to release her.

"After last evening—" Ruby dropped her gaze. "I should wound you."

"You could have ended it with one simple phrase, yet you chose not to do so." Crispin cocked his head and grinned. "So part of the blame lies with yourself."

Ruby fought harder to free herself from his grasp. "Release me, you horse's arse."

He held tight as she struggled against his embrace. "You

belong to me now, Eleanor. Nothing save the devil himself can steal you away from me."

"You treat me like a pet, a whore, a bauble for you to show off to the world." She rounded on him, panting with the exertion of trying to free herself. "And do not call me that!"

"Why? 'Tis your given name, is it not?"

"Aye, but it is not who I am." She licked her lips, and his cock leaped at the innocent action, drawing attention to her luscious mouth.

"You are the notorious thief, the legendary Lady of the Forrest. Or are you Lady Ruby, foster daughter of Baron Skye? How about the orphan Ruby taken in and raised by strangers and former outlaws?" Crispin arched his brow. "You are all of these things, but as of today, there is only one designation you hold which concerns me." He grasped the back of her head and brought her lips close. "You are *mine*."

When he kissed her, it served as not only a branding and a binding contract, but as an enticement and a promise. He wanted her desperate and panting beneath his touch. When he saw her approach in the hall outside the throne room, the pride and possessiveness which consumed him left him reeling. Her lips softened as he tasted her. Crispin curled his fingers into her hair, holding her fast as he feasted upon her mouth. His other arm locked around her waist. When he broke the kiss, her panted breaths caressed his lips. Ruby opened her eyes.

"Yours," she murmured against his mouth before drawing his lower lip between her teeth.

He growled and kissed her harder, pushing, punishing her. She snaked her arms around his neck and grabbed a fistful of his hair, snapping his head back. He gasped as pleasure surged through his body at her taking command. His warrior queen emerged with a victorious gleam in her eyes.

"Fire with fire, my husband." Ruby arched against him, her breasts pressing against his chest.

Crispin's blood heated as his cock thickened. "I should take you right here, bend you over the cool stone, and let your moans of pleasure echo through the bailey." He pulled her arms down, gripping her wrists in his hands. Spinning her around, he wrapped an arm around her waist and drew her skirts up. "Shall we allow the country to watch as we consummate our union beneath the heavens?"

Ruby moaned as his hand traced along her bare thigh. When he touched her center, she murmured something he could not understand.

"Louder next time." He slipped a finger inside her cunt. She bucked in his arms, threatening to collapse as he toyed with her sensitive nub with his thumb. "Mmmm, I love when you melt beneath my touch."

"Crispin, please." Her plea sent a bolt of lust straight to his cock.

He released her. "Place your hands flat."

She leaned forward, pressing her palms flat on the waist-high crest of the battlement.

"Good girl." He lifted the back of her skirt and bared her arse. Unfastening his breeches, he drew his cock out and rubbed it along her moist cleft. "Is this what you wanted?"

Ruby glanced over her shoulder, her eyes dark. Without a word, she pressed back against his cock, and he slid deep into her warmth.

Her body welcomed him as it had the night before. He gripped her hips and thrust into her, over and over. She squirmed beneath him, meeting his thrusts. The gentle brush of her fingertips against his balls made him grin. Crispin slapped her arse. She yelped in surprise, her body clenching around his cock.

"I did not grant you permission to move your hands. Disobey me again, and I will leave you without release." He reached around and pinched the swollen nub she ached to caress. Her body shuddered at the assault. He fucked her harder as he teased her, pinching and rubbing the tiny pearl. When her climax took hold of her, she trembled beneath him, her moans echoing off the battlements. He thrust into her, her body gripping his cock tight. He came with a shout and gathered her against his chest. They clung to each other as muted cheers drifted up from the bailey below.

"Do you think they heard us?" Ruby glanced at Crispin.

"Does it matter?"

"I suppose not." A wicked grin curved her plush lips.

He stroked her hair and kissed tenderly. "Do not concern yourself about last evening."

Ruby tensed in his arms. "I do not wish to discuss it."

"Henry does not remember a thing."

She shook free from his grasp. "He—what?"

Crispin chuckled. "When Henry drinks too much, he forgets much of the time he was under the seductive spell of the alcohol."

"So he...then..." Ruby stumbled over her words and finally sighed. "'Tis better this way."

"Aye." Crispin held his hand out to her. She hesitated before taking it. "Let us retreat to my chamber. The morrow will be here soon enough, and I have not yet finished with you."

"Is that all you think of?" Ruby tugged her hand from his, but Crispin pulled her against him.

"With a woman like you to warm my bed, I would be a foolish cur to not fuck you thoroughly and often. I should be surprised if you can walk at all on the morrow." He tugged the lobe of her ear with his teeth. "Come, my queen, let me show you how wicked I can truly be."

The End
Book One

Hello again,

Thank you so much for reading this book. If you enjoyed it, even a little, would you do me a huge favor? Please take a few minutes and write a review, and if you know someone who would enjoy this book, send them a little note and tell them about it.

If you're intimidated by writing a review, here's a blog post I wrote a few years ago to help readers formulate a helpful review: **https://kirstensblacketer.com/2018/01/11/how-to-write-a-helpful-review/**

An honest review is like a love letter to the author. It helps us grow and lets us know our hard work is appreciated. Though it may seem simple and insignificant, it means the world to hear your thoughts. Thank you for taking the time to show your love.

Also, if you'd like to be the first to know when I have a new release or get some sneak peeks into my current WIPs, then sign up for my monthly newsletter. When you subscribe, you'll get a free steamy historical short story. You can only get it as a loyal subscriber to my newsletter. I'll be offering other special short stories and giveaways as well. You won't want to miss it. You can find the sign up form on my website:

https://kirstensblacketer.com

Thank you again for your love and support! I look forward to chatting with you soon.

Sincerely,

Jen Bradlee/Kirsten S. Blacketer

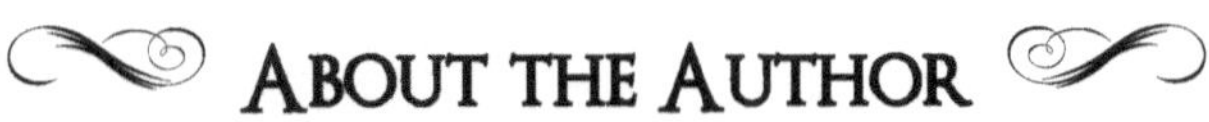# ABOUT THE AUTHOR

Jen Bradlee is the alter ego of author Kirsten S. Blacketer.

Jen Bradlee can get away with murder, metaphorically speaking of course. She enjoys people watching, belly dancing, and taking walks in the rain. Give her a man who isn't afraid to get his hands dirty and plays hard. The ones with rough edges and a little scruff are the best. Comes with a warning label. "Too hot to handle."

Inspired by Tom Hiddleston and Benedict Cumberbatch, she creates characters who have multiple facets to them. The gentleman in the streets but with a wild, dangerous side behind closed doors. She loves villains and anti-heroes, bad boys and irredeemable men. We all have a dark side. Sometimes it must be freed.

http://kirstensblacketer.com/jen-bradlee